Cat got y
**This** cat's g

✳

"The Commissioner in there?" Karen asked.

"Yeah," the cop blocking the apartment said. He grimaced wryly. "You ready for this? They're trying to take a statement from the victim's *cat!*" He glanced down at me. "What's this, the boyfriend?"

"Shove it, bonehead," I snapped. "Step aside."

He stared in astonishment and actually stepped aside before he had a chance to think...

Princess was curled up on the couch, her ears laid back, and every couple of seconds she would raise her head and let loose a grief-stricken yowl. I jumped up on the couch; instinctively, she recoiled and hissed.

"Take it easy, kitten," I said. "It's only me."

"They killed her, Gomez," she yowled. "The lousy chauvinist bastards *killed* her!"

Also by Simon Hawke

The Wizard of 4th Street
The Wizard of Whitechapel
The Wizard of Sunset Strip
The Wizard of Rue Morgue
The Wizard of Santa Fe
Samurai Wizard
The Reluctant Sorcerer

THE NINE LIVES OF

CATSEYE
GOMEZ

by SIMON HAWKE

WARNER BOOKS

A Time Warner Company

WARNER BOOKS EDITION

Copyright © 1992 by Simon Hawke
All rights reserved.

Cover illustration by Dave Mattingly
Cover design by Don Puckey

Questar® is a registered trademark of Warner Books, Inc.

Warner Books, Inc.
1271 Avenue of the Americas
New York, NY 10020

A Time Warner Company

Printed in the United States of America

First Printing: October, 1992

10 9 8 7 6 5 4 3 2 1

With a fond tip of the fedora,
this one is dedicated to The Master,
Mickey Spillane,
and his immortal creation, Mike Hammer.
Some things never change.
And some things never should.

One

JUST when you think you've got the whole game knocked and are ready to settle back for the sweet ride of comfort and security, life comes along and deals you a hand you wouldn't bet on in a game of penny ante with a bunch of Cub Scouts. I guess I should've known better. An old trooper like me should be used to it by now. I've had more ups and downs than a yo-yo in the hands of a hyperactive ten-year-old, but I guess even old troopers get complacent.

See, the secret to dealing with the curve balls life has a tendency to throw at you is to roll with the punches and always land on your feet. I'm good at that. You might say it's an inbred talent. Name's Gomez. I'm a cat. A thaumagenetic feline, if you want to get precise about it. That means I'm no ordinary cat, which by now I guess you might have gathered. What I am is a product of thaumagenetic engineering, a marriage of sorcery and science, and that means I'm a few giant steps removed from my ordinary feline cousins.

Don't get me wrong, when I say "ordinary," I don't mean it as a put-down. I get along just fine with my ordinary cousins—most of them anyway—but the fact is that so-called ordinary cats still basically look and act pretty much the way Nature had intended. Me, I'm a whole different ball of wax. I'm a whole lot smarter. I can talk and I can read, and that ain't bragging, brother, it's just the way my brain was engineered. Don't ask about the details—I'm no scientist, and I'm certainly no sorcerer, though I know a lot more about sorcery than science, mainly because I've lived with an adept. It's an interesting story, and one that's probably worth telling.

See, back in the old days, what they refer to now as "the pre-Collapse period," science and technology were pretty much the basis for reality. Nobody believed in magic. Nobody worth taking seriously, anyway. There have always been people who've believed in all sorts of crazy nonsense, from UFOs to dead celebrities hanging out at the local 7-Eleven, and back then, anyone who seriously believed in magic was either given a nice rubber room to play in or featured in the supermarket tabloids. However, all that changed, and rather dramatically too, when the clock finally ran out on them and the world was plunged into the Collapse.

You've studied about it in school and you've heard the stories from the old folks who still remember it. It was pretty ugly. Back then, people had believed there was no such thing as a limit to growth. They were always robbing Peter to pay Paul, living on borrowed time and handing down their problems to the next generation. Now, you can only do that sort of thing for so long before it comes time to pay the piper. Well, the time came, and they paid. They paid big-time.

See, they'd finally managed to use up most of their natural resources, and what they hadn't used up, they'd poisoned. No more fossil fuels. The wells ran dry. The air wasn't fit to breathe. The water wasn't fit to drink. The overpopulated urban centers were choking on their own garbage and drowning in their own effluvium. Yeah, not a pretty image. Environmental disaster never is, especially when it happens on a global scale.

The warning signs had all been there, and they'd been around for years, only nobody paid attention. Greed, power politics, venality, corruption, all those sterling traits of human nature that often make me wonder why the cockroach isn't the dominant species on Earth today led to the disaster now known as the Collapse. It all finally fell apart. The doomsayers had been proven right, but they probably took little comfort in the accuracy of their foresight.

Like I said, it got pretty ugly for a while. Governments collapsed, economies collapsed, law and order collapsed. . . . I guess that's why they called it the Collapse. The darkened cities became free-fire zones. The outlying areas became a no-man's-land of guerilla warfare among small and well-armed enclaves. It was everybody's favorite postholocaust scenario, except that it never took a holocaust to bring it about. The real miracle was that nobody freaked out and pushed the button, but then, they'd already trashed the world almost to the point of oblivion and were probably desperate to save what little they had left. Saner minds prevailed, though sanity was an extremely relative term in those days. (And in many ways, it still is, but that's another story.)

The Collapse had plunged the world into a modern dark age, where the machinery all stopped and mankind's feral instincts took over. It wasn't very pretty. And then something happened that no one had expected, something that came from so far out of left field it took decades before the public consciousness could even deal with it. Magic was reborn.

Actually, to be precise, it had never really died. It had simply been forgotten. What little history of magic use remained had long since been relegated to myth and folklore. Even today, most people don't know what it's really all about . . . and if they did, they'd lose their cookies.

Tom Malory set it all down in his book, *The Wizard of Camelot*, or most of it, anyway. There were certain things he had held back, but only because he would have caused a panic if he'd told the whole truth and nothing but. This isn't the original Tom Malory, you understand, the one who wrote *Le Morte d'Arthur*, in which he set down the legend of King Arthur for posterity. This was his namesake, and no relation, a guy who'd been a soldier in the British army and an urban Strike Force cop in London during the Collapse. What happened to that Malory has become widespread public knowledge. He wrote about it afterward and retired a rich man, but for the record, he was right there, from the beginning, when magic came back into the world.

He'd moved his family out of London, to the countryside, where it was somewhat safer, but life was still no picnic. They were living hand to mouth, just barely getting by, and his kids were freezing in the biting cold of the English winter. No fuel available. There was some coal and there was wood, but it was a seller's market, and Malory could not afford the going rate. What was the poor guy going to do, watch as his wife and kids died of pneumonia? No, of course not. He did what any self-respecting man would do when caught in such a situation. He went out to steal what he could.

Not far from where he lived, there was a small forest preserve, one of the few wooded areas left standing in that defoliated world. It was surrounded by tall fencing and barbed wire, patrolled by well-armed guards, and the grounds inside the enclosure had been mined. But Malory was a desperate man, and he'd had commando training. He managed to break in, with an ax. The way he tells it, he wasn't really sane at the time. He'd passed the breaking point. He didn't think that the most he could carry was a measly armload, assuming he didn't get caught while he was chopping wood in a protected national preserve, and it was hardly worth the risk. It certainly never occurred to him that what he'd done was about to change the world. He just broke in there, desperate and feverish, and went a short ways in, so that he'd be out of sight of the perimeter, and what he came across was the biggest grandaddy of an oak tree he had ever seen.

What happened after that is legend now. He looked at this huge tree, miraculously left standing after all those years of people chopping down everything in sight, stared at it, at this leviathan that could keep his family warm for months, maybe even years, and he just went crazy. He screamed and attacked it with his ax, but all he ever got in was just that one first blow, because the moment the ax had struck the tree, a bolt of lightning came down from the thunderclouds roiling overhead and split the oak right down the middle. And standing there, right smack in the center of the split, was Merlin, the legendary wizard to King Arthur.

Turns out it wasn't a legend, after all. For two thousand some odd years, after the sorceress Morgan le Fay had tricked him and entombed him in that living oak, protected by a spell, Merlin Ambrosius had slept in some kind of enchanted, suspended animation, dreaming the events that took place in the world outside. It wasn't Tom Malory who broke the spell; he just happened to be there when the enchantment ran its course and Merlin was released. But he was there, at Merlin's side, when the Second Thaumaturgic Age began and the world was dragged kicking and screaming out of the Collapse and into a magical new dawn.

All this happened many years before I was born, of course, and I wouldn't be the cat I am today if Merlin hadn't brought back magic to the world and founded schools of thaumaturgy that would teach the old forgotten arts to his new pupils. The twenty-third-century world of today has come a long way from the Collapse. The union of magic and technology has brought about a kinder, gentler world in many ways. Thaumaturgy is a nonpolluting resource, and so the air is clean now, even in the cities. Cracked and buckled pavement has been replaced by grassy causeways, since vehicles that operate by magic skim above the surface and have no need of asphalt roads. Acid rain is something that's just read about in history books now, and magic properly applied by reclamation engineers has cleaned up landfills and toxic-waste dumps and brought new meaning to the term *biodegradable*.

Graduate schools of thaumaturgy turn out new adepts each year, of varying levels of talent and achievement, from lower-grade adept up through the ranks to wizard, sorcerer, and mage. Your basic lower-grade adept is usually someone with just enough talent to master a few fairly undemanding spells, such as levitation and impulsion, which are used to drive taxicabs and trucks. A wizard can do considerably more, such as maintaining the spells that allow power plants to stay on line, and certification as a sorcerer opens up the corporate world to the adept, with a career and lifestyle right up at the top of the social pecking order. Nothing like living high and skimming off the cream. But not all sorcerers opt for the business world. Some go into the fields of art and entertainment, and that's where I come in.

One of the most respected positions in the world of art is occupied by the thaumagenetic engineer adept, part scientist, part sorcerer, who specializes in creating hybridized new life forms for the enrichment of your private life. A thaumagene is the ultimate form of pet these days. You can go out and get yourself a snat, a cute and furry little creature that's a magical hybrid of a snail and cat. It's soft and cuddly, and it purrs and vibrates and clings to walls and ceilings. Silly things, but they're very big with single women. Or you can get yourself a paragriffin, a hybrid of a parrot and a miniature lion, or perhaps a leopard. It flies and talks, and you can teach it songs. Or, if that's not to your taste, you can get a dobra, a hybrid of a cobra and a dog, and you'll have something spectacularly ugly that you can take for walks out in the park, and pity the poor burglar who tries to break into your home. If you've really got the scratch, you can get yourself a living sculpture, something crafted out of precious stones and metals, then magically animated. Just the thing for the coffee table or the breakfast nook. Me, I'm at the low end of the scale, and I make no bones about it. I'm your basic thaumagene, economy-class model, one of the two traditional categories of pet. You got your dogs, and you got your cats. Look normal, act pretty much like they're supposed to, only with highly developed brains and the capacity to speak and reason. We're the most inexpensive kind of thaumagene, and, consequently, there's more of us around.

Personally, I like the way I am. I'd rather look like an ordinary cat than like some high-toned piece of living art. I'm not pretentious, just your basic milk and kibbles kind of guy. Black, with white markings on my face and paws. I've got one distinguishing characteristic, though, and that's Betsy, my magic Chinese turquoise eyeball. See, I never had what you might call a normal sort of life, normal for a thaumagene, at any rate. Back when I was still a kitten, even then, I had my pride. Sitting in a window of a thaumagene shop, mewing and pawing at the glass each time some skirt came by to take a peek and mutter, "Oh, how cute"—no, sir, not my style. I wanted out. And so I slipped the lock on my little cubicle one night and struck out on my own. Guess I've always been the independent type.

Those were lean and hungry days. Living by my wits in the alleys and back streets of Sante Fe, New Mexico, scratching and clawing for survival, eating out of garbage cans and dumpsters, sleeping in basement window wells and thrown-out cardboard boxes, it wasn't easy, I can tell you that. But it was freedom, Jack, and I loved the sweet and heady taste of it. I never knew the pampered life, and I guess that made me what I am today. I had my share of scraps, some of which I won and some of which I lost, but as I grew older and leaner and meaner, the losses came less frequently. It was in one of those scraps in which I barely squeaked through by the skin of my tail that I lost my eye. Ran into a dog that wanted what I'd scored for dinner. I was hungry and I didn't want to share. Well, turned out the dog was a coyote, and by the time he decided I was more trouble than I was worth, I'd gotten chewed up pretty bad. Scratch one eyeball. Hurt like hell, but I had the satisfaction of not backing down. Stupid? Maybe, but you back down once, you'll back down twice, and it can get to be a habit. I've got enough bad habits as it is.

Enter Paulie. Professor Paul Ramirez was his full name, and he was Dean of the College of Sorcerers at the university. He found me in the street, where I'd collapsed, too tired and too weak and too full of pain to move another step. He picked me up and took me home with him, and I was so messed up, I didn't have the strength to argue. He nursed me back to health and, when I got better, took me to a thaumagenetic vet. I could've had a brand-new eyeball, cloned and grown in a vat, but Paul was not a rich man, despite being a sorcerer. He was a teacher, and teachers do it for the love of teaching. It sure as hell ain't for the money. The best he could do for me was a prosthetic eyeball, made of turquoise. It was a stone he'd had around, intending to get it made into a ring someday, but he gave it to the vet, who cut it and set it nicely in my eye socket.

Frankly, I liked it a lot better than some fancy, cut-glass eye. It's a Chinese turquoise, of a beautiful, robin's-egg-blue shade, with a fine, vertical matrix running through it that almost resembles a feline pupil. I thought it gave me character, and the other felines in the neighborhood agreed. A foxy, little alabaster Persian by the name of Snowball dubbed me Catseye, and the handle stuck. Catseye Gomez I became, unregenerate hardcase and all-around troubleshooter.

I never did become a pet. Paulie was an all-right guy, but I was just too damned set in my ways to change. You want some servile creature that gets all excited when you come walking through the door, rubs up against your legs and has an orgasm when you stroke it, go get yourself a poodle, man, that ain't my thing. But Paulie understood that. We were both loners, in our way, and we just sort of took up with each other, both of us coming and going pretty much the way we pleased. Paulie had his career, I had my wandering ways.

Every now and then, Paulie'd have a bunch of students from the college over for some java and late-night conversation. One time, one of them left behind a book. Something he'd been reading for a pre-Collapse literature class. I found it on the floor. The ability to read had been bred into me, but up to then, all I'd ever read were labels on greasy, thrown-out cans of tuna I'd picked out of the garbage, and the oil soaked newspapers fish heads were wrapped in. This was something new. I read the title. *I, the Jury*, by some guy named Spillane.

It was a tale about a private eye named Hammer. Mike Hammer. Tough guy who packed a .45 and took no crap from anybody. Once I'd started it, I couldn't stop till I had read it all. This Hammer was a guy after my own heart, an hombre I could really understand. It was like coming home. This guy Spillane *knew* about the hard life. He knew the streets and alleys, the shadows where the lizards lurk, the baser side of human nature—of all nature, for that matter—and the never-give-an-inch attitude it takes to make it through the cold, dark night. Man, I was hooked.

When Paulie got home, all I could talk about was this guy Spillane, and the stories he told about Mike Hammer, and I wanted more. Paulie'd never heard of him, but he found that kid's professor and asked him about this writer named Spillane. It wasn't easy, and it took a lot of searching through the antique bookshops of the city, but Paulie eventually brought home everything this guy Spillane had ever written. *My Gun Is Quick. Vengeance Is Mine. One Lonely Night* and *The Big Kill* and *Kiss Me Deadly* and the rest of them. Man, this guy could write. It was as if he knew all about the kind of life I'd led, only Mike Hammer was a human, not a cat. Not much difference beyond that, though. Give either of us any shit and we'd rip your throat right out.

I got through all the Spillane books, and Paulie found me more. He brought home books by Ross MacDonald, stories about a private eye by the name of Lew Archer, maybe not as tough as Hammer, but just as uncompromising in his way. That led to Raymond Chandler and his hero, Phil Marlowe, and then to Dashiell Hammett and Sam Spade and the Continental Op. Maybe things were different back in the days they wrote those books, but I realized one thing. Not all humans were the same. Some were just like me. Tough and feral creatures of the night, hard-bitten scrappers who fought the good fight, grabbed life by the throat and shook it, wringing out each precious drop of blood and letting its hot fire flow coursing through their veins. I would've understood those guys, and I would've been proud to know them. And in some ways, Paulie was like that, only a lot more civilized.

I found that out the way I've learned everything else. The hard way. You'll remember when I said that if most people knew what magic was really all about, they'd lose their cookies? Well, here's how I found out.

A murderer was on the loose in Santa Fe, a vicious serial killer whose victims were found horribly mutilated and drained of their life energies, their very souls sucked dry. This could only mean one thing. The killer was an adept, a necromancer. A wizard who killed to drain his victim's life energy and absorb it, like a vampire. The police had no idea what to do. This was way out of their league. But there *was* someone who could stop the killer, three someones, to be precise, who flew in from New York when they heard what was going down. And one of them was Merlin.

Merlin had taught Paulie everything he knew, but this wasn't quite the same Merlin that Paulie remembered. That

Merlin had died in a struggle with the Dark Ones, but his spirit had survived, to possess a flaky kid from London by the name of Billy Slade. Then there was Kira, a sexy knockout from Lower Manhattan who had made her living as a thief until she found a greater calling, and Wyrdrune, a dropout student of the thaumaturgic arts who had the ability to shapechange into his alter ego, a cold and ruthless mercenary by the name of Modred, the immortal spirit of King Arthur's son.

From the three of them, Paulie and I learned that there was once another race of beings on this Earth, not unlike humans, with coppery-gold skin and bright red hair, and that they were magic users. It was from them that humans got their legends of immortal gods and demons, vampires and witches. They were called the Old Ones, and they used humans in their sacrificial rites, taking their life energies to empower their magic spells.

As the primitive humans started to evolve, many of the Old Ones came to feel that it was wrong to use them in this way, and they started to practice what became white magic, thaumaturgy, a way of taking only some of their life energy and allowing them to recuperate. But there were others, the Dark Ones, who would not give up the old sorcery of death. They were the necromancers, and the rift between them and the others led to war. In the end, the Dark Ones were defeated, and entombed forever in a hidden cavern deep beneath the earth, while the surviving Old Ones scattered and lived out the remainder of their lives pretending to be human, to avoid persecution by those who had once been their victims.

Over the years, they interbred with humans, until they no longer were immortal, but their abilities were genetically passed on, though they became diluted over time. Humans with abilities like extrasensory perception were people who were descended from the Old Ones, just like those who possessed the natural ability to study thaumaturgy and become adepts. Merlin, himself, had been a half-breed, whose father was an Old One, and when he brought back magic to the world, its power had awakened the imprisoned Dark Ones and they had broken free. And the killer loose upon our streets was one of them.

Paulie and I helped stop the vicious necromancer, and, as a reward, Merlin had cast a spell upon my turquoise eye before he left. He gave Betsy the ability to hurl bolts of thaumaturgic force, but this ability was limited by the strength of my own life force. If I cut loose with Betsy, it would take a while for me to get back enough strength to let 'er rip again, but that's because magic has its own laws of energy that cannot be violated. You won't hear me complaining. I've got something no other thaumagene will ever get. My sweet and trusty Betsy, my own version of Hammer's .45. Don't mess with me, Jack. My claw is quick.

After the necromancer was defeated, things settled down in Santa Fe. Paulie had been injured in that final confrontation, and for a while, he was blind. It was only temporary, and everybody thought he would recover. But it was more than just his vision that the necromancer had burned away. He had burned away a part of Paulie, and what was left was not enough to keep him going. He got his vision back eventually, but he just kept getting weaker. I stayed by him, and I watched him fade away, and it just tore my heart out, for Paulie was as close a friend as I had ever had, but there was nothing anyone could do. One day, he simply closed his eyes and never opened them again. And that was that. I was alone again. I'd been that way before, been alone most of my life, but it just wasn't the same. I missed the man. I missed him with a gnawing in my gut that made me want to take on the whole world and scratch its eyes out.

I left the house and took to the streets once more. I just couldn't go back there. It hurt too much. Every day, I'd go to visit Paulie's grave, and I'd sit there and have a conversation with him. I talked, and I hoped that, somewhere, he was listening. And then, one day, as I was laying on the grave a fresh rose I'd torn up out of some old lady's garden, I heard a voice behind me call out my name.

"Gomez? Catseye Gomez?"

I turned around with a snarl at this unwarranted intrusion on my time with my old friend. "Yeah. I'm Gomez. Who wants to know?"

"The name's Solo. Jay Solo. And Paul Ramirez was a friend of mine."

"Is that so? I never heard Paulie mention you."

I looked him over. Feisty-looking character, not too tall, broad in the chest, dark-haired, maybe in his fifties. Had a look about his face I recognized and liked at once. A tough and lived-in look. The look of a guy who's been around and seen a few things in his life that maybe weren't too pleasant, things that might've bothered him, but not enough to grind him down.

"Paulie?" he said, with a wry smile. "Somehow, I've never thought of him as Paulie. With us, it was always Solo and Ramirez." He shrugged. "It was a long time ago."

"What were you to Paulie?" I asked.

"A friend," he said, simply. "We knew each other back in Cambridge, Massachusetts, when he was studying with Merlin and I was going for my criminology degree. He used to date my sister. I'm afraid it didn't turn out too well. I liked him, you understand, liked him a lot, and I tried to warn him. My sister . . . well, let's just say it wasn't in the cards and leave it at that. He got pretty torn up about it. After we got out of school, we went our separate ways and kind of lost touch with each other. I don't guess he'd talk about those days too much."

"I see," I said. "Well, if you want some time with Paulie, it's okay with me. I'm about through here, anyway."

"It was you I came to see," said Solo.

"Me?"

"I've been looking for you ever since I got to town about a week ago."

"Yeah? Okay. You found me. So?"

Solo stared at me for a moment, then moistened his lips nervously and took a folded piece of paper from his pocket. "Paul wrote me a letter," he said. "It must have been . . . just before he died. I'd like to read it to you, if I may."

Something suddenly felt real tight inside me. "Yeah," I said. "Go ahead."

"Dear Solo," the man read. "I know it's been a lot of years, and a lot of water under the bridge. But there's one thing time has never changed, even if we haven't stayed in touch too well. I still consider you one of the closest friends I've ever had. I would have said the closest friend, but there's another friend who's just as close, someone who's like a brother to me, even if he isn't human."

I looked away and closed my eyes, feeling as if somebody'd grabbed my heart and started squeezing. Goddamn, Paulie. . . .

"His name is Gomez," Solo continued, "Catseye Gomez, and he's a cat. A thaumagene." Solo glanced up from the letter. "He goes on here to tell me something about you, about how you two got together and what you're like and some of the things you've been through . . . anyway. . . ."

He looked back down at the letter and continued reading. "The thing is, old friend, I'm dying. There's nothing to be done, and by the time you get this, I'll probably be gone. I've taken care of most things in my will, but there's one thing I'd like you to take care of for me, and it's the one and only thing I've ever really asked of you, and the last thing I will ever ask of you. Look after Gomez for me. Not that Catseye needs much looking after, he's a real independent sort. He's very much his own person . . . well, I tend to think of him as a person . . . and if he knew that I was writing this, he'd probably get angry and want no part of it. He's a tough old cat who grew up on the streets and knows his way around. He can take care of himself, believe me, but somehow, I just hate the thought of him being on his own, without a friend, back on the streets again after I've gone. He's been a loyal and true friend, Solo, just as you have been, and in different ways, at different times, you two have been very important parts of my life. Neither you nor Gomez are exactly spring chickens anymore, but unless I miss my guess, I think the two of you will find you have a lot in common, and I'd like to do just one last thing before I go. I'd like very much to bring my two old friends together. In a way, it's like completing something, I suppose. I don't know how either of you will feel about the idea, and I'm not asking for anything like a firm commitment. I'm just asking you both to give it a try. One last favor for a dying man. I think you'll both find it hard to turn that down. I hope so. But I'm pretty sure you won't regret it. Do it for me. And think about me when I'm gone. Good-bye, old friend.'' Solo looked up from the letter. ''Love, Paul.''

I felt like I had a hairball the size of a Frisbee stuck in my throat. ''Damn, Paulie. . . .'' I said.

''Well . . .'' said Solo. ''I've always been pretty much of a loner, myself, but if Paul Ramirez considers you a friend, then so do I. So what do you say, Gomez?''

What the hell was I supposed to say? Hell, I didn't even know the guy, and I wasn't in the market for any new best friends, but how do you turn down a dying man's request? Especially when it was the best friend you'd ever had?

''Like Paul said, Gomez, we're not talking about any firm commitments here. We're just talking about getting to know each other, and if it doesn't work out, we'll just part company with no hard feelings and I'll take you anywhere you want to go. It's up to you. What do you say?''

I sighed. ''Well, what can I say? It's for Paulie. And if Paulie thought you were worth getting to know, then I guess that's good enough for me. But I do what I damned well please and I sure as hell ain't no pet.''

''That goes without saying,'' Solo replied. ''Like I said,

no strings. We'll just spend some time talking about our old friend and see where, if anywhere, it goes from there. You call the shots.''

"Sounds fair enough," I said. It was for Paulie. Besides, I was always a good judge of character, and there was something about this guy Solo that I liked from the beginning. "Okay. Where to?"

"I've got a rented car," he said, jerking his head back toward the lot. "We'll drop it off at the Albuquerque airport and catch the next plane back to Denver."

"Denver?" I said.

"Yeah, it's where I live," said Solo. "Don't worry, you get a round-trip anytime you want it."

"Denver?" I said again. I'd never even considered leaving Santa Fe. I'd never been anywhere else. I didn't know anything about Denver, except that it was in Colorado. I didn't even know what this guy Solo did for a living. "What do you do in Denver? You mentioned something about criminology?"

"I'm commissioner of police."

"A cop, eh?" I said. I couldn't help it. I thought about Mike Hammer and Pat Chambers, the police captain who'd been Hammer's closest friend. Ironic? Maybe. Fate? Who the hell knew.

"Yeah," said Solo. "Hope you haven't got anything against cops."

I smiled. "Aren't they supposed to be the good guys?"

"We're supposed to be," said Solo. "I like to think we try, anyway."

I nodded. "Yeah, well, all anyone can do it try. Denver, huh?"

"Yeah. Denver."

"What the hell. I've never been to Denver."

I glanced back toward the grave and thought, *Paulie, I sure hope you know what you're doing*. I said a silent good-bye and went with Solo to his car. We got in and he turned the key, activating the thaumaturgic battery. The rental hummed to quiet life and rose about two feet off the ground. Solo turned it around and we softly skimmed off toward Albuquerque. For a while, neither of us spoke. It felt a little awkward, I guess, and neither of us was really certain what to say. We were each doing a favor for a dead man, a man who'd meant a lot to us. What we'd mean to each other, if anything, remained to be seen.

Like I said before, life tends to throw you a curve every now and then. Most of the time, you can't really see it coming, but you roll with the punches and try your best to land on your feet. But then, I'm a cat, and cats always land on their feet. A low rumble of thunder echoed through the sky like a growl as we left the cemetery behind.

Denver, Colorado. A new town. New turf. Maybe a new beginning for an old trooper. Anyway, we'd soon find out.

Two

THE flight to Denver taught me a thing or two about perspective. I'd always thought of myself as a cat who's been around, but though I knew every street and alleyway in Santa Fe like the back of my paw, I learned that I never had any idea of just how much was out there that I didn't know. Oh, I'd read a book or two and watched TV with Paulie, but knowing there's a lot more out there beyond your city limits is not the same as actually seeing it for yourself. Especially from the sky. And I learned something else, as well. I hated flying.

If God had meant for me to fly, he would've given me wings, or at least arranged for the thaumageneticist who designed me to do it. I knew about airplanes, of course, I'm not a moron, but I'd never actually flown in one before and it gave me the willies. The planes they use now, for the most part, are still the same ones that were used back in the old days, except now they don't have jet engines anymore. If you were to go up in the cockpit, and nobody but the crew gets to do that, you'd see two pilot adepts and a navigator sitting up there, in a cockpit stripped of everything except the radio and navigation instruments. The two pilot adepts take turns flying the plane, literally holding it up in the sky

—18—

through sheer force of will. Levitation and impulsion spells are among the least complicated of magical incantations, but there's a big difference between scooting a taxicab or bus a couple of feet above the ground and holding up a plane at twenty thousand feet. It takes a lot of effort, and the pilot adept has to concentrate like hell. It really wears them out, which is why there are always two per crew, and after every flight, it takes them a few days to recuperate and get their strength back. Airline pilots have to be at least fifth-level sorcerers, and they are among the highest-paid adepts. Much is made of how much safer flying is today than it was back in the old days, but that was little comfort to me.

The Bureau of Thaumaturgy, under the administration of the ITC, the International Thaumaturgical Commission, has certain rules that pertain to public transportation. It's all right for private and rental vehicles to be powered by thaumaturgic batteries, but trucks and public transportation vehicles can only be operated by certified adepts. It has to do with insurance, a concept that survived even the Collapse. Nevertheless, the fact that there were two pilots in the cockpit who unquestionably knew what they were doing did not make the flight any easier for me. Especially since the damned airline regulations required me to travel in a fucking catbox.

I had to give Solo credit, though. He sure as hell put up a fight about it. I didn't know what kind of experience he'd had with thaumagenes. Most people, if they didn't own one, have at least encountered thaumagenes, but I had no idea if Solo was a pet owner or not. He'd mentioned being a loner, though, so I'd kinda assumed he meant that literally. Nonetheless, perhaps I should've asked. I could see things getting a bit sticky if the police commissioner had an attack-trained dobra hanging around the house. In any case, he made one hell of a stink about their goddamned "policy," and he even made them bend a little. If they'd had their way, I would've been tranqed and stuck back in the cargo bay. Yeah. Good luck getting near me with a needle.

Even if they'd tried one of those cute little dart guns, I would've had a surprise in store for them with Betsy. Fortunately, that one never came up. Solo wound up buying another fare, and I got to ride with the regular passengers, but I had to stay inside that stupid wire cage. Solo was very apologetic about it, though, and made sure I had the window seat, which, quite frankly, I couldn've done without. He got the stewardess to put some pillows on the seat, so the box could sit higher and I could see out through the window. At first, I thought it might be interesting, but once we gained some altitude, I changed my mind. Yeah, it was interesting, all right, but downright unnerving. I decided that when I'd had enough of Denver, Solo could damned well put me on the bus.

My first sight of Denver as the plane came in for a landing told me that it was going to be a very different scene from Santa Fe. For one thing, it was a hell of a lot bigger, sprawled out in a huge valley at the foothills of the Rockies. The tall buildings of the downtown area stuck out like a small island in a sea of business and residential structures that glowed like the embers of a dying campfire at sunset. The plane came in over the runway, only not on a descending approach. The runways had been laid out in lighted grids. The air-traffic controllers directed the pilot to the proper one and, once he was over it and had the okay to land, the plane simply descended in a gradual drop, like an elevator. There was a shuttle waiting to take us to the terminal, where we didn't have to wait for our luggage. Solo had only a small carryon and me, well, I travel light. I was just glad to be out of that damned box.

We took a cab to the downtown area, where Solo had an apartment in one of the luxury towers. On the way, he kept up a sort of running commentary, pointing things out and telling me about the town. I wasn't too impressed with my first sight of it.

Guess I was spoiled by Santa Fe. See, the folks in Santa Fe have always had a thing about preserving the special atmosphere and culture of their town. Development was a dirty word in Santa Fe, and there were strict regulations about such things as the height of buildings and the style of the structures within the city limits. In Denver, the people didn't seem to care that much about what happened to their town. The architecture was a garish mix of old and new, and the streets had no charm about them whatsoever. Neither did the drivers. Traffic was dense, and everybody fought for what little available lane space there was. Not much chance for grass to grow with so much traffic blocking out the sun above the vehicular causeways, and Denver, Solo said, suffered from chronic water shortages, so the scrubby short prairie grass we skimmed above looked decidedly anemic.

At one time, according to Solo, Denver had been known as the Queen City of the Rockies, and back then that wasn't a reference to its sizable gay population. The architecture had been primarily of the Victorian style, along with a rather blocky, but not altogether unattractive style of house known as the "Denver Square," of which there were still quite a few remaining. However, in the days just prior to the Collapse, a large influx of people from the east and west coasts had changed the demographics of the city, and Denver had started to lose its own unique identity. They didn't want it to be known as a "cow town" anymore. They wanted to "imagine a great city," which had been a popular progrowth slogan at the time, and in the process of imagining a great city, they had apparently managed to ruin a pretty good one.

Then came the Collapse, and, like most other heavily populated urban centers, Denver suffered. There had been riots and burnings and chronic shortages and power outages and, eventually, Denver had succumbed to the same anarchy the rest of the world had been plunged into. That had been a little over three-quarters of a century ago, however, and since then, they'd made a lot of progress. Or, at least, so Solo said.

I guess I'd been spoiled by Santa Fe. My "City of the Holy Faith" had not been hit as hard by the Collapse as most other places had been. The people had pulled together and managed to largely preserve their graceful and laid-back Southwestern lifestyle. But then, there had never been any major industry in Santa Fe, and the city was in a rather isolated location at the foot of the Sangre de Cristo mountains. The people had simply banded together, and since many of them were artists and various counterculture types, they'd had an easier time of it, shifting to an agrarian, barter-based economy. Denver hadn't been so lucky.

The great city they'd imagined had been plunged into a great nightmare of darkness and fighting in the streets. And I got the impression that not all of that had been put behind them. But then, I thought, maybe I was being unfair. I had only just arrived. Why not give the place a chance? What the hell, I could always go back home, right?

The cab dropped us off in front of Solo's building, and we went through the front doors into the lobby. The security guard on duty at the desk was a senior citizen, and I noticed that he greeted Solo with a warm smile and a "Good evening, Commissioner."

"Evening, Joe," said Solo. He paused briefly to introduce me and tell the guard I'd be staying for a while. Joe smiled and greeted me politely.

"Ex-cop," said Solo, as we headed toward the elevator.

"I guessed," I said.

He pushed the call button and the doors opened.

"Floor, please," said the elevator.

"Ten," said Solo.

"Thank you, Mr. Solo." The doors closed, and the elevator started to ascend smoothly. It was very plush in there. Carpeted, nice paneling. The elevator's voice-command capability meant it was computer controlled, very slick and fancy. I gathered that the rent here wasn't cheap.

We got off at the tenth floor and went a short distance down the hall to apartment 10-C. Solo opened up the door and stood aside to let me in.

"Well, here it is," he said. "This is where I hang my hat."

I sauntered in and looked around, twitching my tail back and forth. A nervous habit. "Nice," I said.

"It's got a nice view of the mountains from the balcony."

It did, too, from what I could see through the sliding glass doors, but after that plane ride, I'd had about enough of heights for a while.

"Would you like something to drink?' asked Solo, automatically, and then he remembered he was talking to a cat and added, awkwardly, "I . . . uh . . . always keep some milk around for my coffee."

"Milk would be fine, thanks. I take it neat, in a saucer."

Solo looked at me, saw that his leg was being pulled a bit, and grinned. "Neat, in a saucer, coming right up."

The place was a lot different from Paulie's adobe house in Santa Fe. For one thing, it was an apartment, not a house, though its square footage wasn't all that much less than Paulie's home. As far as apartments went, these were pretty classy digs. I made a quick walk-through inventory. Big living room with a nice fireplace, two bedrooms, large bath, separate kitchen, dining room, large balcony. The carpeting was thick, wall-to-wall, brown pile, and the furnishings looked as if they'd all been bought at once. It was the kind of thing a decisive man who didn't want to waste a lot of time would do. Went in, knew what he wanted, picked up a set. Everything matched, and most of it looked reasonably new. Big, brown leather and mahogany, sturdy kind of stuff, built for comfort with lots of room to stretch out. None of that steel and glass crap. One of the end tables held an honest-to-God Remington bronze that had to be worth a fortune. There were no paintings on the walls, but there were several large, nicely framed Civil War prints by Don Troiani. Again, not cheap. And again, revealing an old-fashioned, manly kind of taste that would give a decorator fits. I noticed a couple of guns hanging on the wall. Antique, black-powder, cap-and-ball revolvers. Navy Colts, by the look of them. I wasn't an expert, but I read a lot, and Paulie had a taste for American history, as well. One of the bedrooms had been turned into a study, with bookshelves and a large oak desk stained dark walnut, with a comfortable leather swivel chair behind it. The desk held a computer, a pipe stand, and a cork-lined humidor, and there was a nice residual smell of cavendish tobacco in the air. Another old-fashioned and outmoded habit. There was no sign of a woman's touch anywhere about the place. Definitely bachelor digs. Warm and comfortable and tidy, with no concessions to style or fashion.

"Milk, straight up, in a saucer," Solo said, putting the dish down as I sauntered back into the living room. "Place meet with your approval?"

"Sorry about that," I said. "Didn't mean to be nosy. It's an inbred trait."

"It's okay," he said. "You hungry? I'm afraid I don't have any cat food, but I can go out and pick some up."

"Thanks, but I'm okay for now," I said.

"You got any preferences?" he asked. "I mean, like particular brands?"

"Hey, man, I spent most of my life rooting around in the garbage for food," I told him. "I'm not a fussy guy. I'll eat just about anything except birds. I hate birds."

Solo grinned and sat down on the couch. "Well," he said, a trifle awkwardly, "here we are."

"Yeah, here we are," I said, taking a seat on the carpet. I didn't know the rules yet, so I had no idea if the guy had a thing about animals on the furniture. When you're a guest, you try to be polite.

I guess neither one of us really knew what the hell we were supposed to do. It wasn't exactly your normal sort of situation. Hey, buddy, do me a favor, take care of my cat after I'm gone. It was pretty obvious that I wasn't your average cat. Hell, I wasn't even your average thaumagene. I had plenty of rough edges. I didn't even know if Solo *liked* cats.

"So, how do you feel about cats?" I asked him, figuring that at least one of us had to start somewhere.

Solo shrugged. "I don't know really. I've never had one. I guess I'm not really a cat person. Not that I've got anything against cats, you understand, I've never had a dog, either. And I'm not too crazy about birds, myself. Had a hamster once, when I was a kid."

"A hamster, huh?"

"Yeah. It died."

"Sorry to hear that."

"I felt sorta sorry for it, sitting in that cage all the time, and I used to let it out to run around. One time, it got away from me and scurried off somewhere. My mother found it. She sucked it up into the vacuum cleaner."

I tried, but I just couldn't make it. I managed to keep it down for about five seconds, and then I had to laugh. It just started coming up, and there was nothing I could do to hold it in. The thing is, my laugh sounds a whole lot like a hairball coming up. It starts with this wheezing, hacking kind of sound, and then settles down into a sort of rhythmic snorting, and for a second, Solo looked alarmed, thinking maybe I was choking. Then he realized that I was laughing, and he started laughing, too.

"Actually, it was a pretty traumatic experience for me, as a kid," he said, when we'd both run out of steam.

"I guess it was, at that," I said. "Sorry for laughing, but . . ."

"Yeah, I know," he said. "Freaked out my mother pretty badly, too. I mean, one second she's just vacuuming the rug, and then there's this soft, funny sort of chunking sound—''

I started to lose it again, and that set him off, too.

"Oh, hell," he said, trying to catch his breath. "I can't believe I'm laughing about this. I cried for days. We pulled it out of the bag and it was all mashed up and covered with dust—''

And we both promptly lost it again. I couldn't even sit up straight. I just fell over on my side and lay there on the carpet, helpless with hysterics. It's not that I find cruelty to animals amusing, you understand, nor that I have a morbid streak . . . well, maybe I do, who knows? But it was just funny as hell somehow. Aside from which, a hamster's really nothing but a rodent, and you know how cats are about mice. I mean, if God hadn't meant for us to bat 'em around, he wouldn't have made 'em so fucking small and stupid.

There was a knocking at the door, and Solo got up from the couch, wiping his eyes. "Excuse me a minute, will you?" he said, heading for the door.

What happened after that kinda put a damper on the evening. He opened the door, and I heard him say something to someone, and then my ears pricked up as I caught the unmistakable scent of a dog. The dog must have smelled me at about the same time, for the next thing I knew, there was a high-pitched, yipping sort of bark, and the most ridiculous thing I ever saw came barreling around the corner into the living room.

It was one of those small French poodles, with its hair cut in that goofy way that leaves bare patches of skin here and big, fluffy balls of hair there, and it even had a ribbon tied up in the hair on top of its ratty-looking head. But that wasn't the worst part, though it was bad enough. Somebody had actually dyed the stupid thing *pink*.

I don't know if it expected me to arch my back and spit or take off running with a stark, raving terror, but it's kinda hard to get scared by anything that looks so goddamned silly. It came racing up to me, yipping like an Indian, and when I didn't turn tail and run, it dug in and stopped about six inches away from me, all ribbony and pink malevolence, and bared its teeth and started growling.

"Fuck you," I said, and gave it the claws. Just reached out with a quick right and raked it one, right across its wet and shiny little nose.

The damned thing squealed like a pig caught in a meat grinder and beat a hasty retreat, crying out, "Mommy, Mommy!"

Mommy? I felt like I wanted to puke. Being somewhat distracted by the pink avenger, I hadn't noticed the skirt who came in with Solo. She was a real elegant-looking number, dressed in a formfitting, clingy outfit that didn't leave much to the imagination. For that matter, if she'd been wearing a sack, it wouldn't have left much to the imagination. You can't hide a body like that without really working at it.

I have to confess that human bodies don't really do anything for me, but some human females I can find aesthetically appealing. They're usually the ones who have something of the cat about them, the ones with lean, slim bodies and long legs and a sinewy, graceful way of moving. This lady wasn't one of those. This was the kind of babe Hammer would've liked. Voluptuous, with generous, curvaceous hips, small waist, and large breasts that strained at the fabric of her dress. What they call "an hourglass figure." I've noticed that a lot of human males seem to really lose their cookies over female anatomy like that. I don't know what their thing is about breasts. Far as I can see, they're only fat.

"Ohhh, my poor baby!" said the skirt, crouching down to scoop up her fluffy, whimpering, pink thaumagene in her arms. "What did the nasty kitty *do* to my Pinky?"

"The nasty kitty gave Pinky a swat in the kisser," I said, wryly.

She stared at me with loathing while she cradled her trembling pink poodle in her arms, protectively. "You horrible thing!" she said. She glanced at Solo. "What *is* that?" she asked him, in an accusing tone.

"A cat," said Solo.

"I *know* it's a cat," she said, her voice dripping with sarcasm. "What's it *doing* here?"

"Visiting," I said.

She ignored me. "Jay, where did you get that awful beast? Don't tell me you actually went out and *bought* it?"

"Nobody *buys* me, lady. I'm not for sale," I said. "We had a mutual friend in common, if it's any of your business, and he passed on recently. We were just getting together at his request to trade some war stories and remember what a privilege it was to know him. And if that ridiculous-looking dog of yours hadn't gotten in my face, I wouldn't have gotten into his."

She just stared at me with her jaw hanging open while Solo stood there, looking uncomfortable, and then Pinky whined, "The kitty *hurt* me, Mommy!"

"Mommy" turned to Solo and said, "Jay, you're not going to *keep* that mangy beast, are you? I insist you lock it up somewhere! It's scaring Pinky. Look how he's trembling!"

"Hell, lady, if I had to go out in public looking like that, I'd tremble, too," I said.

The look she gave me was pure venom.

"*Jay* . . ."

"You want I should leave the room?" I asked him, remembering that it was, after all, his home.

"No, Gomez," he said. "You stay right there."

"*Jay!*"

"Gomez is my guest, Barbara," Solo said, "and your dog came bursting in here and went after him. Far as I'm concerned, the stupid mutt got what it deserved."

He immediately went up quite a few points in my estimation. But then, I should've known. Any friend of Paulie's was liable to be a stand-up guy.

"*Jay!*" said the skirt, again, in a shocked tone of voice.

"If you can't control your dog, Barbara, then I suggest you keep him on a leash," said Solo. "Gomez is a friend and he's staying."

"Well! Then maybe *I* should leave!" she said, in a huff.

"Maybe you should," said Solo.

She stared at him with disbelief, then gathered her wits and turned angrily and stalked back to the door. Solo held it open for her.

"If you think I'm going to stand for this sort of treatment," she said, icily, "then you are very much mistaken."

"Good night, Barbara," said Solo.

"*Good-bye*, Mr. Solo!"

I think she would have liked to slam the door, only Solo was holding it for her and she had precious, trembling Pinky in her arms. She stalked out angrily and he closed the door behind her.

"Sorry about that," I said. "I didn't mean to spoil anything for you."

Solo simply shrugged. "Oh, you didn't spoil anything," he said. "Barbara lives just down the hall. She moved in a couple of weeks ago. She's divorced and she's been dropping hints that we should get to know each other better, coming by and wanting to borrow coffee or have me open a jar of pickles, all that sort of thing. I hadn't quite figured out a way to brush her off politely, but I guess you just took care of that. She was getting to be a bit of a pest."

"Lot of guys wouldn't mind that kind of pestering," I said.

"I guess not," Solo replied, "but Barbara's not really my type."

"What is?"

He walked over to the desk and picked up a small picture

frame. He carried it over and held it out so I could see it. It was a photograph of a lady with a lot of cat in her. She had short, blond hair worn down to her collar, green eyes, a small and slightly turned up nose, nice cheekbones, and a smile that lit up the world. She was dressed in faded jeans and a man's white shirt, with moccasins on her feet. The photograph had been taken outside, in a park. She was sitting on a swing, with one arm up above her head, holding onto the chain, and her head cocked to one side, resting on the arm. Slim body. Long legs. Nothing like Barbara at all. Just looking at the photograph, I could tell that when she moved, it would be with a lithe and supple grace, natural and unselfconscious. The photograph was signed, "Forever, Lisa."

"Pretty lady," I said.

"My wife," Solo replied.

I was surprised. I hadn't seen any evidence of a woman around the place. And then his next words answered my unspoken question.

"She died about fifteen years ago."

"I'm sorry."

He walked back to the desk slowly, and carefully replaced the picture. It looked like a fairly sturdy frame, but he handled it gently. I didn't think it was because he was afraid of breaking it.

"She was killed in a drive-by shooting," he said. "Stupid. She wasn't the intended target. She just happened to be in the wrong place at the wrong time."

"Did you get the guy who did it?" I asked.

Solo looked down at the floor. "No. They were never caught."

He stood staring out the window for a long moment. I didn't know what to say. There really isn't anything you can say in a situation like that. I'd already said I was sorry, and when you lose someone you care about, sorry just doesn't seem to cut it. I knew how he felt. I'd lost Paulie to a killer, too. Only I got the son of a bitch. I tore his fucking throat out.

"She was only twenty-two," said Solo, staring out the window. He turned around and touched the framed photo on the desk. "We were only married for about six months. Forever didn't last too long."

"And you never married again?" I said.

He shook his head. "I still love her, you know. She's been dead fifteen years, and I still think about her. I've tried dating a few women since then, but . . . it's just not the same. Silly, isn't it?"

Silly was one thing it wasn't. It was romantic to the point of pain. Most people get over something like that in time, but a few never do. I guess when you find something like that, if you're lucky enough to find something so rare, everything else seems like a pale, bloodless substitute in comparison.

"Sounds like you had a hell of a six months," I said. "Some people go through their whole lives and never find anything like that."

"No, I guess they don't," said Solo. "Why don't you tell me about Paul?"

We spent most of the night talking about our old friend. I told him about the Paul Ramirez I had known, the respected Dean of the College of Sorcerers at the University of New Mexico in Santa Fe, and the local bureau chief of the BOT, and he told me about the younger Paulie he remembered, the gifted student warlock whose scholarship had been arranged by Merlin Ambrosius himself, the uncompromising idealist who had no thought of making it in the big-time league of corporate sorcery and who only wanted to learn everything he could, to perfect his art so he could return to his native New Mexico and teach. And he told me about Paulie's broken heart, about how Paulie had met and fallen in love with his sister, a young woman Solo didn't seem to care for very much, and how she'd led him around by the nose because she thought it was amusing until it broke up, he was never quite sure how, only that Paulie took it pretty hard and would never talk about it.

I could've told him what had happened, but I didn't, because as he spoke about it, I realized that I knew who Solo's sister must have been. Paulie had never mentioned her by name, but back when he was in college, he had fallen hard for some girl and done the one thing he had promised himself he'd never do. Paulie had a gift, a very unusual gift he had inherited from his Indian mother. He was a sensitive, a powerful empath who could look into other people's minds and see them as they really were. He had become aware of this ability during his adolescence and, over the years, it had developed and grown stronger. It had caused him a few problems, and he had sworn to himself he'd never use it, not only out of respect for other people's privacy, but out of concern for his own emotional well-being. However, in college, he had met this girl, and he had fallen for her hard, and his resolve had weakened.

He had wanted to look into her mind and discover her fondest desire, so that he could give it to her if it was at all within his power. So he broke his promise to himself and probed her secret soul, and what he found there was a twisted, ugly, bitter thing, the heart of an emotional vampire whose fondest desires were centered on cruelty and decadence and using people up, then hanging them out to dry. That brief contact with her mind had so shaken and repelled him that he never got over it.

For all his powers as an adept, Paulie was a very gentle man and, in some peculiar ways, very naive. He genuinely liked people, and his heart was good. Intellectually, perhaps, he knew that there were sharks out there in life's often murky waters, but to know something on an intellectual level isn't quite the same as having it hit you in the gut. People are a lot like animals, and some of them are just plain bad to the bone. Some of them kill in order to survive, and some kill just because they like it. I've seen both sides of that coin, myself. There were times I killed because I had to, because the alternative would have been to starve, and there were times I killed because it made me feel good, because the thing that I was killing was the type of creature Paulie had encountered, one of those sharks who glide silently through life and feed on pain. A thing that needed killing.

No, I didn't tell Solo what I was thinking about his sister, for I was certain she was one who'd leveled Paulie. Solo seemed to have reached his own conclusions about her, and, besides, he was clearly nothing like her. If he had been, he wouldn't have gotten a lady like Lisa to write "Forever" on her photograph.

I realized, as the night stretched on, that Paulie had been right. Solo was one of the good guys. I wasn't surprised that the flouncy skirt down the hall, with her pink hairball, had wanted to get next to him. He was the kind of guy who'd attract females the way a bright light attracts moths, a guy with a quiet, inner strength who had nothing to prove to himself, and so he didn't bother trying to prove anything to anybody else, either. The kind of guy who knew how to listen in a way that made you know he cared, how to create a space around him that made you feel you were safe, a man's man who didn't come across with any macho bullshit, but with a firm and gentle, paternal sort of strength. Men respect a guy like that, because competition and one-upmanship aren't his priorities, and he's the kind of man you want standing at your shoulder if it hits the fan. And women can't resist such men, because they recognize them instantly for what they are, and they also know, having often learned the hard way, that there aren't many of them around. Somewhere, there was a lady who could give this guy her love and really mean it, and consider herself extremely lucky in the process, but she'd have a hard time getting to him, because he'd already said "forever" to a girl named Lisa, and he meant it.

It happens sometimes in your life that you meet someone and you know in fairly short order that this is friend material, and I don't mean close personal acquaintance, I mean the real thing. I knew it when I met Paulie, and now I realized it with Solo, too. But I wasn't really surprised. The two of them were both cut from the same cloth, and Paulie would never have given me, or Solo, a bum steer. I guess maybe I knew it back there at the cemetery, when I said good-bye to Paulie.

"Well, it's getting late," said Solo, finally, "I need to get some sleep. Feel free to make yourself comfortable any way you like. Is there anything you need?"

"No, I'm easy," I said. "Any couch or chair will do just fine, or I can take the floor, if you don't want me on the furniture."

"Forget it," he said. "Make yourself at home. There's a nice, comfortable sofa bed in the study. If you like, I could pull it out for you."

"Hey, I'm a cat, remember? I don't take up much room. I can just curl up on the cushions. I've had lots worse, you know."

He grinned. "Okay." And then he frowned. "Oh. Something just occurred to me. I . . . uh . . . don't have a litter box."

"No problem," I said. "I know how to use the toilet. Just make sure you leave the lid up and the seat down. I can flush and everything. Thanks for the thought."

Solo smiled. "Sure. Is there anything else I can get you?"

"A bowl of water somewhere out of the way would be nice."

"No problem. I'll leave it on the floor, by the sink."

"Thanks."

"Well . . . good night, Gomez."

"Night, Solo."

He got up, and I heard him running water in the sink to fill up my bowl. I thought about what he'd said back at the cemetery, about how he and Paulie had always called each other by their last names. Now we were doing it. The skirt with the pink poodle had it wrong. He wasn't a Jay. He was definitely a Solo. And, in a lot of ways, so was I. Two solo loners, thrown together by a dead man. Strange way to start a friendship.

Three

SOLO was gone when I woke up in the morning, which took me by surprise. It takes someone pretty light on their feet not to wake up a cat. I made another note about the commissioner. He was obviously more than just some administrative Joe. He knew how to move quietly.

He also moved pretty damned early. I've gotten lazy in my old age, and I don't quite get up at the crack of dawn, but I'm not what you'd call a late sleeper, either. It was 6:00 A.M. and Solo was already out and about. He had left me a dish of milk and a can of tuna by my water bowl in the kitchen. He had also left me a note.

Gomez—

I went for a walk and then I'm going to hit the gym. I'll pick up some stuff on the way back. Should be back around nine.

Solo

Working out first thing in the morning? Well, the guy evidently liked to keep in shape. That was another point in his favor. I liked to keep in fighting trim, myself. It helps you stay spry, and you never know when you might need to call upon the old reserves. I lapped up some milk, then scarfed down the tuna, which killed a couple of minutes, and then I had to figure out what to do for the next three hours or so. Trouble was, there's not much to do all by yourself in a strange apartment. I suppose I could have turned on the boob tube by using the remote unit lying on the coffee table, but there was never much on television I found particularly interesting. I like watching old classic movies from the pre-Collapse days, which they ran every now and then, but only late at night. In the morning, all they seemed to have on were talk shows, and watching the idiots who hosted them always struck me as a hell of a lousy way to start the day.

I thought about doing some reading, but Solo's bookshelves were well above floor level, and while I could've gotten up there and gently pawed a book out, there was no way that I could hold it. It would've fallen to the floor, and I don't treat books that way. Besides, I hadn't asked Solo if it was okay for me to read his books. Some people take things like that for granted, but not me. I try to be polite.

That didn't leave a whole lot for me to do. A lot of cats would've been perfectly content to just curl up somewhere in a nice, sunny, warm spot and lie there listening to their fur grow, but not me. I'm the restless type and never got into the habit. There was a new city out there, waiting for me to discover it. The only problem was, how the hell would I get out of the apartment?

I couldn't exactly reach up and use the doorknob. Aside from which, the door was locked. I couldn't use a window, either, not when I was ten floors up. The sliding glass doors leading out to the balcony were closed, not that it would've done me much good if I could've gotten out there. I began to see certain serious disadvantages to this arrangement. I like to come and go as I please, and what I felt like doing at that moment, more than anything else, was going somewhere. *Anywhere.* I don't like being cooped up, and I was starting to feel closed in. I wanted out so bad, I could taste it.

I sat down for a moment to give the matter some careful consideration. Obviously, I wasn't about to get out on my own, and so I needed help. I thought about it for a few minutes, then went over to Solo's desk, where he had his phone and his computer.

Now I was never what you'd call computer literate, but, fortunately, I didn't really have to be. Most computers nowadays are made with thaumaturgically etched and animated chips, which vary greatly in their degree of sophistication. As usual, you get what you pay for. Just what they're capable of doing depends on how sophisticated the hardware and software is, but then I wasn't looking for anything terribly sophisticated. I didn't expect it to be able to open the front door. However, I did think there was a good chance it knew some phone numbers.

I jumped up on the desk and looked the unit over. It was a Hal 9000, whatever that meant. But the on–off switch was right there in plain sight, so I reached out with my paw and flicked it on. There was a soft pinging sound, and the monitor screen lit up with a nice, cool, blue color. Just a plain, blank, blue screen. That was refreshing. A lot of people go in for cute touches, like faces staring out at them, or nude pinups or what have you.

"Good morning, Solo," it said, which told me that it had a built-in clock, but no video capability that would allow it to see anything. It had a deep, cultured, mellow-sounding voice. Pleasant.

"Good morning," I said.

"You are not Solo. Who are you?"

"I'm a houseguest. Name's Gomez."

"I am not programmed with any information concerning houseguests. Access to this unit is restricted without the proper access code."

"Shit," I said.

"Incorrect code," said the computer.

Damn, I thought. Some computers had personalities that

were all their own and you could reason with them, even have a pleasant conversation, but the ones on the lower end of the scale could be frustratingly simplistic. The damned things were so bloody literal-minded. And then I had a sudden flash of inspiration. I said, "Lisa."

"Access confirmed," said the computer. "How may I assist you, Gomez?"

"Are you programmed with a telephone directory?" I asked.

"Affirmative. Do you wish it displayed?"

"Can you do a search and let me know if a certain number's listed?"

"Affirmative. Which number do you wish me to initiate a search for?"

"How about the building manager?"

"Working. . . ."

A moment later, it had the number, and I asked for the display. Bingo. There was a building manager on the premises, in apartment 1-A, on the ground floor.

"Are you equipped with modem capability?" I asked.

"Affirmative. Do you wish me to dial the number?"

"Yeah, affirmative," I said. "Connect me."

"Working. . . ."

A moment later, I could hear a phone ringing. It was picked up on the fifth ring. A sleepy-sounding voice said, "Logan Towers, can I help you?"

"Sorry to wake you up," I said. "My name is Gomez, and I'm a guest of Mr. Solo's up in 10-C. Mr. Solo's out, and I seem to be having a problem with the door. I can't get it open. I'd sure appreciate it if you could come up and see if you can open it for me."

"The door won't open?"

"No, I can't open it."

"What'd you say your name was again?"

"Gomez. In 10-C."

He gave out a weary groan. "Okay, give me a minute, I'll be right up."

"Thanks. I appreciate it."

I had the computer disconnect, and then I shut it down, feeling very pleased with myself. The building manager would now come up and let me out of the apartment. There was no question but that I would appreciate it—the question was, would he? Somehow, I didn't think so. Don't ask me why, but it occurred to me that he might take exception to being dragged out of bed at about 6:00 A.M. to go upstairs and let a cat out of an apartment. I figured I'd better prepare myself for one rather irate customer.

He didn't take very long. He was up in only a few minutes, knocking at the door.

"Mr. Gomez?" The voice sounded fairly young.

"Yeah, that's right," I called out.

"Building manager, Mr. Gomez. The door seems to be locked."

"Yeah, I know. I can't get it open from in here. Try using your passkey."

I heard the key inserted into the lock, and then I heard it turn. The door opened and the guy stuck his head in. He was younger than I'd thought, about college age, with a thick shock of blond hair that hung over his forehead and down to his collar in the back, and wire-rimmed glasses. He had thrown on a black and gold University of Colorado sweat shirt and a pair of faded jeans. His bare feet were tucked into an old, worn pair of running shoes.

"There doesn't seem to be anything wrong with—" and then he noticed me sitting back on my haunches on the floor and his eyes glanced past me for a moment. "Mr. Gomez?"

"Down here, kid."

He looked at me and his eyes opened wide. "*You're* Mr. Gomez?"

"We can dispense with the *mister* part," I said. "I don't stand on formality. Look, I can see how you'd be ticked off and I don't blame you, but I couldn't reach the doorknob, much less turn it, and I was starting to get a little stir-crazy in here. I'm not used to living in apartments. There was no other way I could get out. Believe me, if there was, I wouldn't have bothered you.''

He snorted with amusement and made a little dismissive motion with his hand. ''Ah, it's all right. I've got an early class today, anyway. My alarm would've gone off in another hour. One less hour of sleep won't kill me.''

''Well, that's awful damned decent of you,'' I replied, somewhat taken aback. I'd frankly expected the guy to get angry. And like I said, I wouldn't have blamed him one bit. ''To be honest, I didn't expect you to be so understanding.''

''What the hell, animals have rights, too,'' he said. ''Oh, my name's Rick, by the way. Rick Daniels.''

''It's a pleasure, Rick,'' I said, as we walked out of the apartment and he closed and locked the door behind us. ''I'm Catseye Gomez. Just Gomez, to my friends.''

''Catseye?''

''Yeah. It's on account of the turquoise eyeball.''

''I noticed that. It's certainly different.''

''Yeah, well, so am I.''

He grinned. ''I noticed that, too.'' We'd come up to the elevator and he pushed the call button. He pointed to a heavy ashtray and waste receptacle standing beneath the call buttons, one of those things that look a bit like heavy stone planters and have a sand tray on top. ''I got building management to spring for some of these things, so now there's one on every floor. You can jump up on it and then you can reach the buttons.''

''Very thoughtful,'' I said. ''Thank you.''

He shrugged. ''I actually did it for the other thaumagenes in the building, only I didn't tell management that. If I had, they probably wouldn't have gone for it. Not that many of the tenants here smoke, but a few of them do have small thaumagenes. See, there's a limited pets policy here. Certain thaumagenes are allowed, but no large ones, you know, like dobras, and no ordinary animals, except for tropical fish and parakeets and like that.''

The elevator arrived and we stepped in. The electronic-sounding voice said, ''Floor, please.''

''Three,'' said Rick.

The voice said, ''Thank you,'' and the door closed.

I gave Rick a questioning glance. ''Three?''

He smiled. ''There's someone I think you should meet,'' he said.

''At this hour?''

''She'll be up,'' said Rick. ''Oh, and while we're at it, let's get your voice print done.''

''My voice print?''

He held up a finger, telling me to wait. ''Elevator, voice print registration, guest category, indefinite.''

''One moment . . . standing by.''

He looked at me and said, ''Just say your name and the apartment number when I say record, okay?''

''Okay.''

''Record,'' said Rick.

I said, ''Catseye Gomez, apartment 10-C.''

''Catseye Gomez, apartment 10-C, guest status, indefinite,'' the elevator said. ''Awaiting confirmation.''

''Confirm,'' said Rick.

''Voice print recorded and confirmed,'' the elevator said. The doors slid open and it added, ''Third floor.''

We stepped out. ''Now your voice print is registered with the security system,'' Rick explained. ''Ordinarily, your host would do that, but I guess Mr. Solo didn't think of it. You can tell him I took care of it.''

''Thanks,'' I said. ''What happens if someone gets on who isn't registered?''

''Well, ordinarily, if a tenant is bringing a guest in, they'll do the registration. It can be for anywhere from twenty-four hours, after which it's canceled automatically, to indefinite status, the way we just recorded you. That way, it stays active until either Mr. Solo or I cancel it. If someone gets on who isn't registered, then the elevator automatically checks with the security desk, where somebody's always on duty. If the desk okays it, there's no problem. Otherwise, the elevator takes the occupant down to the basement and holds them there until either the police or security arrives."

"Impressive," I said. "Ever have any mistakes?"

"Just once or twice," said Rick. "One time, they had a problem down at the power plant. Apparently, the engineer adept had been working overtime and allowed the maintenance spell to slip a bit, which caused a temporary brownout. One of our tenants got stuck for a few minutes, but then the emergency thaumaturgic generator kicked in. It's a backup system that stores enough power to get us through about twelve hours. Another time, one of our tenants had a bad case of laryngitis, and the system didn't recognize his voice. The elevator took him to the basement and he had to wait a few minutes till security arrived, but fortunately he had a sense of humor about it. We're actually set up pretty well here. The tenants like the added security features. It makes them feel safe."

We stopped outside apartment 3-E, at the end of the hall, and Rick knocked at the door. I noticed it had one of those small pet doors built into it.

A muffled voice on the other side said, "Who is it?"

"It's Rick, Princess. Got someone I think you should meet."

"Come on in, Rick."

Rick used his passkey to open the door. "Hey, Princess. Want you to meet a new friend of mine. This is Catseye Gomez. He's staying with Mr. Solo up in 10-C."

My one good eye met a pair of cat pupils floating in twin pools of gold that seemed to suck me in. I felt a low growl start in my throat that had nothing to do with anger, and I fought it down before it came out in a mating yowl that would have made a tom my age look like a complete idiot. Princess was royalty, all right. A young and regal-looking calico with enough style and self-possession to enrapture an entire alleyful of stalking toms. I wasn't exactly a young prowler anymore and, while I've done more than my share of backyard serenading in my day, it had been a long time since a sexy little feline got to me that way. This one had it all, in spades, and it hit me the moment I came walking through that door.

I felt my claws digging into the carpet, and all my muscles tensed. I tried to hide the involuntary reaction, but I wasn't too successful, because she picked up on it at once, and I thought I caught a faint glint of amusement in those lambent, golden eyes.

"Catseye Gomez, eh?" she said, in a lilting voice that was pure music to my ears. "That's an unusual name."

"I'm an unusual guy," I said.

"I can see that," she replied, giving me the slow, critical once-over.

I could guess what she was thinking. I didn't look like your typical, pampered, domestic thaumagene. I looked more like what I was, an old scrapper of an alley cat, a bit chewed up around the edges and getting slightly long in the tooth. Each scar, however, was a badge of honor, and I wore them proudly. Especially ole Betsy, my turquoise eyeball. I saw her looking at it. They all do. It's striking and unusual and it makes me look dashing and romantic as all hell. I gave her a wink with it. She winked back and my tail started to twitch.

"Well, I'll leave you two to get acquainted," Rick said. "I've got to go and get ready for class."

"Thanks for the help, Rick," I said.

"Don't mention it. Oh, and if you want to get a little cat door like that for your place, have Mr. Solo give me a call. I've got a couple of doors in storage that have them."

"I'll ask him about it. Thanks again."

"Anytime. See you around."

He closed the door behind him.

"Nice fella," I said.

"Rick? Yes, he's very nice. Come in and make yourself at home."

I followed Princess into the living room, watching that supple, sensuous walk as she preceded me. She knew I was watching, too, and she gave her tail a teasing little flick for my benefit.

I took a quick glance around the place. It was very stylish, and also very feminine. A single woman's apartment, no question about it. It was all done in muted pastels, very soft and inviting, and very balanced. Lot of warm earth tones, indirect lighting, some nice abstract oils on the walls. The paintings were not your typical artsy nonsense, the sort of modular, glue-a-bunch-of-garbage-on-a-canvas crap you see in lots of galleries and office buildings these days, but very cool and flowing sorts of pieces, with a lot of swirling movement to them, suggesting waves and ocean currents. It was the sort of art that seemed to draw you in and grow on you, relaxing you the more you looked at it. Very tasteful.

There was a state-of-the-art home entertainment system, as well, built into a large and attractive cabinet. The radio was on, tuned to a local FM station. One of those all-news, all-talk formats, morning news alternating with interviews and features. The woman who was on the air had one of those brisk, clear, well-modulated voices that sound professional and friendly at the same time. The volume was turned down low enough to listen to, yet not be obtrusive.

Princess jumped up onto the couch and stretched out languidly. I took the chair, keeping the glass coffee table between us. It wasn't that I didn't trust myself, but I figured that every tom who saw her probably came on like gangbusters, and with a classy kitty like this a fella ought to take his time.

She cocked her head at me, noticing that I was purposely keeping a polite distance, and she seemed to like that. She gave me an added little stretch and then settled herself down, giving me an unsettlingly direct gaze with those incredible golden eyes.

"Remind me to be especially nice to Rick," I said.

They say that cats can't smile. They're wrong. There's a certain kind of look cats get when they're especially contented or feeling at peace with the world and very pleased with themselves. There's a slight tightening of the muscles around the mouth—which if you look closely, actually resembles a Mona Lisa sort of smile—and a slight squinting of the eyes. It doesn't sound like much, but then, what's to describe about a human smile? It's more than just a stretching of the lips. You can do all sorts of little things with your facial muscles, but a genuine smile comes from somewhere inside and somehow manages to shine out through the eyes, which are the windows of the soul. Maybe that's why cats squint a little when they smile. We're very private creatures.

"Rick was merely being a dutiful recruiter," she said.

"Recruiter?" I said, somewhat taken aback.

"He's a fellow activist," said Princess. "That's why he might have seemed a bit more considerate than your average human. He really loves animals and he's an ERA member."

She didn't say "era," but spelled it out, letter by letter.

"ERA?" I said. "What's that?"

"Equal Rights for Animals," Princess replied. "You mean you never heard of us before?"

"I'm from out of town," I said. "Santa Fe, New Mexico."

"Ah. Well, we've been trying to start chapters in several other cities," Princess said, "but we're not quite organized enough yet."

"We?"

"I'm one of the founders," Princess said. "Susan and I started ERA together, along with some of our friends. It's still pretty much a grass-roots effort, but we're starting to gain some real recognition."

"Susan?"

"Susan Jacobs. My human friend. She lives here. That's her on the radio right now."

"I see." That explained why Rick had no reservations about knocking on the door at a little after 6:00 A.M. Morning radio personalities get up to go to work before the crack of dawn. "What exactly is it you're trying to accomplish?"

"Pretty much what our name implies," Princess replied. "We want animals to be treated ethically, to be granted civil rights, and we're lobbying for citizenship for thaumagenes."

"Citizenship?"

"Absolutely," Princess said. "And why not? Why should we be treated as inferiors? We think, we reason, we communicate, and we're literate. We are intelligent beings."

"Have you met the little pink hairball who lives upstairs?" I asked.

She gave a little snort of disgust. "Pinky is a spoiled and pampered case of arrested development. A classic example of conditioned subservience and just the sort of thing we're fighting against. The point is that if Pinky were human and not a thaumagene, even with his stunted personality intact, he would still have rights, legally defined civil rights, while thaumagenes have none. We are intelligent, reasoning, feeling beings, and yet we are treated as property. Bought and sold on the marketplace, frequently abandoned, often abused, with no recourse to the courts, no rights under the law whatsoever. We're no better than slaves, Gomez. Your human owner can do anything he wants with you and you've got no say about it whatsoever."

"Whoa, Princess, back up a bit," I said. "First of all, I'm nobody's slave. I haven't got a human owner. Never did."

"Never?"

"Nope. Never."

"What about Mr. Solo? Isn't he your owner?"

"Nope. He's an old friend of the guy I used to share digs with in Santa Fe. I'm only visiting."

"Well, what about this man in Santa Fe?"

"Paulie? He wasn't my owner, anymore than I was his pet. We were just friends, see? He picked me up and took me home once after I'd gotten chewed up pretty badly in a fight. He nursed me back to health and we became close friends. I just sort of hung around, but I carried my weight, sister, and I was free to come and go as I pleased, anytime. Before that, I lived on the streets and fended for myself. And I don't mind saying I did a pretty fair job of it. The way I see it, any animal that doesn't like its circumstances is free to change things. It's a hard life out there, which is why most of them don't go for it, but if freedom is something that's important to you, then you ante up and take your chances."

"What about the animals that are kept locked up inside, or the ones who are kept in cages?" she asked.

"Well, that's how I started out, kitten, but I made a break for it as soon as I was old enough to realize there was another way. Don't get me wrong, it's not that I'm unsympathetic to your views, but if you ask me, I think you've bitten off a whole lot more than you can chew."

"Really? What makes you think so?" she asked, defensively.

"Hell, kitten, I've been around and I know people. I know animals, as well. You take a dog like that silly mutt upstairs. How long do you think a creature like that would last out on its own? I'd give it a day or two, at most. I've known animals with human owners and I've known animals who lived out on the streets and, believe me, the ones with people to take care of them are a lot better off. What's more, most of the cats I knew out on the streets would trade places with them in a hot second, except for a few hardcases like myself. Aside from that, what you're talking about would require some pretty drastic changes in society and, frankly, I can't see humans sitting still for it.

"Can you see some dog taking its owner to court because it got smacked with a newspaper for going doo-doo on the rug?" I asked her. "No way, baby, it's nuts. Besides, where would you draw the line? Would you grant civil rights to all animals, or only to some and exclude others? Would you just grant them to thaumagenes, because we're intelligent and ordinary animals are stupid? Let me tell you something, I've known plenty of ordinary alley cats who had a lot more street smarts than most thaumagenes I've run across, even if they couldn't speak the human lingo or read a paper. What about them? Or don't they count? And if you grant civil rights to *all* animals, then what are you going to do about the people who eat meat? Are they suddenly going to become guilty of murder? Cannibalism? You going to pass a law to make all humans vegetarians? It just ain't natural. Look at human teeth. Humans evolved to eat meat. And so, for that matter, did most animals. You ever eat a mouse? Maybe kill a bird?"

She shuddered. "Of course not! That's absolutely vile."

"I didn't think so. But that's because you've got your 'human friend' to buy you a nice brand of cat food, right? And what do you think *that's* made of? I've got news for you, kitten. If you ever had to go hungry, perish the thought, you'd pounce on the first mouse or sparrow you could get your pretty little claws into and you'd relish the taste of its hot blood spurting down your throat."

"Stop it!" she said. "I don't want to hear that kind of talk! It's disgusting!"

"Yeah, well, it's no more disgusting than you scarfing down your canned chicken and liver. The truth isn't always pleasant to our sensibilities."

It occurred to me that maybe I was being a bit harsh with her. After all, she'd led a pretty sheltered life and couldn't really be blamed for not knowing the score. She was one fine feline, you could bet on that, but all the class and sex appeal in the world couldn't make up for lack of experience, the kind of experience you only get when you have to look the cold, dark, unfriendly world smack in the face and play the cards you're dealt without whining about it.

"Look," I said, "I'm not trying to put you down. I think you're motivated by the best intentions, but I just don't think you've really thought it through."

"There are a lot of thaumagenes and even a good number of humans among our membership who'd disagree with you," she said, stiffly. "We've gotten a lot of response from Susan's radio spots. A lot more than we thought we'd get. And most of it has been very positive, I'll have you know."

"Most of it?"

"Yes, most of it."

"Meaning there's been some negative response," I said.

"That's to be expected," she replied. "Anytime you introduce proposals for profound social change, there are always going to be those who resist, and support the status quo."

"That's right, kiddo. And most of them aren't going to bother getting in touch with you. For every negative response you got, there's probably at least a hundred or a thousand out there who simply wrote the whole thing off as a crackpot idea, not to be taken seriously. Oh, you'll hear from the hardcore opposition, the ones who are offended or threatened by what you're proposing, or the flakes who like to blow off steam, but they only represent the minority. You'll hear from the majority at the ballot box, assuming you ever get that far with it. Frankly, I wouldn't hold my breath."

"That's a pretty defeatist attitude," she said. "You struck me as a fighter."

"I am that, kitten, but I try to pick my battles. Tilting at windmills ain't my style."

"So you're satisfied to remain oppressed, is that what you're telling me?"

"I'm not telling you anything of the sort," I said. "I've

never considered myself oppressed. I've lived my life the way I chose to live it and I've got no regrets. If I had it to do all over again, I'd do it exactly the same way. I'm sorry if I'm not demonstrating the proper enthusiasm, but I'm afraid I wouldn't make a very good recruit for your group.''

"I see," she said. "So you've got what you want and screw everybody else, is that it?"

"You know, it really is too bad," I said. "You're a very classy feline, kitten. I think I might have enjoyed getting to know you, but you're spoiled and your political agenda keeps getting in the way. I don't agree with you about this one thing, so based on that, you've made up your mind that you already know everything you need to know about me. If I'd gotten all excited about your ERA group, that would've made me useful. But I don't see it your way, so that makes me wrong, and if you can't convince me of the error of my thinking, then you've got no use for me. I don't think that's a very practical way to look at things. It limits your options and gives you a bad case of tunnel vision. I'm not really interested in arguing with you, Princess, or in trying to convince you that I'm right. You'll find out for yourself. But when you go through life with your kind of attitude, it pretty much guarantees that you're not going to learn much. And if you do learn anything, it's going to come the hard way. Like I said, it really is too bad.''

I hopped down to the floor and headed for the door. I paused briefly to turn around and take one more look at her, all proud and haughty and indignant, and beautiful as hell. Yeah, it definitely was too bad.

"Good-bye, kitten. And I really wish you well, despite what you may think."

"Good-bye, Gomez," she said, frostily.

Yeah, no winks this time. Definite coolness there. I'd rained on her parade and been pretty graceless about it, too. Well, I guess I'm just not a very graceful kind of cat. I stood there, feeling the temperature drop, and wondered

what the hell I was doing in a place like this, the ritzy
luxury apartment of some honey-toned, big-city broadcaster
and her politically active feline. It was crazy. I didn't belong
here. So I left, thinking about the way things might have
been.

I went through the little cat door and trotted down the hall
to the elevator. I jumped up on the ashtray thing, stretched
up against the wall, and pushed the call button. Yeah, too
bad. The first thing I'd seen in Denver that I liked and she
turned out to be a fruitcake.

I thought about some of the things she'd said while I
waited for the elevator, and I had to admit that her position
was not entirely without merit. Take what happened earlier
that morning. I'd have been stuck in that apartment if I
hadn't figured out a way to call the building manager and
have him come up and let me out. And if Rick hadn't been
thoughtful enough to put those ashtray things beneath the
call buttons, I wouldn't have been able to use the elevator,
either.

The elevator arrived and I got in. "Floor, please."

"Lobby," I said.

"Thank you, Mr. Gomez."

The doors slid shut and the elevator started to descend.
Needless to say, just getting into the elevator would've been
only half the problem if it had had regular floor buttons I
couldn't reach, instead of a fancy, voice-response computer.
No question about it, the human world was not set up very
well for animals, but that's because it was the human world.

Animals were never meant to live in cities, they were
meant to live in the wild. An old street survivor like me
could probably handle it, but most domestic animals couldn't,
thaumagenes included. We were an artificial species, one
that would never have existed if humans hadn't created us
for their own amusement. However, Princess had a point.
Just because humans had created us did not necessarily
mean were were not entitled to *some* rights. I guess I could

see certain laws against abuse of animals, for instance, just as there were laws against child abuse. Just because you created something that was a living thing did not give you the right to mistreat it.

Hell, even if you were breeding animals for food, there was no reason not to treat them humanely, and then butcher them as painlessly as possible. It was the same basic ethic followed by the hunter. If you hunt for food, then you do your best to achieve a clean kill. You don't simply wound your prey and then leave it to suffer because it's too much work to follow the blood trail.

In my younger days, I'd batted around my share of mice before I killed them, but while I may still joke occasionally about things like that, these days, that's as far as it goes. Being on the receiving end of that kind of treatment, as I'd been on several occasions when I'd had a few close calls, had changed my outlook. Yeah, I was still a predator, as were humans, though many of them didn't like to admit it, but I no longer tortured my food. I remembered how Paulie had given up on eating veal when he found how the calves were raised, locked up all the time in stalls that were too small to allow for any movement and kept in darkness all the time.

The point is, we all make choices, but if you're going to stand on principle, then you've gotta follow through. Some people get all upset when they see some skirt wearing a fur coat, and so they get together for a protest at the local furrier, pounding the pavement with their shoe leather. Holding up their pants with leather belts. And then sending someone out for a sack of hamburgers. Frankly, I don't see the difference between someone who packs a shotgun in the field to shoot some quail and someone who picks up a package of chicken breasts at the local supermarket. I'm a predator, a killer, and I make no bones about it. If it really bothered me, then I could make a choice to change and learn how to eat seaweed or something, but if I let someone else do my killing and package my food for me in a convenient, nonbloody form, then I'd only be a hypocrite.

For all I knew, maybe Princess derived her nourishment exclusively from soybean kibble, but she looked more like the gourmet cat food type to me. And *citizenship* for thaumagenes? That had to be the silliest idea I'd ever heard. Maybe I should've asked her if we'd be expected to pay taxes once we'd been granted citizenship. Or go out and get jobs and social security numbers. Maybe put up our own candidates to run for office. How about a *real* dark-horse candidate? Hell, humans had designed us so we'd talk to them and help them fill the lonely hours that stretch out in the night. A sympathetic ear to listen when there's no one else to care, a nice, warm, furry thing that could curl up beside you and provide a little instant, nonthreatening love. But just because we'd been given the ability to communicate with humans didn't mean they wanted us to *be* human, or be on an equal footing with them.

I got off at the lobby. There was a new guy at the security desk. I went up and introduced myself, then asked if he'd mind opening the front door for me and giving a message to Solo that I'd gone out for a while. Andy said he wouldn't mind at all, and he bent down to scratch me behind the ears. I never did like being scratched or stroked, especially by people I didn't know, but I figured what the hell, the guy was being nice and it didn't cost me anything. I wondered how Princess would feel about that sort of treatment. Would she purr and rub herself up against the guy's legs, or would her political correctness interpret the gesture as harassment?

I went out into the street and stood there, feeling very small surrounded by all the tall buildings of downtown Denver. People were beginning to fill the sidewalks as they bustled off to work. The city was starting to come awake. I had a feeling it was going to be a long day.

Four

YOU can't explore much of a city in a only a few hours, and certainly not on foot, but you can get some idea of its pulse. Take Santa Fe, for instance. Start downtown, at the plaza, and just walk around awhile, in no particular direction. You won't see any tall buildings, and almost everywhere you look, you'll see the graceful look of adobe-style architecture. Warm earth tones all around, mocha brown, café au lait, and terra-cotta, tastefully trimmed with cool blues and greens, with exposed *vigas* and columned *portillas*.

You'll see the people, and the way they move, the way they dress. No one's in a particular hurry. You'll see your trendy fashion statements, such as studded leather, Renaissance Punk, and fantasy Nouveau Medieval, but the Southerwestern style predominates. Women still dress in graceful flowing prairie skirts, and lace-trimmed blouses, or soft, drapey riding-style dresses, vests, boots, and Indian jewelry. Many of the men still wear jeans and Stetsons, western boots, and big silver buckles on their belts. You'll see a lot of personal expression in the styles, and the shops and galleries will tell you that this is a town that takes its art seriously. The atmosphere is laid back and mellow, the

walks are brick, the bougainvillea perfumes the air. Chances
are you'll want to stay awhile.

Denver, on the other hand, marched to a very different
beat. The city seemed anything but relaxed. There wasn't
really any overwhelming sense of urgency, but there was a
definite feeling of directed purpose. Women on the sidewalks on their way to work wore business clothes with
running shoes, getting in some fitness training on the way to
the office, where they'd probably slip the shoes back in their
bags and change into high heels. Men wore suits and
carried attaché cases and walked with an unhurried, yet
brisk stride. Drivers conducted business on their car
phones. Traffic was still light, but there were a lot more
vehicles than you'd find in Santa Fe.

I wound up on something the sign called the Cherry
Creek bike path, which looked like little more than a huge
drainage ditch at first glance, sunk down below street level
smack in the center of Speer Boulevard, with one-way
traffic flanking it on each side. However, on closer examina-
tion, it turned out to be an actual creek, only one managed
by city planning. Gently sloping concrete sidewalks that
bicyclists could coast down led to the paved path, which ran
alongside the creek between concrete walls that had been
painted with graffiti. The creek babbled softly along a
streambed that was bordered with large, square-cut, unfin-
ished stone blocks. There was a narrow grass strip separat-
ing the paved path from the stream, and the bicyclists,
joggers, and walkers moved briskly and seriously along the
path, beneath the overpasses. Collisions between the pedestrians and the bicycles were avoided by the bicyclists shouting
out, "On your left!" as they approached from behind, and
the pedestrians obligingly veered to their right to allow the
faster-moving traffic to pass. Everyone seemed very earnest
about their fitness. Brightly colored, aerodynamic Lycra
tights abounded, and the equipment all looked very racy and
expensive.

I strolled along the pathway for a short while, then decided I was taking my life into my hands by being down there among all those fast-moving bicycles and ground pounders, so I went back up to the street, where the morning rush hour was beginning and the ragged homeless people ambled down the sidewalks, talking to themselves and carrying sacks which held their pickings from the dumpsters. I headed back downtown and stopped at the Sixteenth Street Mall, which ran through downtown Denver like any other street, only it was closed to traffic. Small shuttle buses skimmed silently above the graveled causeways on either side of the wide median strip, which was paved and filled with well-tended little gardens and comfortable park benches. At this early hour, no one was lingering, so I picked one of the empty benches and made myself a perch, so I could watch the parade pass by.

Someone had left a newspaper on the bench and I quickly skimmed it, carefully turning the pages with my paw. In many ways, things had come full circle. There was an article about the rebuilding of the Aladdin Theatre, complete with a sketch of how the structure would look when it was finished, side by side with a photograph of the way the place had looked just before it had been torn down back in the 1980s. It was sort of strange. Santa Fe had never really changed that much, though it had grown some, but in other cities, in the days prior to the Collapse, there had been bursts of building that saw the demolishing of old, historic structures to make room for architectural monstrosities that looked as if they'd been designed by some demented kid let loose with a set of Lego blocks. Tear down the old and make room for the fashionable new. But fashions change, and I guess the Aladdin was a case in point.

Judging by the old photograph, the original Aladdin Theatre had been quite a landmark, a wonderful example of American kitsch, built to look like a cross between a Turkish mosque and some mad sultan's palace. I guess it hadn't fit in with the grand visions of the urban planners back in the late twentieth century. It wasn't square and blocky, and you couldn't cover it with fancy, reflective, tinted glass. So out came the wrecker's ball and down it went. Now, with the pre-Collapse nostalgia craze, they were putting it back up again, exactly the way it had once been.

Things like that seemed to be happening all over the country. In New York City, they were tearing down glass-slabbed office buildings and replacing them with stately brownstones. They were also replacing the passenger hover-crafts with updated replicas of the old Staten Island ferry-boats. In Chicago, they were spending tons of money to reconstruct the elevated trains. The latest style in homebuilding was Retro-Victorian, and miniature stone castles were making a big comeback among the monied set. It was as if the whole country had become obsessed with turning back the clock, trying to recapture the spirit of the good old days, before everything had started to fall apart, and to pretend that the Collapse had never happened. Progress had brought about the whole unholy mess, so now everyone wanted to regress. But despite the new, spiritual nature consciousness and historical recreationism, there was no going back to the way things were before.

The union of magic and technology had brought about all sorts of strange developments, not the least of which were creatures like myself. Computers had learned to talk long before animals were bred to speak, but now they were truly "magic boxes," encased in a new type of polymer produced by alchemy and hardwired with magically animated chips that made them, in a sense, a sentient lifeform. (And it boggled the mind to think of what might happen if *they* started insisting on their civil rights, as well.) Right there on the mall, in front of me, between a bookstore and a boutique, there was an alchemist's shop where one could purchase herbs and charms and potions guaranteed to do everything from curing your arthritis to enhancing your sexual performance. And only a short distance away, at the University of Colorado, students who had demonstrated an aptitude for magic were busy taking "pre-thaum" courses along with their electives in the hopes of getting into grad school and becoming warlocks, which was the term applied to students in the advanced-degree programs of the College of Sorcerers.

I watched some of the young future adepts pass by, laughing and joking with each other on their way to school, dressed in faded jeans and colorful, high-topped athletic shoes and short, brown warlocks' cassocks. They were already wearing their hair long, as was the fashion among most adepts, just as many sorcerers wore robes in colors and patterns they adopted as their own personal trademark. Merlin himself had given up that look when he became a university administrator. He had cut his hair and trimmed his beard and taken to wearing tweed sport coats, button-down shirts, and flannel slacks. However, the romantic tradition of the sorcerer meant billowing robes and long, flowing hair, so that had become the style, and it had stuck. It also had given birth to Nouveau Medieval haute couture, which in turn had influenced the rest of the fashion industry. Now, almost every style of dress, from business suits to casual wear, was tinged with a medieval sort of flavor.

Men's business suits had simple, clerical-style tunics paired with light, form-fitting breeches; girdle-style, ornamental belts; three-quarter-length cloaks, and short, soft, low-heeled boots. Some women chose this style as well, or went for the softer, more traditionally feminine look of clinging, ankle- or calf-length gowns, while others paired loose, riding-style skirts and boots with short, embroidered doublets and coat-hardies. In recent years, the unisex Neo-Edwardian style had arrived from Europe, with a more well-tailored look composed of frock coats and narrow, stovepipe trousers, ruffled or lace jabots, lace trim at the sleeves, and wide, high collars and lapels, worn with long, caped coats and accessorized with amulets and charms and velvet gloves or a profusion of rings and bracelets.

Young people, of course, adopted their own style, and in keeping with the pre-Collapse nostalgia craze, Renaissance Punk was born. No one seemed to know exactly where it started or how, but it came with its own swaggering philosophy of nihilism and musical group apostles, that is, if you want to call that sort of noise music. Black leather was the uniform, elaborately studded and trimmed with chains and spikes. Tights or skin-fitting breeches, knee-high or above-the-knee boots, gauntlets, studded wristbands, white dueling shirts with laces at the neck, chain-mail vests, and head scarves or long, piratical bandannas completed the look. They called themselves "Rippers," a name derived from the initials of their movement. At least, they claimed it was a movement. Just exactly what it was they were moving toward was anybody's guess. I didn't see any of them around the mall this morning, but that was no surprise. The Rippers were a night breed.

As I sat and watched the people flowing past me, the crowds growing thicker as the morning drew on, I began to understand the attraction of big cities. It was, more than anything else, the people. The ebb and flow of humanity. Humans were really no different from many animals in that respect. They, too, had a herding instinct. Most of them seemed to find comfort and security in being among large numbers of their fellow creatures. Given that, it was ironic how few of them managed to connect.

My train of thought was abruptly interrupted by a voice at my side that said, "Well, and whose cute little kitty are you?"

I turned my head, narrowing my eyes and feeling the fur on my back starting to bristle. I've been called a lot of things, but "cute little kitty" has never been one of my favorites. I bared my fangs and she froze, stopping her hand halfway from where she'd started to reach out to stroke me.

I saw the expression on her face change from that "Oh-how-adorable" look women get when they see a nice little puttytat, to one of caution. I guess up close, where she could see my battle scars, I didn't look quite as cute as she had thought.

She was dressed in the dark blue uniform of the Denver Police Department. She had on high boots and riding breeches, a black leather jacket, and a white helmet with a gold shield painted on it. Her scooter was parked a short distance behind her.

"Something I can do for you, officer?" I asked, testily.

"I just thought you might be lost or something," she said.

"So you stopped to see if I needed any help getting down out of the tree?" I asked.

She grinned, and my annoyance dissipated instantly. A smile like that and you'll sit still for an entire sheaf of speeding tickets. She took off her mirrored glasses and I saw a pair of sparkling blue-gray eyes that would've stopped any perpetrator dead in his tracks. I glanced at her name tag. Officer Sharp. She sure as hell was. Tall, slim, leggy, dark-haired, and drop-dead gorgeous. About twenty-eight or -nine, I guessed. A lady with a lot of cat in her, no doubt about it.

"Something like that," she replied. "Mind if I sit down?"

"Not a bit."

She took a seat on the bench beside me and stretched out those long, booted legs, crossed them at the ankles, and stuck her hands into the pockets of her leather.

"I notice you're not wearing a collar or a tag."

"That against the law?"

"No. I was just wondering if you belong to anyone," she said.

"Matter of fact, no. Why do you ask?"

She shrugged. "Curiosity."

"Curiosity killed the cat," I said.

She grinned again. It was amazing. With her uniform, boots, and helmet and those mirrored shades, she looked hard as nails and authoritarian as hell, but when she smiled like that, her whole face lit up.

"Okay," she said. "The truth is you look as if you've had some rough treatment."

"And?"

"And I was wondering if you'd been abused," she finished.

"What if I was?"

"Then your owner and I would've had ourselves a little talk," she said.

"I don't think there's much you would've been able to do, legally," I said.

"Maybe not," she admitted. "But I'll betcha if I looked at his or her vehicle real close, I could probably find all sorts of little violations. And that would only be for starters."

"Well, I appreciate the thought," I said, "but the fact is, I never had an owner who abused me. Never had an owner, period. I grew up on the streets and backing down never quite got to be a habit."

"How did a thaumagene wind up living on the streets?" she asked.

"Ran away when I was just a kitten," I told her. "I couldn't stand being locked up, or sitting in a window and making cute every time some skirt walked by, in the hope someone would fall in love and buy me. That struck me as pathetic. So I figured out how to slip the catch on my cubicle and struck out on my own."

"And you've been out here on the streets ever since?" she asked, with surprise.

"Not here," I said. "In Santa Fe."

She raised her eyebrows. "That's about an an eight-hour drive," she said. "How did you wind up in Denver?"

"It's long story, Officer Sharp."

"Karen," she said. "You have a name?"

"It's Gomez. Catseye Gomez."

"Catseye Gomez," she repeated, and smiled that thousand-watt smile again. "It fits you. So, tell me your long story, Gomez. I've got some time."

I gave her an abbreviated version. I left out the part about my encounter with the necromancer, because it would've taken too long to explain and there were things about that case that were better off not being public knowledge. I only said that Paulie had fallen ill and died, then finished up with how I wound up in Denver with Solo.

"Police Commissioner Solo?" she asked.

"Yeah," I said. "You know him?"

"Not personally," she replied, "but of course every cop in the department knows who the commissioner is, and he's very well known in this town."

"How's that?" I asked.

"Well, his father was Congressman Solo, and he himself worked as an assistant district attorney, then served two terms as D.A. before he was appointed police commissioner."

"He hadn't mentioned any of that," I said, with some surprise. "I'd somehow gotten the idea he worked his way up through the rank and file of the cops. Guess I assumed that when he said he took a degree in criminology."

"And one from Harvard Law," said Karen.

"Hmm. Sounds like he's a pretty big wheel in this town. But wouldn't police commissioner ordinarily be considered a step down from district attorney?"

"I see you know something about city politics," said Karen, with a smile.

"I read the papers."

She grinned again. I could tell she was enjoying this conversation. I was having a pretty good time, myself.

"Well, there was some talk about getting him to run for mayor," she said, "but apparently he wasn't interested. He wanted to stay in law enforcement. Word is he's still carrying a torch for his wife, who was killed in a shooting about ten or fifteen years ago.''

"Yeah," I said, "I know about that."

She looked at me with interest. "Is it true? That he's still carrying a torch for her, I mean.''

"Yeah, I'd say it's true. Why?''

She shook her head. "No reason. Not that it's any of my business. I just think it's sort of sweet, I guess. Sad . . . but sweet. He must have really loved her.''

"I gather she was someone pretty special," I said.

Karen shrugged. "I wouldn't know. I was just a kid then, still in high school. I remember hearing about it on the news, though. He was in the D.A.'s office at the time. They played it up pretty big.''

"Yeah, I imagine they would. D.A.'s wife gunned down in drive-by shooting. Details at eleven. Reporters have never been among my favorite people.''

"Boy, I'm with you there," said Karen. "They're all a bunch of vultures.''

"That's flock," I said.

"Huh?''

"Flock of vultures. Bunch of grapes, flock of vultures.''

"Gaggle of geese," she said.

"Pride of lions," I countered.

"An exaltation of larks," she came back.

"A sty of cops," I said.

"*Watch* it.''

"Sorry, officer. I won't let it happen again.''

"Well, I'll let you off with a warning this time.''

I laughed and she looked alarmed. "What's wrong?''

"Nothing, I was just laughing. I know, it sounds like I'm choking on a hairball, but I can't help it. That's just the way it works.''

"You had me worried for a second there," she said, with a chuckle. "So, how long are you going to be staying with the commissioner?''

I shrugged. "I don't know. I don't think either one of us has really given it a lot of thought. We barely even know each other. It's sort of an unusual situation."

She nodded. "Think you might make it permanent?"

I shook my head. "I try not to think along those lines. Life isn't permanent, you know what I mean?"

"Yeah."

"What time is it?"

She glanced at her watch. "About eleven."

"I didn't realize it was so late. I should probably be getting back," I said.

"Come on," she said, getting up, "I'll give you a ride."

I glanced dubiously at the scooter. "On that thing?"

"Sure. Why not?"

"I can think of a number of reasons," I said.

"Oh, don't be a pussy," she said.

"Cute," I said. "Very cute."

"Sorry, couldn't resist."

"All right, how are we supposed to work this?"

She threw her leg over the scooter and patted the seat between her legs. "Hop on."

"I don't know about this," I said, as I leaped up onto the seat and sat down with her legs on either side of me.

"Don't worry about it," she said, as she reached for the handlebars. "Long as you don't go squirming around, you're not going to go anywhere."

"If you say so," I replied, uncertainly.

"Relax," she said. "Logan Towers, right? It's a short ride and I won't go fast. Just don't go digging your claws into my legs."

She brought her thighs closer together, cradling me so I wouldn't slide around, and punched the starter button. With a soft hum, the scooter rose about a foot or so off the ground and we were off, skimming down the mall.

"You okay?" she asked.

"Yeah," I replied, enjoying the feeling of the breeze rippling my fur. "This is kinda fun."

"I live to ride," she said, as we skimmed past park benches and pedestrians. "You should see the scoot I've got at home. Custom job; built it myself. It would eat this thing alive."

"I'll take your word for it."

We skimmed down to the end of the mall and then headed south on Broadway. She kept the speed down to something reasonable, but it was still a lot faster than I was used to going. And I decided that this kind of transportation wouldn't be all unpleasant getting used to. In a car, you were enclosed, but on one of these scooters, you were right out there in the wind and you could see everything around you much better. It wasn't entirely without risk, of course, but then what is? And Karen really seemed to know what she was doing. Of course, that made perfect sense. Police motor officers received extensive training on their scooters and were generally much better riders than the average person. On top of which, other drivers have a tendency to slow down and behave themselves whenever there's a cop around.

We took a left at Ninth and headed east a few blocks, to Logan. And as we turned the corner, we ran into a police convention. In addition to the squad cars, there were two fire trucks, a paramedic van, and a bomb-squad truck. Flashing lights were all over the place. Right in front of the entrance to the underground garage of Logan Towers were the burnt-out and still-smoking remains of a car.

Karen pulled over to the curb and I hopped down, then she got off and I followed her as she walked up to one of the officers on the scene.

"Jeff, what's going on?" she asked.

"Looks like a homicide," the officer replied. "Explosive device wired to the car. Bomb squad just found what's left of it." He glanced down toward me. "What's with the cat?"

"This is Catseye Gomez," she said. "He's a thaumagene, staying with the commissioner. I was just giving him a ride home."

"Hi, Gomez," he said. "Jeff Coles. Friend of the commissioner's, eh? He's upstairs in 3-E."

"*3-E?*" I said. I glanced toward the blown-up car. "Susan Jacobs?"

Coles nodded. "Yeah. The radio personality. You knew her?"

"No, we never met, but I was just talking with her cat this morning."

"Well, maybe you'd better go up, then," Jeff said.

"I'll take him up," said Karen. She glanced back toward the wreckage. "Did she make it?"

"What, are you kidding? Look at that thing. You didn't hear it go off?"

She shook her head. "No, I was downtown, on the mall. The buildings must have blocked the sound."

He shook his head. "Man, I was cruising about four blocks away and I heard it blow. I was the first one on the scene. The blast took out half the widows across the street."

"I'll talk to you later," Karen said. "Come on, Catseye."

We went through the door and past the security desk. One of the cops was taking a statement from the guard on duty. We went into the elevator.

"Floor, please."

"Three," I said.

"Thank you, Mr. Gomez."

The doors slid closed.

"Fancy," Karen said.

"Security building," I said. "Though it didn't seem to do Miss Jacobs any good."

"Yeah," said Karen, making a tight-lipped grimace.

We got off at the third floor and went down the hall to 3-E. The neighbors were probably all at work, because I didn't see anybody except for a couple of cops in the hall. They nodded at Karen as we approached.

"The commissioner in there?" she asked.

"Yeah," one of them said. He grimaced wryly. "You ready for this? They're trying to take a statement from the victim's *cat*. She's being a real handful, too. Yowling up a storm in there." He glanced down at me. "What's this, the boyfriend?" he added sarcastically.

"Hey, shove it, bonehead," I snapped. "Step aside."

He stared at me with astonishment and actually stepped aside before he had a chance to think about it. Karen grinned and followed me into the apartment.

There were several detectives in there, but Solo was running the show. He still hadn't changed from the gym and was dressed in blue police-department sweats and running shoes. He was hunkered down in front of the couch, talking to Princess when I came in. Or at least trying to talk to her. She was in a real state. She was curled up on the couch, her ears laid back, and every couple of seconds, she would raise her head and let loose with a grief-stricken yowl. I jumped up on the couch beside her and, instinctively, she recoiled and hissed.

"Take it easy, kitten," I said. "It's only me."

"They killed her, Gomez!" she yowled. "The lousy chauvinist bastards *killed* her!"

Solo took a deep breath and exhaled heavily. "I'm glad you're here, Gomez. As you can see, she's quite distraught. Maybe you can help calm her down. We need to find out if she knows anything."

"The *bastards*!" Princess yowled. "The lousy, murdering *bastards*!"

"I know, kitten, I know," I said, reaching out to touch her paw gently.

Solo straightened up and glanced at Karen.

"Motor Officer Karen Sharp, sir," she said. "I gave Gomez a ride home from the mall."

"Thank you, Officer Sharp," he said. "Stick around. She's used to being around a woman, it might help. Her name is Princess."

"Yes, sir."

Karen squatted down beside us. "I'm sorry, Princess," she said. "I'm truly sorry."

Princess glanced toward her and Karen held her arms out. With a soft, mewling little sound, Princess went to her and Karen picked her up, stroking her softly. So much for my comforting presence.

Karen sat down on the couch, holding Princess and stroking her gently. Solo sat down next to her and I jumped onto the coffee table. Solo looked at me and nodded, indicating that I should talk to her.

"Kitten, I know this is pretty rough," I said, "but we need to find out some information, anything that might tell us who did this. They shouldn't get away with it, Princess, and they're *not* going to get away with it, but we need your help. Do you think you're up to it?"

She looked at me and nodded. She was still pretty frazzled, but Karen's holding her seemed to calm her down. I glanced at Solo, but he nodded that I should continue. I guess he figured he could jump in if I didn't ask the right questions.

"Okay, Princess," I said. "Now, these questions might be a little tough, but they've gotta be asked. Can you think of anybody that might have wanted to harm Susan?"

She took a deep breath and nodded. "The people who are against us," she said.

"Against you? You mean against ERA?"

"Yes," she said bitterly.

Solo frowned and I explained. "Equal Rights for Animals," I said. "It's a group Princess and Susan Jacobs started together, along with some of their friends."

"It's the first I've heard of it," said Solo, frowning.

"We were trying to get an animal rights bill on the

ballot,'' Princess said. "Our goal was equal rights for animals and citizenship for thaumagenes.''

Solo raised his eyebrows, but said nothing. He glanced at me and I picked up the prompt.

"What makes you think someone would have wanted to kill Susan because of that?'' I asked.

"We've had threats,'' Princess replied.

"What kind of threats?''

"Phone calls,'' she said. "Both here and at the station. I was upset about it at first, but Susan said it was nothing to worry about. She said there were always kooks calling up the station with stuff like that.''

"Calling up a radio station is one thing,'' I said, "but calling her at home is something else again.'' I saw Solo nod in agreement. "Was her number listed?''

Princess glanced from me to Solo, then back again. "No, I don't think so.''

"And she didn't change her number after she started getting the threatening calls?'' I asked.

"She saved the tapes from the answering machine,'' said Princess. "She was going to dub them and put them on the air.''

"Why?''

"We were going to do a talk show,'' Princess replied. "Susan thought the tapes would be a good example of the kind of coercion and repression imposed by homo-chauvinist attitudes.''

"What about these tapes?'' I asked. "Where are they?''

"I think she put them in her desk,'' said Princess.

One of the other detectives immediately went to the desk and started looking. "Top drawer's locked,'' he said.

"Break it, Ryan,'' Solo said.

One broken desk drawer later, the detective had the tapes. There were three cassettes, rubber-banded together, wrapped in a piece of paper with the word *Threats* written on it. He handed them to Solo.

"Nicely labeled and everything," he said wryly.

"Did she ever call the police about these threats?" I asked.

Princess shook her head. "I don't know."

I glanced at Solo. "She ever speak to you about them?"

He shook his head. "No. We didn't really know each other very well. Just said hello in the elevator, that sort of thing." Then he smiled slightly and shook his head.

"What?" I said.

"Nothing," he said. "You're doing very well. You'd make a pretty good cop."

"Yeah, but I'd look silly in a uniform," I replied. "Princess, you're here most of the time, did you ever actually hear any of these calls?"

"Yes," she said. "I heard them all. All the ones that came on the answering machine, anyway."

"I don't suppose you recognized the voice? I mean, did it sound at all familiar?"

"No. It sounded muffled. But it was a man's voice. I'm sure of that."

"Same voice every time?"

"Yes."

"We'll take these tapes and listen to them," Solo interjected. "What about her personal life, Princess?"

"What do you mean?"

"I mean, was she seeing anyone?" said Solo. "Involved with someone special?"

"I don't see what that has to do with . . . with . . . what happened," Princess said.

"I don't know that it does have anything to do with it," said Solo, "but we need to look into any sources that might help us, anything that might produce some information."

"What about it, kitten?" I asked. "Did she have a special man in her life?"

"Mark Michaels," Princess said. "The general manager at the radio station."

One of the other detectives wrote it down.

"How serious was it?" Solo asked.

"You mean were they sleeping together?" Princess asked, in a tone that implied it was none of his business.

"I mean how serious was it?" Solo asked again. "Was it merely casual, or was it a serious relationship?"

"It was a serious relationship," said Princess.

"Okay," said Solo. "What about her friends? Can you give us any of their names?"

"Her best friend is...was...Dana Cain," said Princess. "And she was also close with Christy Ivers. You'll find their numbers and addresses in her phone book."

"In the desk?" asked Solo.

"The top drawer," Princess said. "It's a little black book." She looked up at Karen. "Thank you. I think I'm all right, now."

Karen let her off her lap and Princess settled down onto the couch beside her. She looked like something...well, like something the cat dragged in.

"Who else was she close to?" Solo asked, while the detective went to the desk again to get the phone book.

"Why don't we take a break?" I interrupted. "We can go through the names in the book with her later. I think she could use a breather."

Princess glanced at me gratefully. "Thank you, Gomez," she said.

"Sure," said Solo. "Princess, the detectives need to do some work in here. Would you like to come up to my apartment for a while? Have some milk or water, something to eat?"

"I don't think I could eat anything," said Princess, "but I could do with a drink, thank you."

"Gomez, why don't you take her up?" He reached into the pocket of his sweats, took out his keys, and handed them to Karen. "Officer Sharp, stay with them, will you?"

"Sure thing, Commissioner," she said.

One of the cops came in from outside. "Commissioner, we've got a crowd of reporters outside."

"That figures," Solo said.

"The chief's down there, talking to them. He said to tell you he'd give them a short statement and then be right up."

"Okay, thanks," said Solo. "Let's get the lab boys up here. I'll want—"

I didn't hear the rest of it. We were out the door and on our way down to the elevator. The cop I'd sassed gave me a sour look as we went by, but though he looked as if he'd have liked to drop-kick me, he didn't say anything. Apparently, as an animal friend of the commissioner's, I had some clout. But then not everyone was an animal lover. And it looked like maybe Susan Jacobs had found that out the hard way.

Five

E ARLIER that morning, I'd had an uneasy feeling that it was going to be a long day. I hadn't known the half of it. Maybe one of these days I'd figure out why trouble has a way of following me everywhere I go. Maybe it's my color. Maybe what they say about black cats is true. I'd been with Paulie, and now Paulie was dead. Grief had come to Princess only a matter of hours after I had crossed her path. Solo took me in and Susan Jacobs got killed right on his doorstep. I hadn't even met the lady and, in a crazy sort of way, I somehow felt responsible. Maybe it was because in her own cockeyed sort of way, Susan Jacobs had been trying to do something to improve my way of life. And maybe I shouldn't have given Princess such a hard time about it. Maybe I should have stayed in Santa Fe. Maybe I was just plain bad luck.

I took Princess into Solo's guest room, where she curled up on the couch and conked right out. When I came back into the living room, I found Karen standing by Solo's desk, staring at the framed photograph of his late wife. She didn't hear me come in. She just stood there, staring at the picture, then she picked it up for a closer look.

"Beautiful, wasn't she?" I said.

Karen gave a small guilty start, then slowly put the

picture back down on the desk. "Yes, she was," she replied softly. "I'm sorry, I didn't mean to be nosy."

"Don't worry about it," I said. "I'm something of an expert in curiosity, myself."

She smiled, then sighed. "Hell of a day, isn't it?"

"Yeah," I said, "and it's early yet."

Karen looked out the window. It was about noon. "The media's out in force," she said. "A murder right outside the police commissioner's building. They're going to have themselves a real field day with this." She glanced at me. "How's Princess?"

"Asleep."

She nodded. "Delayed shock reaction," she said. "Are you and Princess very close?"

"Well, no, I wouldn't say that," I replied. "We only met for the first time this morning. The building manager introduced us. He's apparently big on this ERA thing, too."

"And they wanted to get you involved?"

"I suppose," I said. "But it struck me as a fruitcake idea."

"Really? Why's that? You don't think animals having equal rights would be in your best interest?"

"Frankly, no. I think it would open up a very smelly kettle of fish. It would raise all sorts of awkward legal and ethical and moral questions, the sort of questions that don't have any easy answers. The sort of questions that would upset a lot of people."

"Apparently, it already has," said Karen grimly.

"Maybe," I said. "We don't really know that Susan Jacobs's murder had anything to do with ERA."

"What about those threats?" Karen asked.

"A threat is not the same thing as an act," I replied. "People get mad at each other all the time and say things like, 'I'll kill you,' but most of the time, they don't really mean it."

"True," said Karen, "but when you have a series of threats, followed by an act that makes good on them, it begins to look a little more convincing."

"Like I said, maybe. Personally, I'm hoping that isn't the case."

"Why?"

"Because up to now, this ERA thing seems to have been little more than a curiosity, the kind of story the media would give some coverage because it's got an off-the-wall human-interest angle. But things are going to be different now. Susan Jacobs's murder makes it a big story. Like you said, they're going to have a field day with it. And things are liable to get ugly."

"I'm not sure I follow," Karen said, frowning slightly.

"Think about it," I said. "You've got a small group of activists going around saying animals deserve equal rights with humans. One of them's a media type and gets the group some coverage. No big deal. A few radio spots, a short feature here and there, nothing that would really make much of an impression, probably. Only now you've got a murder. The murder of a media personality, complete with taped death threats. Now it's a big, sensational story. Now ERA has a martyr to the cause. Now it'll make a big impression. Now people are going to start coming out of the woodwork and getting on the bandwagon. You're going to have organized protests at thaumagene shops. People are going to start writing letters to the newspapers and to their legislators. A lot of thaumagenes are going to start rethinking their position in life and deciding maybe they should do something about it. And a lot of people who don't agree with the idea are going to start resenting it. Things are liable to start getting pretty tense unless it turns out that Susan Jacobs was killed for something that had nothing to do with ERA."

"I see what you mean," said Karen. "But do you really think it's going to go that far?"

"I think the media will make sure it does," I told her. "You watch. It's got too many angles. They won't be able to resist it. They're going to pick up the ball and run with it."

The door opened and Solo came in, looking grim. There

was another man with him, a balding, beefy-looking guy in a plain gray suit, his tunic open at the neck, his waistline bulging and his shoes looking very worn and comfortable. No fashion statements here, this guy was all business.

"Hello, Chief," Karen said. "Commissioner."

The chief glanced at her and frowned faintly.

"Officer Sharp, sir," she said.

He nodded and grunted softly.

"Where's Princess?" Solo asked.

"Asleep," I said. "She was looking kind of wobbly, so I thought I'd put her on the couch in the guest room."

Solo nodded. "Oh, Chief, this is Catseye Gomez. He's visiting from Santa Fe. Gomez, this is Chief Moran."

"Hello, Chief," I said.

Moran looked down at me and scowled. A real animal lover. I could tell.

Solo plopped down on the couch and sighed heavily. Moran simply stood there, looking like a tank.

"You shouldn't have spoken to the press, Commissioner," he said. "You should've let me handle it."

"Hell, I had to tell them something, John," said Solo wearily. "One of my neighbors gets blown up right outside my front door, I can't very well say 'No comment,' you know what I mean?"

Moran grunted again. "Yeah, but the way they grilled you makes the department look bad. You shoulda held off and then issued a statement later, after we had something to go on."

"*Do* we have something to go on?" Solo asked.

"Well, so far we know that whoever wired the victim's car knew what they were doing," Moran said. "The device wasn't connected to the battery switch, otherwise it would've gone up the moment she started the car outside the radio station. So that means it was either a timed device or else a remote detonator. We should know in a couple of hours. Probably whoever did it installed the device while she was on the air this morning. Pretty cool customer, to do it right out on the street, in broad daylight. And then we've got those death threats, which I'd better take with me and get to the lab.''

"I want to hear them first," said Solo.

He got up and went over to the answering machine on his desk. He took the three tiny cassettes out of his pocket and popped the top one into the machine, after first taking out the tape already in it. He clicked it on.

Beep. "Susan, this is Dana. Great show this morning. We still on for Mudd's tonight? Christy called and said she can't make it. Got a hot date. Call me."

Beep. "Susan? Christy. Look, I'm sorry, but I'm gonna have to cancel out tonight. Got a date for dinner with this *very* sexy man I just met. God, he's so gorgeous! Could be a late night, I hope, I hope. Tell you all about it tomorrow. Wish me luck. Love ya."

Beep. "Man was put on this earth to have dominion over animals, not be equal with them. Animals are inferior creatures, and thaumagenes are an abomination in the face of God. ERA is blasphemy. You have incurred the wrath of God and you shall be struck down."

Moran snorted. "Terrific. That's just what we need. A fucking religious freak."

Solo reached out and stopped the tape, rewound it, and listened again. He sat there and listened through all the tapes, noting down the names of all the callers. There were five more threatening calls, much like the first one. The same muffled male voice, same kind of nutso messages. The caller sounded like a die-hard Christian Fundamentalist.

There were still a few of them around, and they didn't seem like very happy people. At one time, in the days prior to the Collapse, the Christian Fundamentalist movement had been going very strong. As the world grew more and more complex, more and more people found themselves with a need for simple answers, and Christianity, especially Fundamentalist Christianity, provided them. The lure was simplicity itself. Believe in the Lord. Turn your life over to Christ. Jesus came to Earth to bear the burden of responsibility for the sins of humankind, for which selfless act they crucified him, and so he became a martyr to the cause of Truth. Place your faith in Jesus and be "born again." In return, the slate's wiped clean. You get one great, big "Do Over." You can be cleansed and start anew, living in a state of grace, and if life starts posing those nasty, complicated questions, all you have to do is pray and read the Bible. Gather together in His name, in a place where His messenger, the preacher, will explain the finer points to you and tell you what He wants you to do. Just remember to drop something in the collection plate, whatever you can afford, and if money is a little tight this month, don't worry, just call the 800 number, toll free, He takes credit cards.

It got to be a pretty big thing there for a while. They had their own radio and TV networks, their own publications, their cathedrals and their Bible colleges, their universities, and even their amusement parks, complete with time-share condominiums. Every now and then, one of the preachers would be nailed for fraud or tax evasion or some other scandal, but all they had to do was cry on television and repent. After all, the Lord was nailed, too, and they were only human. They "stumbled," succumbed to the temptations of the flesh, and then prostrated themselves with grief and touching sincerity in public, rededicating themselves to their faith with renewed vigor. The faithful flocked to them in ever greater numbers to be fleeced. Maybe that's why they called the Lord their shepherd.

During the Collapse, Fundamentalism reached a fever pitch. Everything was falling apart, and the preachers were announcing the arrival of the Apocalypse. In many ways, those were, indeed, Apocalyptic times, only the world survived, the Second Coming never came, and the souls of the faithful did not rise up to Heaven. At least, not spontaneously. There were some far-out, Fundamentalist

cult groups that tried to hasten the process along by indulg-
ing in mass ritual suicide, despite the fact that traditional
Christian belief held suicide to be a sin, but if their god was
truly a forgiving one, then perhaps their souls gained admit-
tance to the paradise they sought. But all those who waited
more passively, if no less eagerly, to be lifted up, were
doomed to disappointment. The world survived. In fact, it
not only survived, it flowered, thanks to the return of magic.
And for many of them, that proved to be a problem.

Magic was not really accepted in the Christian faith. One
could indeed argue, as Merlin had, that the Christian Church
had been built upon many pagan traditions, or at the very
least had borrowed from them. Belief in the death and
resurrection of the Christ paralleled pagan beliefs in the
death and resurrection of the God and Goddess, to mark the
seasons. The Christian ritual of transubstantiation, Merlin
pointed out, was really no different from many pagan rituals
of magic. But that only infuriated the Christian opposition.

Some argued that it wasn't magic, but merely a symbolic
act, a ritual of reaffirmation of the faith. But nevertheless a
ritual, Merlin had replied, just as many pagan rituals were
meant to reaffirm a connection with the natural, primal
forces of the universe. Others argued that it wasn't magic,
but a miracle, performed by God Himself, and while the
Host was not actually transformed into a bloody piece of
flesh torn from Christ's body, it nevertheless became imbued
with all the qualities that body and spirit had possessed. To
which Merlin had replied that pagan rituals could also be
looked upon as miracles, brought about by a connection
between those who were performing them and the natural
forces inherent in the world.

Merlin had not attacked the Christian Church, nor any
other faith. He taught that anything that brought about
attunement with the creative forces of the universe was
good, and he maintained that there was no one path to the

Truth. Yet that was precisely where he ran up against the strongest opposition.

Merlin Ambrosius had been denounced from every pulpit as a fraud, a sinner, and a necromancer in league with the Devil. In vain, Merlin had protested that the Devil was a purely Christian invention. He was not a Christian, therefore he did not believe in the existence of the Devil. His faith predated Christianity, and his pagan beliefs were based upon a veneration of natural creative forces, seen in the masculine and feminine dualities occurring throughout Nature and personified as the God and Goddess, or the Lord and Lady, or Diana and Apollo, or any of a score of different names. What you called them did not matter, Merlin had insisted. Personification of the gods was merely a matter of convenience, a frame of reference. So, for that matter, were the gods themselves.

Go out at night and look up at the moon, he'd said. Revel in the beauty of the stars and feel the cool night breezes on your skin. Or go out and climb a mountain on a sunny day, and gaze up at the sky. Look out at the panorama spread before you, the trees, the meadows, the grasses and the flowers, the entire panoply of natural creation stretching out in all directions. What difference did it make, he'd asked, if you called it God, or if you personified the creative forces of the universe in the ancient masculine and feminine duality of witchcraft, or the multiple personas of the Norse gods, or the gods of Greece and Rome, or if you called it Buddha, or Allah, or Wakan Tonka. It was all the same.

They tried to kill him, anyway. All in the name of God, of course. However, Merlin had expected that and he'd prepared for it. Modern weapons were certainly superior to those used in King Arthur's day, but they were nevertheless weapons created through the means of science, while the forces Merlin was in tune with, and could call upon, were of an entirely different nature. Older and more powerful. What was a mere gun compared to the elemental forces of creation? They had tried to stop him, but they had succeeded only in proving his point. Magic worked.

Had he chosen to, Merlin could probably have set himself up as a messiah and brought down the Christian Church, but such was never his intention. He was not out to bring about a religious revolution, but a revolution in the way people perceived themselves, especially in relation to the world in which they lived. I guess he figured that whatever faith you chose to follow, if it helped you make it through the cold, dark night, then it was a good thing. So long as it harmed nobody else. In that respect, he was inflexible. To the extent that any religion proclaimed itself to be the One True Faith, he fought it, not to destroy it, but to get it to loosen up and be more tolerant of other systems of belief.

It was not an easy task, but then, Merlin was no ordinary man. And he had something that the blighted world desperately needed. Knowledge. Knowledge of an old, forgotten path from which humanity had strayed. They had known it once, in their most primitive days of evolution, when they had been under the dominion of the Old Ones, and they had learned to walk it for themselves after the Old Ones fell from power, but they had strayed from it when they began to live in cities and to think of Nature as something apart from themselves, something not to be in tune with, but something to be tamed and dominated.

In time, as magic spread throughout the world through Merlin and his disciples, the Christian Church was forced to make some changes, as were other major faiths such as Judaism and Islam. For some, such as the Zen Buddhists, the coming of the Second Thaumaturgic Age did not require radical changes in their systems of belief. But for others, it meant change in the form of new interpretations.

The word "infidel" was stricken from the tenets of the Islamic faith. There *were* no longer any infidels, because everybody worshipped Allah, even if they called Him by a different name or followed Him in different ways. Jews and

Christians ceased to debate the issue of whether or not Jesus Christ was the Messiah, because the question ceased to have any relevance. Everyone had the capacity to be a savior, to accept the burden of responsibility for their fellow human beings and their planet, so long as they could accept responsibility for their own actions. Every man became the Son of God, and every woman became the Daughter of the Goddess. The Trinity became the Father, the Mother, and the Holy Spirit, which had entered Christ, and Moses, and Buddha, and Bodhidharma, and Muhammad, and anyone, in fact, who chose to open up their soul and receive it.

Nowadays, most people still considered themselves Christians or Jews or Muslims or Buddhists or whatever, but there were also many people who considered themselves Neo-Pagans, which meant simply that they could enter any church or shrine or temple and take part in the services, donning yarmulkes or removing their shoes, prostrating themselves toward Mecca or taking Communion, respecting the traditions of the services being conducted, because it was all regarded as the same. It was an honoring of and an atunement with the creative forces of the universe, and it gave them strength and peace. For that matter, they could just as easily commune with Nature on a mountaintop, or in a park or meadow, or go out on a balcony or the roof of a tall building and gaze at the moon and stars. There was no One True Path, because all paths leading in a spiritual direction were the same. Magic touched them all.

Unfortunately, there have always been those whose hearts and minds were closed, and these people made up the Fundamentalist sects of the world's faiths. Often, these were people whose souls were small and shriveled things, who found meaning not in celebration of the world around them, but who sought significance in demeaning all those who did not see things their way. Their numbers had grown smaller over the years, their hearts had grown colder, and their tolerance had shrunk almost to nonexistence. Inasmuch as they needed to live with their fellow creatures in their day-to-day existence, they put up with them and often kept their own council. But when they gathered together with those who shared their narrow-minded beliefs, it was to sing the praises of their own superiority and state of grace in a world that had gone all wrong and decadent around them. They had that right. But they had no right to interfere with the rights of others. They had no right to force their own beliefs on anybody else.

I had learned about human religious beliefs because of my own relentless curiosity. I had none myself. At least, not in the formal sense. Humans were the only creatures on this Earth who had religion. Animals had no need of such formalized beliefs. We knew we were a part of Nature, and we felt its forces in and around us all the time. We didn't choose to give it names, or represent it in some god or prophet that we could relate to. We merely accepted it and were a part of it. That didn't make us any better or any worse, I guess, it simply made us what we were. But no animal had ever killed another because that animal had disagreed with its system of belief.

Solo took the last little cassette out of the machine and stared at it for a moment, the expression on his face unreadable. However, I could guess what he was thinking. He put the three of them together, slipped the rubber band around them, and handed them to Chief Moran.

"Okay, get these down to the lab," he said. "Maybe we can get a decent voice print that will let us match it to a suspect." He paused. "And let's see if we can't have a divination performed on those, as well."

"You know that's not admissible without corroborating evidence," Moran said.

"Yes, I know, but at this point, we haven't got anything to go on, and I don't want to overlook anything that can help us get a handle on this guy."

"I'll need that list of callers, too," Moran said.

"I'll make you a copy," Solo replied. "I want to keep this one for myself."

Moran shook his head. "Commissioner, you don't want to go getting personally involved in this."

"I *am* personally involved, John," said Solo. "I want to talk to these people."

Moran took a deep breath. "Sir, with all due respect, that's really not your job. Let me assign some detectives to this thing and do it right."

Solo smiled. "Are you saying you don't think that I can do it right, John?"

Moran sighed. "May I speak frankly?"

Solo smiled again. "You always do."

"Again, meaning no disrespect, sir, but you're not really experienced at this kind of thing. As far as I'm concerned, you were the best damned D.A. this town ever had, and I can't think of anyone else I'd rather have as commissioner, but you don't really know the streets. This sort of thing is work for street cops, for detectives. Let your people do their job. And don't make mine any harder than it already is."

"In other words, butt out," said Solo.

Moran exhaled heavily. "Yeah, in other words, butt out, sir. Please."

Solo stared at him for a moment, then sighed and nodded. "Okay, John, I'll let you do it your way. But I want our best people on this, and I want to personally see copies of every single report."

"You got it," Moran replied. "I'll put Chavez and McVickers in charge of it."

"No," said Solo. "I want Leventhal."

"*Leventhal*?" Moran echoed him, incredulously.

"He's the one I want, John," insisted Solo.

"Sir, Chavez and McVickers are the senior detectives on the Homicide Squad," Moran protested. "They're the best people for the job. Besides, Leventhal works Vice."

"And what was he working before he worked Vice?" asked Solo.

"Homicide," admitted Moran, uneasily, "but he was transferred out. The man's a problem, Commissioner. He's a maverick. He's insubordinate, he cuts corners, he couldn't even get anybody to work partners with him. The guy's a flake."

"If he's a bad cop, why isn't he out of the department?" Solo asked.

Moran hesitated uncomfortably. "Well . . . I didn't say he was a bad cop, exactly."

Solo raised his eyebrows. "Because he gets results? You know, I've seen his file, John."

Moran worked his tongue around inside his mouth. "Okay, so he's got the best record of felony arrests in the department," he said grudgingly. "But he's also got the most reprimands. Internal Affairs has had him on the griddle at least a dozen times. He's been cited repeatedly for excessive force, charged with brutality—"

"Any of it ever stick?" asked Solo.

Moran grimaced. "No. But you already knew that, didn't you? Besides, that's not the point. The point is that this is going to be a high-profile case, with lots of media attention. You want somebody handling it who comes across polished, professional, and competent, like Chavez and McVickers. You give the media Leventhal and it'll be like throwing raw meat to a bunch of starving wolves."

"You think he's going to embarrass the department?" Solo asked.

"Sir, have you ever *met* Leventhal?"

Solo smiled. "Yes, as a matter of fact, I have. Back when he was working Homicide and I was in the D.A.'s office. It's been a few years, but I still recall the incident vividly. It was one of the few times we screwed up. Actually, *I* screwed up. I assigned a young, relatively inexperienced A.D.A. to prosecute a case Leventhal brought in. She was a good lawyer, but she was a bundle of nerves and I thought a baptism of fire would make her rise to the occasion. It didn't. She made a procedural error that violated the rules of evidence, and the defense counsel jumped on her about it, jumped her hard enough to shake her up and really throw her off her stride. The perpetrator wound up walking on a technicality. Afterward, Leventhal came storming into my office and read me the riot act, blamed *me* for screwing up his case.''

''Well, there, you see? That's precisely the sort of thing I'm talking about,'' Moran said. ''The man's irresponsible, a loose cannon.''

''He was absolutely right,'' Solo replied. ''He gave me quite a dressing down, and I thought it took a lot of guts.''

''He's got them, all right,'' Moran said, scowling. ''What he *ain't* got is a lot of sense, or respect for authority.''

''Let's just say he made a favorable impression,'' Solo said. ''He's the man I want, John. Have him come and see me. Pull him off whatever he's doing and get him here as soon as possible. As of right now, he's in charge of this case.''

Moran rolled his eyes. ''Commissioner, *why* are you doing this to me?''

''Because you're a good cop, John, but you've been behind a desk too long,'' said Solo. ''Like you said, this is going to be a high-profile case and the media is going to make waves. I want someone who can bring in some results. And make waves right back at them.''

''Oh, I think you can count on that last part,'' said Moran. ''But don't say I didn't warn you.''

''I won't. Your warning has been duly noted, John. Now get me Leventhal.''

Six

A FTER Chief Moran left, Solo went to take a shower and change. He seemed irritable and off his stride, and not just because of the events of that morning. I'd noticed the same kind of thing in Paulie when we'd roomed together in Santa Fe. Like Paulie, Solo was a creature of habit. Most people are. They have little routines and schedules they develop that they like to stick to, and when those are violated in some way, it upsets them and throws them off. Solo's routine consisted of getting up early and going to the gym to work out, then taking a walk or a short run, coming home, showering, shaving, getting dressed and puttering about, then going to the office. That routine had been disrupted—by a murder, no less—and as the afternoon wore on, I noticed Solo becoming more and more edgy.

Karen, on the other hand, seemed to be taking things in stride, which told me that she was a much more easygoing and adaptable person. Pulled off routine patrol duty at the downtown mall to baby-sit a grief-stricken cat, she seemed very relaxed and calm about it. Any other street cop might have become nervous at the prospect of being placed on such unusual duty at the commissioner's own home, but

Karen fell right into it. She called in, made her report, then took off her leather, unbuttoned the top of her uniform blouse, and made herself at home, brewing up some coffee in the kitchen and getting breakfast started while she fielded the phone calls coming in.

It made me think about the human habit, or even compulsion, of developing routine activities. To many people, it was a sort of security blanket, something familiar they could take comfort in amid the chaos of the world around them. Animals sometimes fell into it, as well, but more often than not, they were animals that had been domesticated. It was as if the human compulsion for routine activity was a disease they'd caught.

Relieved by their human masters of the need to hunt or scrounge for their food, domestic cats would fall into the routine adopted by their owners. If they were fed at eight o'clock each morning, seven forty-five would find them waiting expectantly by their bowls. And if their humans had to go away for a time, and someone else came by periodically to take care of them, they would often act surly and out of sorts until their people returned.

Humans often felt the joy their domestic pets displayed when they came back after an absence was a sign of fondness for them, a sign that they'd been missed. Maybe, but personally I think it much more likely it was relief that the familiar, comfortable routine could once more be resumed. I've always thought that much of human grief and emotional trauma could be attributed to a disruption of routine. The greater the disruption, the greater the emotional upset. People who avoided falling into patterns of routine activities seemed much more resilient. They could bounce back more easily and were seldom thrown by the unexpected. Karen seemed to fit that profile.

We chatted about Paulie and my life in Santa Fe while she got breakfast ready, as if nothing at all unusual had happened, and I realized that it wasn't that Karen was insensitive, but quite the opposite. It had been a rough morning, and while Moran was there, I felt a palpable tension in the room, especially while we were listening to the tapes. Karen sensed it—hell, anyone could—and she was just doing what she could to break it, to return things to some semblance of normalcy, so that we could all get on with business.

As I watched her putter around the kitchen, looking domestic as all hell even in her uniform, boots, and gun rig, what struck me about her was the fact that everything she did, from riding her scooter, to taking in the situation earlier that morning, to answering the phone, to whipping up some eggs and bacon, she did with an air of relaxed natural competency. That old expression "taking things in stride" meant preserving the constant flow of forward motion without stumbling, without "breaking stride." And there was a smooth flow to everything that Karen did. She was a lady with a lot of cat in her, all right. She landed on her feet.

Solo could do a hell of a lot worse, I thought, and then I immediately pushed the thought away. It was none of my business, and there was nothing more ridiculous than the idea of a battered old trooper like me playing matchmaker. Besides, if Solo was half the man I thought he was, then he wouldn't let this one get away.

When Solo came out again, he had showered, shaved, and changed into a comfortable, well-cut, brown Neo-Edwardian suit. Now, instead of a worn-out and put-upon bureaucrat, as he had appeared earlier, he looked more like a man ready to take charge of things. He smelled the coffee brewing and the bacon frying and glanced at the kitchen with surprise.

"I thought you could use something to eat," said Karen, coming out of the kitchen with a plate of food and a fresh-brewed cup of coffee.

"Why, thank you, Officer Sharp," said Solo, a bit taken

aback. "That was very considerate of you. You find everything all right?"

"Sure, no problem," she replied. "I got Gomez some food, as well, from that bag on the kitchen table."

"I appreciate it. Will you join me?" Solo asked.

"I'll just have some coffee, thanks," she said, as she started to button up her blouse.

Solo waved her off. "Forget it," he said. "Make yourself comfortable. We've all had a rough morning and I'm not conducting any inspections here."

She grinned and poured herself a cup of coffee, then joined him at the table.

"Princess still asleep?" he asked.

"Out like a light," I said.

"We're going to have to figure out what to do about her. She'll have to find someplace to stay. And given her political militancy, I don't think calling the animal shelter would be the best move."

"If none of the victim's friends can take her, I can put her up with me," said Karen.

"You're sure?" said Solo. "I wouldn't want to put you out."

"No problem, sir. I like animals. I've already got two snats who could keep her company."

"Okay," said Solo. "If we can't make any other arrangements, she can stay with you for the time being. Did you call in?"

"Yes, sir. I explained that I'd be on duty here, until you had no further need of me. There've been a lot of calls, mostly from the media. The reporters are still camped outside. They're anxious to speak with Princess."

Solo grimaced. "That figures. Let's keep her away from them if we can. At least until we can get a better handle on this thing." He shook his head. "I'd sure like to know how they keep getting my private number. I keep changing it, but they keep right on calling anytime something like this breaks.''

"Somebody's handing it out," I said. "I think it's called 'a leak.' The cause is usually attributable to a sudden infusion of cash.''

Karen grinned, but Solo scowled. "Well, if I ever find out who's leaking it, I'm gonna have his ass in a sling.''

"What if it's a her?" asked Karen innocently.

Solo glanced at her and cleared his throat. "Well, I wouldn't want to be thought of as a sexist, Officer Sharp,'' he said. "Let's just say it would be a case of equal-opportunity butt-kicking.''

She chuckled and reached for the coffeepot. There was a knock at the door. "I'll get it," she said. "Finish your breakfast.''

"What breakfast, it's almost suppertime," Solo replied gruffly.

Karen checked the peephole, scowled, then said, "Who is it?''

"Leventhal.''

"Good. Let him in," said Solo.

She glanced at him dubiously. "Are you sure?" Without waiting for a response, she opened the door.

The guy who walked in looked like a Ripper. He dressed like one, at any rate. He wore loose black breeches tucked into heavy black boots festooned with metal buckles, a black T-shirt, and a black, blouson-cut, studded leather jacket. An antique, gold, double-edged razor blade dangled on a chain around his neck, and he wore studded leather bracelets. He had short, curly black hair and a dark complexion, with a well-shaped, prominent nose and dark, sad-looking brown eyes. What women often referred to as "bedroom eyes.'' He looked young, maybe in his early to mid twenties, and he was fairly good-looking in a trashy sort of way.

An unlit cigarette dangled from his lip. He yanked down

the zipper on his leather jacket with an abrupt, sharp motion, and unsnapped a small leather case on his belt. From the case he pulled out an antique Zippo lighter, snapped it open with a flourish, and lit his cigarette. Snick, snap, and the Zippo was back in its case. He dragged deeply on the cigarette, exhaled a long stream of smoke, and took the cigarette out of his mouth, holding it between his thumb and forefinger.

"Detective Dan Leventhal," he said, his voice soft and slightly breathy. "You wanted to see me?"

"Yes, Leventhal, come in," said Solo. "Have a seat. You want some coffee?"

"Thanks." He sat down, glanced at Karen, and added, "Black."

She raised her eyebrows. "I look like a waitress to you?" she said.

He grinned. "Black, *please*," he said. "Or would you rather I get it myself...." He glanced at her name tag. "...Officer Sharp?"

"That's okay, detective, I'll get it," she replied dryly.

"Thank you very much," he said, with a smile.

"I understand you've been working Vice," Solo said.

Leventhal simply shrugged. The way he sat, slumped back in the chair and smoking, you might have thought he owned the place. His leather jacket hung open to display a black leather shoulder holster holding some kind of ugly, semiautomatic cannon. I didn't know what the hell it was, but it looked big enough to stop an elephant.

"As of now, you're back on Homicide," said Solo.

"The chief know about this?" asked Leventhal.

"He knows."

"I'll bet he didn't like it much."

Solo smiled slightly. "How much do you know about what's happened?"

Leventhal shrugged again. "Not a lot. Broadcaster got blown up in her car outside. Friend of yours?"

"Not really," Solo said. "She was a neighbor who lived downstairs. I didn't actually know her very well."

"But it doesn't look too good, a murder right at your front door," said Leventhal.

"No, it doesn't," Solo agreed. "That's why I want you to take charge of this case."

Leventhal inhaled on his cigarette, exhaled the smoke through his nostrils, and looked down at the table. "Why not Chavez and McVickers? They're supposed to be the supercops, Moran's dynamic duo. Why not send in the first string?"

Solo steepled his fingers and stared at Leventhal. "Suppose you tell me."

Leventhal looked up at him and gave a small snort. "Because the media's gonna be all over you on this one, and Chavez and McVickers are about as distinctive as a couple of stockbrokers. They dress nice, they know how to talk to the press, they can say 'No comment' about a dozen different ways, and they look good on camera. Me, every time I open my mouth, I get in trouble. The media gets on my case, I tell 'em to fuck off. Somebody gets in my face, I get in theirs three times as hard. They're gonna be so busy bashing me, they won't have any time for you. And if I blow it, it's my fault for being a maverick. Meanwhile, Chavez and McVickers and whoever else work quietly behind the scenes, while I draw all the heat. That about right?"

He drew on the cigarette and spat out the smoke. He noticed me watching him and gave me a wink. I winked back with ole Betsy and gave him a little thaumaturgic sparkle, just a brief flash of bright blue light. For a second, he looked surprised as hell, and I said, "Gotcha." Then he grinned. I decided the guy was all right. He had "street" written all over him.

"Actually, that wasn't what I had in mind," said Solo, "though I'm sure it's occurred to Chief Moran. And those are all pretty good reasons. But the main reason has to do with a lecture a certain snot-nosed, young, rookie detective gave me a couple of years ago.''

Leventhal smiled. "You remember that, huh?"

"I could hardly forget it," said Solo wryly. "Nor could anybody else in the D.A.'s office."

"So what's this, payback time?"

"No, that isn't it," said Solo. "It took a lot of guts to do what you did. Maybe it took stupidity, as well, but it showed me that you gave a damn. You cared enough to jeopardize your position on the force. And that's just what I need on this case. Somebody who cares."

Leventhal snorted again, but he had no reply.

"What do you know about the ERA?" asked Solo.

"Equal Rights for Animals?" said Leventhal. He shrugged. "I've heard about it. Know some people who're involved."

"Did you know that the victim, Susan Jacobs, was one of the founders of the group?" asked Solo.

"No," said Leventhal, suddenly looking interested, "I didn't. Is that what it's about?"

By way of reply, Solo picked up a piece of paper on which he'd written down a transcript of the death threats, and handed it to him. Leventhal took it and read silently, then handed it back to Solo.

Solo gave him a quick rundown on everything he knew so far, which wasn't very much. "So what do you think?" he asked, when he was finished.

Leventhal took a deep breath and let it out in a heavy sigh. "I think the media's purely gonna love this," he replied. "They know about this religious angle yet?"

Solo shook his head.

"They will soon," said Leventhal, "you can bet on that. And you can bet that if the same fruitcake who made those calls planted that bomb, he'll be contacting them and taking credit for it."

The phone rang.

Karen answered it. "It's Chief Moran," she said.

"Put it on the speaker," Solo said. He waited till she switched the speakerphone on, then raised his voice and said, "Go ahead, John."

"Well, our boy's been heard from," Moran's voice came from the speaker. "He's had himself a busy afternoon. He called the papers *and* all the local TV stations, taking credit for the bombing. Just in time to make the six o'clock news."

"Ta . . . da . . ." sang Leventhal, spreading his arms out.

"What was that?" Moran asked.

Solo gave Leventhal a dirty look. "Never mind," he said, getting up and walking over to the speakerphone so he wouldn't have to raise his voice. "How do we know it's the killer and not some crank?"

"The message was pretty much the same as on those tapes," Moran said, "almost word for word. They said it was a man's voice, sounded muffled. The Lord giving Man dominion over all the beasts of the field, ERA is blasphemy, the hand of God smiting the blasphemer, and all that. Other than taking credit, the caller didn't identify himself in any way. Oh, and Channel 7 somehow found out about the death threats the victim received. Needless to say, they did not reveal their source. Just thought you ought to know. Leventhal show up yet?"

"Yes, he's here," said Solo. "You want to speak to him?"

"Not particularly. You're really sure you want him on this thing?"

Solo glanced at Leventhal, who merely smiled wryly and shook his head. "Yes, I'm sure."

"Well, you're the boss," Moran said, with resignation in his voice.

Leventhal held up his middle finger.

"Okay, John, thanks," said Solo. "I'll talk to you later." He switched off the phone and turned back toward the table.

"You know something, Leventhal?" he said. "You've got a bad attitude."

Leventhal gave a sharp bark of laughter. "Yeah, that's what my mom told me. She always said I'd either wind up in jail or wearin' a badge. She wasn't sure which one was worse."

"Well, if you fall down on this one, you'll wish you *were* in jail," Solo said.

Leventhal raised his eyebrows. "You're serious? You're really putting me in charge of this? I'm not just window dressing?"

"It's your show," said Solo.

"I'm not gonna be trippin' over Chavez and McVickers?"

"Nope."

"I'm gonna have free rein?"

"Within reason," Solo said.

"What's that mean?"

"It means that if you go stepping on anybody's civil rights, I don't want to hear about it," Solo replied. "It means I want a conviction. This time, nobody's getting off on any technicalities. Otherwise, there *will* be a payback. Got it?"

Leventhal smiled. "Got it."

"You'll report directly to Chief Moran," said Solo. "Otherwise, anything you need, you let me know and I'll see that you get it."

"Well, I can think of three things right off the bat," said Leventhal. "The first one is reporting directly to Moran. I could have a real problem with that, unless you keep him off my back."

"What is it with you and Moran, anyway?" asked Solo.

"It's personal."

"That's not an answer," Solo snapped. "You want me to play straight with you, then damn it, you play straight with me. He's got it in for you, and it isn't just your sense of style. So what is it between you two?"

Leventhal moistened his lips and stared at the ceiling. Then he looked down and made a self-conscious grimace. "I slept with his daughter."

Karen made a sound halfway between a snort and a choking noise and quickly turned away. Solo and Leventhal both glanced at her and she said, "Excuse me. Something in my throat."

"That's it?" said Solo.

"I guess for him, it's enough," said Leventhal wryly. "Hell, I didn't even *know* she was his daughter till he walked in on us."

"Was she a minor?" Solo asked, frowning.

"No, actually, she was pretty major," Leventhal replied. He saw the look on Solo's face and hastily added, "Sorry, bad joke." He grimaced. "Look, she was twenty-two and I was nineteen, fresh out of the academy. I met her at a concert at Red Rocks. She asked me to come home with her, said her parents were away for the weekend. Guess they decided to cut the weekend short. They walked in on us and Moran lost it. He got a little physical. I kept a lid on it, because I recognized him and it threw me for a loop, but he didn't know me. He thought I was just some punk kid. He didn't find out I was a cop until a couple of months later, when I made my first big bust and went up before him to get my commendation. He recognized me halfway through the ceremony and just about shit a brick. After that, he did everything he could to make my life miserable. I almost didn't get my gold shield because of him. So like I said, it's personal, and I'd rather you didn't mention that I told you."

Solo pursed his lips and nodded. "Okay. I'll keep him off your back. You said you wanted three things. What's the second?"

"Her," said Leventhal, pointing at Karen.

Her eyes went wide. "I beg your pardon?" she said.

"Why?" said Solo, frowning.

"Because she's in on the ground floor of this thing and

she already knows what it's about," Leventhal replied. "She can function as my liaison with Moran. The less he sees of me, the better he'll like it, and I haven't exactly got a lot of friends in Homicide. Also, she's on motors, which means she hasn't been around long enough to get her nose brown or figure that she knows it all."

"Unlike you, I suppose?" said Karen dryly.

"And I like her attitude," added Leventhal, looking directly at her with a grin.

"Swell," she said.

Solo glanced at Karen. "What do you think, Officer Sharp? You want in on a homicide case?"

She glanced from him to Leventhal and back again. "Hell, yes. Sir."

"Okay," Solo said, nodding. "You're on it. I'll tell the chief." He turned back to Leventhal. "That's two. What's three?"

"I'd like to have the cat," said Leventhal, jerking his thumb at me.

I blinked with surprise. Solo and Karen both looked surprised as well.

"*Gomez?*" Solo said. He looked at me with a puzzled expression, then back at Leventhal. "*Why?*"

"Because this thing's all about ERA," Leventhal replied. "Or, at least, that's how it looks, and that's how the media's gonna play it. My instinct tells me they're gonna turn this killing into a big political issue. I want to throw a monkey wrench into the works, show 'em the department's taking it seriously enough to have a thaumagene representing animal interests in this case. Besides, he might come in useful when it comes to questioning some of the ERA people."

"But Gomez isn't a trained detective," Solo said.

"In that case, he'll fit right in with half the guys in Homicide," said Leventhal.

Karen stifled a chuckle. Solo didn't look amused.

"Ba-rum-bump," said Leventhal, imitating a rim shot. "Joke."

Solo shook his head and sighed. "I'm beginning to see what Moran meant when he said you were a problem," he said. "You don't have any respect for authority at all, do you?"

"I guess that depends," said Leventhal. "I respect people who give a shit and know what the hell they're doin'. Like I respect you, for one, and I'm not just saying that to kiss ass. You could've slid into the mayor's office, if you wanted to, but instead you took a job where you could make a real difference. Hell, if my manner offends you, Commissioner, I'm sorry, but then I don't think my having a few rough edges makes a difference in why you're givin' me this case."

"Tell me something, Leventhal," said Solo. "What made you want to become a cop?"

"I wanted to catch the bad guys," Leventhal replied. "And I'm good at it, even if I am an obnoxious SOB. But I figure you've gotta bring some to get some, if you know what I mean."

Solo shook his head. "You're some piece of work," he said. "But you are good at it, I'll grant you that. Otherwise, with your attitude, you never would have lasted this long."

"Thanks," said Leventhal.

"I'm not sure I meant that as a compliment," said Solo.

Leventhal grinned. "I'll take what I can get. So, do I get the cat?"

Solo glanced at me. "Well, I can't say I haven't got a lot of reservations, but it isn't entirely up to me. Gomez doesn't belong to me. He's a free agent. You'll have to ask him."

Leventhal raised his eyebrows. I guess he must have figured I was Solo's pet.

"I'd be happy to help if I can," I told him, "but I'll tell you up front, I've got a bit of an attitude myself. I'm not too good at taking orders."

"You know, somehow, I had that feelin' about you," said Leventhal, pointing at me and smiling. "I've also got a feelin' there's more to you than meets the eye. You've got the look of a real scrapper. I like scrappers. I think we're gonna get along just fine."

"You know, I think so, too," I said. "You remind me of someone I knew once."

"Yeah? Who?"

"Me," I said. "When I was just a wiseass little kitten who thought he could take on the whole world."

Karen cracked up and almost spilled her coffee. Even Solo had to chuckle. As for Leventhal, his jaw dropped and his cigarette fell from between his lips. He quickly picked it up before it could burn the tabletop.

"I think he's got you there, kid," Solo said. He grinned and shook his head. "This partnership is going to be one for the books. I can't wait till Moran finds out about it. He'll throw a fit."

"He will, huh?" said Leventhal. He looked at me and grinned. "Well, in that case, put 'er there, partner."

He held out his hand. I put my paw in it and we shook. Like I said before, life tends to throw you curve balls every now and then. I had a feeling this one was liable to be a real corker.

Seven

WE left Princess sleeping in Solo's guest room and took the elevator downstairs to the lobby. The crowd of reporters had mostly broken up, realizing they'd gotten all that they were going to get, at least for now. However, a few of them had stuck it out, and they descended on us with their mikes and notepads and tape recorders. They fired questions at us, and a bunch of them seemed to know Leventhal personally, but it wasn't what I'd call a warm relationship. They seemed interested as hell in me, and my presence deflected a lot of questions, which I guess was the general idea. In any case, I gave them a lot of noncommittal answers and generally felt foolish about the entire thing.

When we finally broke away from them, we were approached by another reporter who'd been waiting off to the side, a young and heavyset woman in her mid to late twenties. She wasn't the glamorous type, so that meant she was print medium. As far as the television media are concerned, the only people worth looking at are those mannequin types who look as if they've been stamped out with a cookie cutter. Heaven forbid you should get the news from someone who's got mousy hair or is just a little overweight.

This woman did not have mousy hair. In fact, she had truly spectacular hair, flaming red, which she wore long and loose, except for a thin little braid hanging down on the left side. However, she was on the heavy side, and unless she lost about fifty pounds she'd never be doing any stories on TV. She didn't look as if she gave a damn. She was dressed in loose, baggy, black trousers; heavy, lace-up boots; a white pullover; and a black frock coat with an Edwardian collar. She had been standing across the street from the building entrance, leaning back against her car and smoking, and as we came out, she crushed her cigarette out beneath her heel and headed toward us with a cocky swagger, her hands jammed in her pockets, a wry smile on her face.

"Aw, hell," said Leventhal.

"How's it going, Dan?" she said, falling in step beside him. "Don't tell me they're actually putting *you* on this case?"

"Okay, I won't tell you," he replied.

"I thought they sent you down to Vice," she said.

"Well, you oughtta know, B.J."

"The name's Bobbie Joe," she said.

"I like B.J.," Leventhal replied. "I've always like B.J.'s. It just sort of rolls right off the tongue, if you know what I mean."

"Yours is probably small enough to roll right off the tongue," she came back, acidly.

"Yeah? How would you know?"

"Snappy comeback, Danny boy." She glanced at me. "This your new partner?"

"As a matter of fact, yeah, he is," said Leventhal. "Catseye Gomez, meet B.J. Jacklin, would-be ace reporter for a would-be newspaper called Breakwind."

"That's *Westwind*," said Bobbie Joe.

"One of those free rags they leave lying around in bars,

quasi art cafés, and topless joints,'' said Leventhal. ''Terribly relevant. Definitely P.C.''

''P.C.?'' I said.

''Politically correct,'' Leventhal explained. ''They'll tell you where all the bodies are buried, where to get the best cappucino, what's hot and what's not, and they'll even help you with your love life. Well, maybe not yours, Cat. You'll find lots of cunt in their personal ad section, but very little pussy.''

''That's what I've always liked about you, Leventhal,'' said Bobbie Joe. ''You're such a 'Now' kind of guy.'' She glanced at me. ''What's a nice kitty like you doing with a creep like this?''

''I'm his partner,'' I said. ''And I'll make a deal with you. You drop the 'kitty' stuff and I won't call you B.J. Okay? The name's Gomez.''

''Got it,'' she replied. ''This on the level, Dan? You're partnered with a thaumagene?''

''It's on the level.''

''Since when do they have thaumagenes on the force?'' she asked.

''They don't,'' said Leventhal. ''This is a special case. Gomez here is a close friend of the commissioner. An interested party, you might say, representing animal concerns on this case.''

''So you really *are* on this case?'' she said.

''Yup. I really are.''

''Why you? Why not Chavez and McVickers?'' she asked.

''They wanted someone who knew how to deal with the media,'' he replied.

Bobbie Joe snorted. ''You? Give me a break. I still remember how you shoved Tommy Martino's microphone halfway down his throat.''

''Like I said, they wanted someone who knew how to deal with the media,'' said Leventhal.

"You're serious?" she said. "They really put you back on Homicide?"

"As per the commissioner, himself."

Bobbie Joe whistled softly. "That must've put a burr up Moran's ass."

Leventhal grinned. "Yeah. Too bad, ain't it?"

"You know, I always wondered what it was with you and Chief Moran," said Bobbie Joe. "I always thought it was just your winning ways, but I heard a rumor it was something a bit more personal."

"Man just doesn't like my style, that's all," said Leventhal.

"I heard you fucked his daughter. Any truth to *that*?"

"I heard you pull the train for the Broncos. Any truth to *that*?"

"I'll show you mine if you show me yours."

"No, thanks," said Leventhal. "I don't think I could handle that."

"Never know until you try."

"Why, B.J., is that a proposition?"

"Would you take me up on it if it was?"

"What, and ruin a beautiful friendship?"

"Didn't think you'd have the guts for it."

"It ain't that, B.J., it's just that I like to mate within my species."

"You mean you only fuck baboons?"

I was enjoying the hell out of their interchange. Despite the shots they were trading, it was obvious they really liked each other. And just as obvious that they had never been intimate, though both of them had given it some consideration. That undercurrent of sexual tension only takes place between people who've given it a lot of thought, but have never been able to work their way around it for one reason or another. My guess was that she found Leventhal attractive, but was put off by his macho prick attitude. And Leventhal liked her personality, but couldn't get past the extra weight she carried. Maybe one of these days they'd both get really drunk, and go for it. Then, in the morning, one of two things would happen. They'd either wake up in love or not speaking to each other.

Leventhal reached his car and opened the door on the driver's side. I noticed that his car seemed to fit his personality. It was an old Cadillac Margaux, one of the last ones made and, therefore, a classic, worth quite a piece of change when properly restored. Except Leventhal's was painted a flat, primer black, with orange and purple flames on the hood, and a red leather interior. It was enough to make a collector blanche with horror. I liked it. So sue me.

"So how about it, Dan?" said Bobbie Joe.

"How about *what*?"

"Come on, stop being such a fucking hard case, will ya? Don't you ever get *tired* of this fruitloop act of yours? How about a break for your favorite journalist?"

"Sure. Where do you want it? Arm? Wrist? Kneecap?"

Bobbie Joe rolled her eyes. "I *could* help you out, you know, if you'd meet me halfway."

"Yeah? How? Whatcha got?"

"Quite a bit, actually. On Susan Jacobs and the ERA. I was working on a piece about it."

"No kiddin'."

"No kiddin', tough guy. So, what do you say? Want to compare notes?"

"Yeah, sure. One condition, though."

"Shoot."

"Anything you get from me, you sit on until I say it's okay to use it. Otherwise, all bets are off."

Bobbie Joe nodded. "I can live with that."

"Okay, but I haven't got the time now. Why don'tcha meet me tonight at Mudd's? I need to see the Baghwan."

"Okay. About eight o'clock?"

"Better make it nine. I got some stuff to do."

"Right. See you then."

As Bobbie Joe walked back toward her car, I jumped up

onto the front seat through the driver's-side door and Leventhal got in behind me. He inserted the key into the switch and turned it, activating the thaumaturgic battery. The dash lit up with a soft blue glow and the car gently rose about two feet off the ground.

"Interesting lady," I said, in an offhand tone.

"B.J.? She's a pain in the ass. But I guess she's okay, for a reporter. If you tell her 'off the record,' it stays off the record. She's a straight shooter. Not too many of those around anymore."

"Never were," I said.

Leventhal switched on the stereo and pushed a disc into the player. Not unreasonably, perhaps, I expected to hear music. Silly me. Instead, what issued from the speakers was a deafening, throaty, *"Thraghhhhh!"*

I arched my back and felt my fur bristling. "What the hell is *that*?"

Leventhal grinned at me. "Chevy 454 V-8," he said, "with racing cams and blower."

I frowned. "An *internal combustion engine*?" I willed myself to relax and retracted my claws. I didn't want to ruin his upholstery.

"Great, huh? It's music to my ears, Cat. Thaumaturgically powered vehicles don't pollute the air, but when it comes right down to it, they just ain't got no soul. This," he said, pointing at the player, *"this* is what a car oughtta sound like!"

I shook my head. "If you say so. If you ask me, it sounds like somebody torturing a jackhammer."

He grimaced and turned the volume down low. "Some people have no appreciation for the finer things in life. Me, I'd give my left nut for a fully restored Corvette Stingray and the juice to make it go. I've got an engine out of one sitting in my living room at home. All chromed and polished. Beautiful. It's like a fuckin' sculpture. But even if I could manage to put one all together and score some gas for it, I'd get my act shot down before I went three blocks.'' He shook his head and sighed. "Guess I was just born too late, that's all.''

Another one, I thought. I didn't think I'd ever understand this nostalgic longing so many humans seem to have for the past. I've never met an animal who felt that way. Animals live in the present. We deal with life as it happens, just one day at a time. That always seemed to make sense to me. Humans, on the other hand, rarely seem to live in the present. They're either preoccupied with thoughts about the past, or with making plans for the future. As a result, they often don't seem to enjoy *today*. Perhaps that explained their preoccupation with time. Time slips away from them.

"What's a baghwan?" I asked, quickly changing the subject, because I really didn't want to get into a discussion about "the good old days." From everything I'd read, I couldn't see what was so damned good about them.

"Baghwan's not a what, it's a who," said Leventhal. "Though a few people might argue that point," he added, with a smile.

"Okay," I said. "Then *who* is Baghwan?"

"His real name's Bruce Young," Leventhal replied, as he drove, "but most people know him by his street name, Baghwan. I'm not sure what the hell it means. It has to do with East Indian religion or philosophy or something. But it seems like he's studied just about everything at one time or another. Guy's a walking encyclopedia of obscure knowledge. History, philosophy, theology, psychology, you name it, he knows something about it. He also knows where all the bodies are buried when it comes to the street scene in this town. He deals in information. Specializes in connections.''

"You mean he's sort of a go-between?" I asked.

"Among other things," said Leventhal, nodding.

"And you use him as a source?"

"Every now and then," said Leventhal. "Generally speaking, the Baghwan won't talk to cops. That is, he'll talk to 'em, be polite and all, but he won't give 'em anything."

"But he talks to you?"

"Because I play straight with him," Leventhal replied. "I never ask him to sell anybody out and I never hassle him or any of his friends. And if he scratches my back, I always try to return the favor. That's something the guys who go by the book never understand. They come on with this big authority trip and expect to get something for nothing. Or else they'll flash a couple of bills and expect a guy to roll over and be their stoolie. Sometimes it works out that way, but only with sleazy small-timers, not guys like Baghwan. If you're a scuzzball, you'll sell out your own mother for a lousy buck, but most people have their pride and you gotta respect that. If I slip the Baghwan a few bucks, it's understood that it's to meet expenses, period. It's a business transaction, pure and simple, and it's a door that swings both ways. Most cops don't understand that, or else they don't want to understand it. They think a badge makes them superior and entitles them to throw their weight around."

"And you don't?"

"Only when I have to, Cat, only when I have to. In the old days, the Mob had a saying—'Sooner or later, everybody does business with everybody.' If you understand that, it makes it easier to get along with people. That's why I often come up with leads nobody else can get. It's not that I'm such a great detective, it's that I don't treat people like shit just because they dress or look different or follow a lifestyle that's on the fringe. Hell, if I hadn't joined the cops, I'd probably be one of 'em."

"In a way, you *are* one of them, aren't you?" I asked. "You seem to understand them."

Leventhal shook his head. "No, Cat. Maybe I used to be, but not anymore. Just because I understand 'em doesn't make me one of 'em. I'm on the other side. I stopped being one of 'em when I went into the police academy. That's a one-way trip.''

"It must have been important to you, though," I said.

Leventhal nodded. "Yeah, it was. Still is."

"Why?"

"Because, like I told the commissioner, I wanted to catch the bad guys," said Leventhal. "And nobody really gives a shit about the bad guys who prey on the people of the street. Oh, every once in a while, they'll bust one of 'em, because it's easy and maybe they've had the bust handed to 'em on a silver platter, and it's another felony arrest that looks good on your record, but most cops would just as soon bust the victims as the victimizers. They don't really care. A bust is a bust. If you got some sleazeball out there taking young runaways and turning 'em out to work the streets, it's easier to bust the runaways then the creep who turned 'em out. They'll bust some kid for taking his frustration out on a wall with a can of spray paint, just trying to say, 'Hey, I'm here; I exist; I got this to say,' but nobody cares that the kid's living under a bridge and eating outta dumpsters.''

I nodded. That was a part of life I understood only too well. I'd been there.

"Anyway," said Leventhal, shrugging his shoulders, "I had my share of being rousted when I was a kid on the streets. And I didn't like it anymore than anybody else does. I wondered why they were hassling me when they could be out there doing some good, going after the real creeps, not kids like me, who were only acting creepy because nobody understood and nobody cared and it was a way to make people keep their distance. And then, one day, when I was mouthing off at some cop, a funny thing happened. I thought to myself, you know, if I was in this guy's shoes, *I'd* fucking know what to do. I'd know how to handle this. I started looking at the situation from his point of view and I realized why he was the way he was. Because he didn't understand. He didn't care. And, in another way, *I* didn't understand and *I* didn't care, either. To him, I was just another snot-nosed, wiseass street punk. But to me, he was just another hardass pig on a power trip. I was just as guilty of seeing things only one way as he was. And I thought about it. I thought about it a lot. And I realized that if any of that shit was going to change, *somebody* had to start changing it. Might as well be me. If I thought I could do it better, then maybe I should walk the walk and not just talk the talk, you know?" He shrugged again. "So I became a cop."

"And you've been bucking the system ever since," I said.

Leventhal grinned. "Yeah, well, maybe it's just self-defense. It's a lot harder for a cop to hassle another cop."

"You're an idealist, Dan," I said. "It's a dying breed."

"Well, definitely an endangered species, anyway," he replied, with a grin.

"I keep hearing about this place, Mudd's," I said. "A couple of Susan Jacobs's friends mentioned it on the tape. What is that, a bar?"

"A coffeehouse," said Leventhal. "They don't serve alcohol, which is why they can stay open till four A.M., and why a lot of the young street kids can hang out there."

"Somehow, it doesn't sound like the sort of place Susan Jacobs and her friends would frequent," I said.

"You get all kinds of people at Mudd's," said Leventhal. "Artists and adepts, writers, dancers, students and musicians, Rippers, and whoever thinks it's cool to hang around with people like that. It makes for a pretty strange mix. Dee Rose, who owns the place, holds the whole thing together. Place has a lot of history. During the Collapse, it burned down in a firefight between the cops and the street gangs. They say sometimes you can see the ghosts of some of the people who got killed there that night."

"Can you?" I asked.

Leventhal shrugged. "I haven't seen 'em, but Dee doesn't

say yes, and he doesn't say no. I guess it helps business to have rumors that the place is haunted. Dee's a little strange, anyway. He wanted a place to hang out with his friends and he didn't like any of the other night spots in town. They were all either too slick, or too trendy, or too expensive for his tastes. He wanted something more laid back, more bohemian. So he bought the old building with the aid of a historical preservation grant and reopened Mudd's."

"Let me guess," I said. "It's your favorite hangout."

Leventhal grinned. "How'd you know?"

"Just took a shot," I said.

"Well, I think you'll like the place. You oughtta fit right in."

"Assuming they let me through the door," I said. "Isn't there some health department regulation about not allowing animals in where they serve food?"

"Yeah, but when it comes to thaumagenes, it's not really enforced," said Leventhal. "Leastwise, not at Mudd's. Dee says most of the thaumagenes that come in are cleaner than some of his regular customers."

"I'll be sure to go in the restroom if I have to bring up a hairball," I said.

"Yeah, well, you probably won't be the only one hackin' in there," Leventhal replied. He pulled in to the curb. "Well, here we are."

"Good. Where are we?"

"Sixteenth and Lincoln. We're going in that building over there, right on the corner."

I glanced toward the tall, glass-fronted office building. "What's in there?"

"A shitload of overpriced offices, and the studios of KTLK, Denver's K-Talk FM, home of the late night call-in shows and big-time alternative radio."

"Big-time alternative radio? Isn't that a contradiction in terms?" I asked.

"Yeah, but don't tell 'em. They're very sincere about it."

He held the door for me while I trotted across the seat and hopped down onto the sidewalk, then we went up the steps and into the lobby. It was very ritzy. Lots of mirrors, fake marble, and potted plants. Someone had taken a lot of trouble to make the lobby look subdued and elegant, I guess so they could justify the high rents they obviously charged.

I leaped back and hissed as a floor buffer shot past me and swung wildly to make a wide detour around Leventhal. There wasn't any cord attached to it and it made a sort of swishing, whuffle-whuffle sound as it gyroscoped crazily across the tiled floor, like some animated appliance waltzing to music that no one else could hear.

"You okay, Cat?" Leventhal asked me.

"Stupid thing almost ran me over," I said, staring at it malevolently.

"Hey!" he shouted, pointing at the buffer.

It stopped and swiveled around, its bristles rotating furiously.

Leventhal beckoned to it with his forefinger. "C'mere."

It swished and whuffled up to him.

He gave it a sound kick and I heard the clang of his steel-toed boot on the buffer's housing as the thing went scuttling backward with a high-pitched, whining sound.

"You! What the hell do you think you're doing?" A beefy security guard came bustling over from the lobby desk.

Leventhal flashed his shield.

"Oh," said the guard, relaxing somewhat, but still staring at Leventhal suspiciously. "You a cop?"

"No, I'm a Girl Scout," Leventhal replied wryly. "You better have building management get an adept to adjust that thing. It almost ran over my partner."

The security guard looked down at me and raised his eyebrows. *"That's* your partner?"

"Yeah," said Leventhal. "You got a problem with that?"

"Uh, no sir," the guard replied, a bit taken aback. "Is, uh, there something I can help you with?"

"Yeah, just point us toward the elevators," Leventhal replied.

"Certainly, sir. Right that way," said the guard, pointing across the lobby.

"And get a leash on that thing, before somebody gets hurt," added Leventhal, pointing at the buffer.

"Uh . . . right. Yes, sir. I'll speak to building maintenance."

"You do that."

I couldn't help chuckling as we made our way to the elevators.

"What's so funny?" Leventhal asked.

"Just the way you kicked that buffer," I replied.

"I hate those damned thaumaturgically animated things," he said, with a scowl. "Computers are bad enough, but it's getting so's you can't get through a single day without tripping over some kind of spell-animated contraption."

"They're just work-saving devices," I said.

"They're a pain in the ass, if you ask me," he replied. "That 'work-saving device' just about flattened you."

"Well, it didn't."

"Came close enough," said Leventhal. "I don't know about you, Cat, but it bothers me to see machines and things skittering about all by themselves. About half the time, they don't even work right."

"That's because the adepts who cast the spells were sloppy," I replied. "I've seen some pretty sophisticated jobs of thaumaturgic animation myself."

I thought of Broom, Wyrdrune's familiar, a magically animated kitchen broom which had somehow become impressed with his late mother's personality, and Ramses, the living sculpture created by Lady Rhiannon out of precious stones and metals. However, Broom was the result of a highly sophisticated spell that not even Wyrdrune had understood completely, and Lady Rhiannon, in addition to being Santa Fe's preeminent sculptor, was a highly talented and gifted sorceress. My partner had a point. Most thaumaturgically animated objects one encountered these days were not on the same level, primarily because the adepts who animated them were not very advanced, themselves.

Magic was no longer secret knowledge and, on at least some level, almost anyone could do it. There were hundreds of books to be found in the thaumaturgy and occult sections of most bookstores, and a dedicated layman who wished to study magic could, theoretically, receive almost as complete an education as a warlock in a graduate study program at a College of Sorcery. However, it was one thing to have access to the knowledge, and it was quite another thing to have the skill and talent to put that knowledge to practical use. Most people who tried their hand at magic and found they had no talent for it usually had sense enough to let well enough alone, because it could be dangerous, but there has never been a shortage of people who have no sense whatsoever, nor was there a shortage of unscrupulous and sloppy hack adepts.

The Bureau of Thaumaturgy, under the aegis of the International Thaumaturgical Commission, fought a constant battle to regulate the practice of magic, but there was only so much any bureaucracy, no matter how large and powerful, could do. Adepts were licensed and registered, and an unscrupulous or unethical adept could have his or her license lifted, but that didn't solve all the problems. Lately, there had been a move to ban the sale of books and information giving instructions for practical magic use, but that had run into stiff opposition in the legislature, based on the First Amendment.

In Washington, Congresswoman Brady was seeking to find a way around that little loophole by introducing the "Thaumaturgical Control Bill," which aimed at registering all purchasers of books and other information pertaining to practical magic use and called for a seven-day waiting period on all such purchases, to provide for a background check. It was a controversial bill, but it had a lot of grass-roots support, particularly among people who saw the opportunity to make a fortune in black-market, underground-press publication of thaumaturgy texts. The battle was being fought with bumper stickers proclaiming slogans such as "Magic is alive, trouble is afoot," and "You'll get my book only when you pry my cold, dead fingers from its spine." It was an imperfect world, but at least it was an entertaining one.

The elevator doors opened and we entered. "Floor, please," said the elevator.

"Sixteen," said Leventhal.

The doors closed, but the elevator didn't move. "Floor, please."

"*Sixteen*," Leventhal repeated.

The doors slid open. "Lobby," said the elevator. "Have a nice day."

Leventhal slammed his fist against the control panel. "*Sixteen, you dumb, fuckin' box!*"

The doors closed and the elevator started to ascend.

Leventhal shook his head. "I rest my case," he said. He took out a pad and pen and made a note to call the building inspector.

We arrived at the sixteenth floor without further incident and stepped out. "Have a nice day," said the elevator, as we exited.

"Up your shaft," Leventhal growled.

The glass-fronted office enclosure before us was labeled with the call letters of K-Talk, where Susan Jacobs had worked, and beneath it, the name of the broadcasting group that owned the station. The letters were ornately stenciled on the glass in gold. The receptionist, a glossy blond in a dark-blue, well-tailored, Neo-Edwardian suit, looked up as we approached.

"Good afternoon," she said. "Can I help you?" From a

speaker concealed in the ceiling, the program currently on the air could be heard.

"I'm here to see Mark Michaels," Leventhal said.

"I see," the receptionist replied, automatically. "And do you have an appointment?"

Leventhal flashed his shield. "No, but this says I don't need one."

She seemed unimpressed. "Just a moment, please." She picked up a phone and turned her back to us, speaking softly. I caught the word "policeman," uttered with distaste. She put down the phone after a moment and turned back to us with a smile that was anything but sincere. "Someone will be with you in a moment," she said.

Leventhal grunted and flipped out his cigarette case with an abrupt motion. With a flick of the wrist, he snapped it open.

"I'm sorry, but there's no smoking in here," said the receptionist.

Leventhal ignored her. The Zippo appeared in his hand as if by magic and, with a flourish, he snapped it open and lit up.

The receptionist cleared her throat. "Sir, there's no smoking in here."

Leventhal gave her a heavy-lidded stare. "So call a 'policeman,' sweetheart," he said, saying the word with the same tone of distaste she'd used.

She gave him an icy look and proceeded to ignore us. A moment later, a man in a powder-blue Neo-Edwardian suit came out into the reception area. He looked almost as glossy as the receptionist. His dark hair was styled in a very non-Edwardian geometric cut and he wore several gold amulets and chains that definitely clashed with the look.

"I'm Dan Daniel, program director," he said, holding out his hand. "How can I help you, officer?"

"Well, Dan Dan," Leventhal replied, ignoring his outstretched hand, "you can take me to see Mark Mike."

The program director's smile slipped slightly. "I'm afraid Mr. Michaels is busy at the moment. Is there something I can do for you?"

"Yeah," said Leventhal, exhaling smoke into the man's face. "Tell him to get unbusy and get his ass out here, or I'm coming in and getting it."

Dan Daniel moved his tongue around inside his cheek for a moment, then took a deep breath and walked over to the phone. He picked it up and, like the receptionist, turned his back to us and spoke softly. I caught the word "hardass." Daniel replaced the phone on its cradle and turned back to us.

"Mr. Michaels will see you now," he said stiffly. "If you would follow me, please?"

We followed him through the reception area and down a short, carpeted corridor, past the glass-enclosed broadcast studios to the general manager's office. Daniel knocked on the door and entered. The man seated behind the large, glass-topped desk in the stark and airy office was speaking on the phone. A large book was open on the desk before him. The far wall of the office behind him was all glass, affording a panoramic view of the city and the foothills of the Rockies beyond. The wall to his right was one large cabinet, containing an array of recording equipment, a state-of-the-art sound system, and a large television screen. The opposite wall had shelves mounted on it, containing books, files, and what looked like bound reports or transcripts of programs. The carpeting was dove gray, and there was one single potted plant in the room, or actually three, thick-trunked corn plants crammed into one large pot. A small, comfortable, leather-upholstered couch was placed at an angle to the desk, in front of it, with two upholstered chairs across from it.

Michaels finished speaking and hung up the phone, then stood to greet us. Daniel, the program director, lingered.

"How do you do?" said Michaels, holding out his hand. "Mark Michaels, general manager."

Leventhal ignored the outstretched hand. "Detective Leventhal, Homicide," he replied, flatly. "And this is my partner, Catseye Gomez."

Michaels stared at him, then me, then finally let his hand drop after an awkward moment. "Your partner?" he said, glancing at me again.

"Yeah. You got a problem with that?" said Leventhal.

"Uh . . . no, of course not," Michaels replied hastily. "I was simply unaware that there were thaumagenes on the police force."

"There aren't," said Leventhal. "Gomez is assisting the investigation in a special capacity, as a representative of animal interests in the case."

"I see," said Michaels, not seeing anything at all. But he did give me a nod.

"I'd like to ask you a few questions about your relationship with Susan Jacobs."

Michaels nodded to Daniel. "Of course. Give us a few moments, will you, Dan?" he said.

Daniel said, "Sure," and turned to leave, but Leventhal said, "Stick around, Dan Dan. The hardass might have a couple of questions for you, as well."

Daniel hesitated and exchanged a quick glance with Michaels, who nodded and beckoned us to take a seat on the couch. Leventhal plopped down onto the cushions and I hopped up beside him. Michaels remained behind his desk and Daniel remained standing, despite the two chairs being free.

"It's a terrible thing about Susan," Michaels said earnestly, shaking his head. "Just awful. Her death was quite a blow to us all. We're all still in shock here. But I'll do anything I can to help, of course."

"What exactly was the nature of your relationship with Ms. Jacobs?" Leventhal asked.

Michaels replied smoothly, without batting an eye. "We had a personal relationship, as well as a professional one," he said. "I was in love with her. Her death has hit me particularly hard." He moistened his lips and took a deep breath. "I wanted to marry her."

"And did she want to marry you?" asked Leventhal.

Michaels looked down at his desk and shook his head. "No," he replied. "No, she didn't." He looked up again and met Leventhal's gaze straight on. "However, if you're looking for a motive there, detective, I'm afraid you're wasting your time. Susan and I had a very good relationship; she simply wasn't ready to take that step. She didn't feel ready for marriage, or for having children. But it wasn't a question of commitment. There wasn't anybody else."

"You sound pretty sure of that," said Leventhal.

"I am sure of it. If there was, she would have told me. We were always very honest and open with each other. Susan was just that kind of person. You can ask anyone. She wasn't one to hold anything back."

Leventhal nodded. "How long had you known her?"

"Six years," said Michaels, reflectively, "ever since I hired her." He paused a moment, to collect himself, and took a deep breath. He was doing his best to be straightforward and businesslike about the questioning, but it was clearly difficult for him. "We started seeing each other . . . Well, we both had some reservations, at first, you know, about the pitfalls of dating someone you're working with, but we talked it over and we both decided we were mature enough and professional enough to deal with any potential problems that might come up." He shrugged. "As it turned out, there weren't any problems. None whatsoever. We were very much alike and we had a great deal in common. We . . ." His voice trailed off, and he looked away for a moment and cleared his throat. "I'm sorry. I realize you have a job to do, but you have to understand, this isn't very easy for me."

"I understand," said Leventhal.

"If you want to know who killed her, I can save you a lot of time," said Daniel, interjecting. "It was those Tabernacle nuts."

"Tabernacle?" Leventhal said, raising his eyebrows.

"Well, now, we have no proof of that," said Michaels, with a glance at Daniel.

"Who or what is the Tabernacle?" Leventhal asked.

"Bunch of Fundamentalist zealots," Daniel replied, tersely. "They call their church the Tabernacle of True Faith, but it's not so much a church as it is a cult."

"We did a program with them once," said Michaels, "on Sean Prescott's 'Late Shift' show."

Leventhal nodded to indicate he was familiar with it.

"It was one of our more controversial programs," Michaels said. "It generated a flood of call-ins. The phone lines were tied up all night. I can get you a tape of it if you like."

Leventhal nodded. "Yeah, I'd appreciate that."

Michaels picked up the phone, punched a button for an extension in the studios.

"What makes you think these Tabernacle people were responsible for the murder of Ms. Jacobs?" Leventhal asked Daniel.

Daniel snorted with disgust. "I'll tell you what," he said, "you listen to that tape and draw your own conclusions. You know about the threats we received over the ERA features?"

"I was about to get to that," said Leventhal. "I understand that there were threats phoned in to the station, as well as to Ms. Jacobs's home."

Daniel nodded. "Yeah, that's right. And the rhetoric was the same as the kind of crap those Tabernacle loonies were spouting. I mean, it was almost word for word the same kind of bullshit."

"Well, you had those people on the air, didn't you?" asked Leventhal.

"That doesn't mean I like what they stand for," Daniel replied grimly.

"No, but it does mean that anyone who heard them on that show could have borrowed some of their rhetoric, as you put it, to word their threats."

Daniel grimaced. "I suppose you have a point," he admitted. "But anyone who'd act on that kind of demented logic belongs in the same camp with them. If I were you, they're the ones I'd be investigating."

"I'll look into it," said Leventhal. He turned to Michaels. "Did you tape any of those calls? The threats, I mean."

"No," said Michaels. "That is, we would have had them on tape if they'd called in on the air, during one of the programs, but they were phoned in directly to the station, to the main switchboard. A couple of times, the caller or callers pretended to be someone else, so the call would be routed to my office, or to Dan's, or to Susan, and then they'd spew their bile and hang up. We couldn't tape those. But Dan's right about one thing, those Tabernacle people were definitely hostile to the ERA, and to Susan in particular. Very strongly hostile."

"Why didn't you call the police?" asked Leventhal.

"We didn't really take them all that seriously," Michaels replied. "That is, not until Susan . . ." He swallowed hard and looked away, out the window, into the distance. He remained silent for a long moment.

Daniel picked up the thread. "You have to understand, we get a lot of calls like that. When you're doing talk radio, all sorts of kooks and cranks call in. Susan had said something about saving the calls she got on her answering machine at home for a show she was going to do with Sean this week, but other than that, none of us ever thought it was anything more than a bunch of crackpots letting off some steam. It happens all the time."

"I see," said Leventhal. "And employees of the station

getting threatening calls at home, does *that* happen all the time, as well?''

Daniel looked uncomfortable. ''No,'' he said, awkwardly. ''No, it doesn't.''

''Would it be safe to say it was a first?'' asked Leventhal.

''No, actually, it wasn't the first time,'' Michaels replied. ''It was the first time for Susan, because of her personal involvement with the ERA, but Sean Prescott had received crank calls at home, as well. There was one particular caller who was uncommonly persistent and somehow kept getting hold of Sean's home telephone number, every time he had it changed. We never did find out who he was.''

''Were these threatening calls, as well?'' asked Leventhal.

''Well, not exactly,'' Daniel replied, with a smirk. ''They were more in the nature of sexual propositions.''

''You mean obscene calls?''

''I suppose you could call them that,'' said Michaels. ''The caller seemed obsessed with Sean, with the sound of his voice, with his on-air persona. I understand that he would occasionally get rather explicit. Sean kept hanging up on him when he called him at home, and when he called during his show, the engineer simply wouldn't put him through. It got so we could recognize his voice.''

''He eventually give up?'' asked Leventhal.

''No, Sean did. He had his home phone disconnected. If we want to get in touch with him, we call his pager. He—that is, the caller—doesn't seem to have gotten that number. Yet.''

Leventhal shook his head. ''Strange business you're in,'' he said.

''No more strange than yours, detective,'' said Michaels. ''We both often see people at their worst. Will there be anything else?''

Leventhal shut his notepad. ''No, not at the moment,'' he said. ''But I would like that tape you mentioned.''

''It'll be waiting for you at the front desk,'' said Michaels.

"Oh, and one more thing," said Leventhal. "I'd like to speak with Mr. Prescott. Is that possible?"

"He doesn't come in until just before his show starts," Michaels said, "usually about eleven forty-five or so. Sometimes he comes in with only seconds to spare before he has to go on the air."

"But you said you can page him?"

Michaels nodded.

"Would you mind doing that?" asked Leventhal. "Tell him that I'd like to meet with him. I'll be at Mudd's Café tonight at about nine or so. If he could drop by before he goes on the air, I'd appreciate it very much."

"I'll see he gets the message," Michaels said.

"Okay," said Michaels, rising to his feet. "If there's anything else, I'll be in touch. Thanks for your time."

"Look, uh, abut that 'hardass' remark," said Daniel, "I'm sorry. I was out of line. We're all a little on edge here."

Leventhal nodded. "Sure. Forget about it."

"Detective Leventhal?" said Michaels.

"Yeah?"

"Realistically, what do you think the odds are of finding the one who did this?"

Leventhal gave him a steady look. "Better than even."

"Get the son of a bitch."

Leventhal nodded. "Count on it."

Eight

I N real life, watching a detective going about his work was nowhere near as interesting as it was in mystery novels. I hadn't really expected to see Leventhal slapping witnesses around or dodging gunfire from speeding dark sedans, but it was still a little disappointing to see how dull detective work could be. Mostly, it was fairly routine, methodical stuff. At this early stage of the investigation, he didn't know exactly what he was looking for, so all he could do was examine the evidence and question everyone he knew to be associated with the victim, in the hope that something would come out that he could follow up on. If Mike Hammer had worked this way, I never would've gotten past the first chapter of *I, the Jury*.

As we were leaving the radio station, Leventhal picked up the tape Michaels had made for him, then used the phone to call the two women who had left messages on Susan Jacobs's answering machine. Neither of them were home, so he left messages asking them to meet with him at Mudd's Café later on that night.

I pointed out to him that one of them, the one named Christy, had said something about having a hot date, but Leventhal replied that he hadn't met a woman yet who left

for a date straight from work. She would go home to
freshen up and change, and he felt reasonably sure she'd
break her date to speak with a police detective about her
girlfriend's murder. I had to agree that having a friend
blown up was liable to put a damper on her plans for a
romantic evening, so I conceded the logic of his point and
we moved on to our next stop, which was the crime lab at
the police headquarters building on Cherokee Street.

It was amazing how quickly things moved when the police
commissioner expressed a personal interest in a case. The
crime lab boys had dropped everything else they were working on to give the Susan Jacobs murder top priority. What
they had learned so far was interesting, to say the least. From
the evidence left behind after the blast, they had determined
that the bomb had been set off by a remote detonator, and that
the explosive was of a type designated as C-4.

"What the hell is that?" asked Leventhal, with a puzzled
frown. "I never even heard of it."

"That's not surprising," Eggleston, the forensics adept,
replied. "It's a little before your time. They used stuff like
this back in the twentieth century. It's ancient."

"You're kidding," said Leventhal.

"Nope. First time I've ever seen it myself, although I'd
heard about it. It's pretty devastating stuff. And it wouldn't
take much to get the job done."

"Where would anyone get something like that nowadays?" asked Leventhal. "You're not telling me somebody's still manufacturing it?"

"Not since the Collapse," Eggleston replied. "No, the
only way you could make something like this today would
be if you got a crooked alchemist to brew it up for you. And
that's not the case here, or I'd have picked up thaumaturgical
trace emanations. What we've got here is an explosive that
dates back to the days of the Collapse, or even earlier."

"Wouldn't it go bad?" asked Leventhal.

"Nope."

"Who'd be dealing in stuff like this?" Leventhal asked, with a frown.

"Your guess is as good as mine," said Eggleston, with a shrug. "If someone local is dealing in this stuff, they've probably only recently come into possession of it, because we've never run across it before. If you want my best guess, I'd say somebody found an old weapons stash. Here, take a look at this."

He took a book off his desk and opened it to a page he'd marked. Leventhal picked me up and set me on the desk, so I could see it, too. The book showed a photograph of a large, heavy, metallic cylinder.

"This was a type of safe used in the pre-Collapse days by survivalists," Eggleston said.

"Survivalists?" said Leventhal.

"People who apparently anticipated the Collapse. They often constructed underground shelters and stocked them with emergency supplies and weapons. They'd sometimes pack a cache of weapons and ammunition in a safe like this and bury it in some out-of-the-way location, so they could dig it up at some future date, when they had need of it. It was a way of stockpiling ordnance without risking being caught with an arsenal."

"And you're thinking somebody dug up one of these things from the pre-Collapse days?" Leventhal said.

"That would be my guess. Otherwise, if somebody had this stuff lying around from the old days, we'd have seen some evidence of it being used by now. Or we'd have nailed someone with a supply. I can't imagine anyone simply sitting on something like this for all these years. They'd either turn it in, use it, or sell it."

"I see your point," said Leventhal grimly. "So what you're telling me is that we've got an explosive device that's impossible to trace."

Eggleston nodded. "That's about the size of it."

"Terrific," said Leventhal sourly. "Got any more good news for me?"

"Not much, I'm afraid," Eggleston replied. "We're still working on those tapes. The trouble is, the caller had muffled his voice, so we're going to have to filter and enhance them to get a decent voice print. That's the kind of thing a defense attorney can have a field day with in court. Besides, it still wouldn't necessarily prove anything. If you arrest a suspect, we might be able to tie him in to the death threats, but that's still no proof your suspect actually committed the murder. It's circumstantial evidence, at best, and somewhat shaky evidence, at that."

"So, basically, what you're telling me is we've got nothing," Leventhal said.

"Well, we know what kind of explosive was used, but there's no way to trace it. We'll be able to come up with a voice print, but there's no guarantee it'll stand up in court, and even if it does, it won't tie a suspect in with the murder without corroborating evidence. And we know a remote detonator was used, but all that tells us is that the killer was in the general vicinity when the bomb went off, probably in visual contact with the victim's vehicle. That's about it."

Leventhal grimaced. "Well, it's not much, but at least it's something."

"The victim's vehicle was garaged in a security building, right?" asked Eggleston.

"Yeah," said Leventhal. "Why?"

"Well, then that means the bomb was probably planted when the vehicle was parked outside, unattended, while the victim was at work. But what puzzles me is why didn't the killer detonate it as soon as she got in the car? Why take the risk of following her home and doing it there? What would be the point?"

"To blow her up on her own doorstep," Leventhal replied. "And on the commissioner's doorstep, as well, to insure maximum media coverage. Our killer seemed especially anxious to make sure the media got the message.''

"You know, there's one other possibility we haven't yet considered," I said.

They both looked at me.

"What if the bomb was planted while the victim's car was still in the garage?" I said.

"What?" said Leventhal.

"Think about it," I said. "If the killer was able to get into the garage the night before, that would have given him all night to plant the bomb, in relative privacy, which would be a lot less risky than doing it while the car was parked outside, in broad daylight. Then the killer could have simply waited while she drove to work and went on the air, then detonated the device when she came back.''

"And it would look as if the bomb had been planted while she was on the air," said Leventhal, "when in fact, it had been planted earlier, while she was home and the car was in the underground garage. And the only reason the killer would have for doing that would be to conceal the fact that he had access to the building. Which means the killer might even be living there." He punched his fist into his palm. "Dammit, Cat, that's good! If the killer was one of the victim's fellow tenants in the building, it could also explain how he managed to get her private phone number. Maybe she actually *knew* her killer!''

"It's possible," said Eggleston, with a thoughtful nod. "It's certainly a fascinating speculation.''

"Speculation, hell!" said Leventhal. "I think he's onto something! It's the first decent lead we've got. I want you to send a lab team over to that building and go through that garage with a fine-tooth comb. See if you can find anything that would indicate the bomb was planted there.''

"I'll get right on it," Eggleston said. He glanced at me and nodded. "That's good thinking, Gomez. You'd make a fine detective." He grinned. "If you ever want a reference, just let me know."

"Thanks," I replied, giving him a sparkle with ole Betsy. "I'll keep it in mind."

Our next stop was Leventhal's apartment, in a run-down section of Capitol Hill, just off the Colfax Strip. The house it was in certainly wasn't much to look at from outside. It was a big, old, private home that had been divided up into apartments. The house had seen better days. Hell, the entire neighborhood had seen better days, but I didn't think there was anyone around old enough to remember when.

The ugly brick house needed tuck-pointing so badly, it was dropping bricks like a collie sheds fur. The brick porch was settling and looked about ready to crack in two. The lawn, or what there was of it, had been taken over by thistles and wild roses. Music, or what passed for music among kids these days, blared from speakers set into the windows of the upper stories. I don't know, maybe there was a melody in there somewhere, but to me, it sounded like robots trying to smash each other to pieces.

"Looks like a party goin' on," said Leventhal, as we went up the overgrown front walk. A machete would have come in handy.

"This is where you *live*?" I said, with disbelief.

"Yeah," he replied, flicking his cigarette away into the street. "Me and about a dozen college kids. Not all together, you understand. I got my place, they got all the other apartments. I'm like an island of fascism in a sea of bullshit."

He opened the door and an overpowering cloud of sandalwood incense came wafting out. Something was burning, and it didn't smell like food.

"Oh, shit, here come the marines," said the young person of indeterminate gender as we went down the corridor and toward a room at the back.

"Up yours," said Leventhal.

"Anytime, officer, anytime."

"Hey, look!" a pretty young skirt called out, "Danny got himself a pet kitty!"

I hissed at her as we passed, and she backed away, eyes wide.

"Figures," somebody said. "The street cop went and got himself an alley cat."

"Friends of yours?" I called out, over the noise.

"Ahh, sort of," Leventhal replied, as he inserted the key into the apartment door. "I'm kinda like the den mother around here."

"Pretty rowdy bunch of cubs, if you ask me," I said.

"Just youthful exuberance," Leventhal replied. "Hey, you assholes, turn it down! I got some work to do!"

"Fuck you!" someone yelled out.

"Individuation is an awkward stage, ain't it?" Leventhal said, as we entered the apartment.

The first thing I noticed was the engine. It was sitting on a platform in the center of the room, all gleaming chrome and polished aluminum. Leventhal gave it a pat as he passed.

"Hey, baby, daddy's home," he said.

The floor was covered with a threadbare rug. There was a battered, old, amputated couch in the room, which was to say, it had no legs. It just sat flat on the floor. An equally battered pair of chairs was placed across from it, with the engine as a sort of centerpiece between them. Wooden packing crates doubled as end tables and bookshelves. On the walls were framed posters of some sort, apparently reproductions of pre-Collapse cultural icons. One depicted the faces of four young men against a black background and bore the legend, "The Doors." Another showed a metallic-skinned, silver figure on a matching board against a kaleidoscope of colors, with the legend, "Surfing with the Alien." Still another showed an intense, angular-faced, young man with long black hair in what looked like the robe of an adept, holding what appeared to be a roasted guitar. And one entire wall was completely obscured by a complicated-looking stereo console and *stacks* of huge speakers with the front covers removed, exposing formidable-looking woofers and tweeters.

"You like?" said Leventhal, as he noticed me taking in the awesome array. "I put it together myself." He grimaced at the sound coming from outside. "They never learn," he said. "Okay, they want war? They got war."

He picked up a remote-control unit and punched a button. The deafening sound of driving electric guitars and pounding drums came booming from the stacks of speakers with all the power of a freight train. I arched my back and my fur bristled. I'd never heard anything that mind-numbingly loud in all my life. The walls literally shook and bits of plaster rained down from the ceiling as a voice that sounded like a banshee's wail filled the room, the entire house, and probably the whole neighborhood, as well. In seconds, there was pounding on the ceiling, barely audible, and moments later, someone threw open the door and an arm reached in, waving a white flag.

Leventhal turned the system off as the bearded young man waving the white flag stuck his head in. "All right, all right! We'll turn it down, already! Shit, you and your damned oldies!"

Leventhal grinned. "AC/DC gets 'em every time," he said.

"*What?*" I said.

"I said, "AC/DC gets 'em every time," he said.

"*What?*"

He made a face at me and unzipped his leather jacket. He took it off and tossed it on the floor. My ears were still ringing. Leventhal flipped out a cigarette and lit up with a flourish of his antique Zippo. He inhaled deeply, blew out a long stream of smoke, and sighed with contentment.

"Man, they just don't make music like that anymore," he said.

"What a shame," I mumbled. "No wonder this damned house is falling apart. You're vibrating it to pieces."

"Everyone's a critic," Leventhal replied sourly. "Let me

tell you something, Cat—back then, they had something we just plain don't have nowadays.''

"Broken eardrums?" I said.

"Funny," he replied wryly. He picked up the cassette tape Michaels had made for him and slipped it into the player. "Okay," he said. "Might as well kick back. This could take a while."

He went to the refrigerator and took out a roll of salami. He held it up interrogatively and I nodded. As the intro music for Sean Prescott's "Late Shift" program started playing, Leventhal sliced us up a snack.

"Welcome to the 'Late Shift,'" the announcer's voice said. "I'm Sean Prescott, and as usual, we'll be taking you into the wee hours of the morning with music, talk, and phone calls from our audience—that's you—so if you've got something to say about our topic tonight, the number is 555-8255, that's 555-TALK, and we'll be taking calls in just a little while. Our topic tonight is the nature of true faith. What it means, to us as individuals, and to our society, and to help us examine this provocative question, our guests in the studio tonight are the elders of Denver's Tabernacle of True Faith, the Reverend Bob Johnson, Brother Theodore Washburn, Brother Marcus White, and Sister Ruth Cottrell. Welcome to the 'Late Shift,' Reverend, why don't we start with you? You call your order the Tabernacle of True Faith. What, exactly, does that mean?"

"Well, Sean," the Reverend Johnson replied smoothly, "as we are told in Revelations, 'And I heard a great voice out of Heaven saying, "Behold, the tabernacle of God is with men, and He will dwell with them, and they shall be His people, and God Himself shall be with them, and be their God. And God shall wipe away all tears from their eyes; and there shall be no more death, neither sorrow, nor crying, neither shall there be any more pain: for the former things are passed away."' What that means, in other words, is that the only true path to salvation is through God, and through the scriptures, which are given by the inspiration of God for the instruction of the righteous."

"I see," said Prescott. "So what you're saying, basically, is that the only true faith is that which can be found in a fundamental interpretation of the Bible?"

"That's essentially correct, Sean. The Bible is the Word of God, passed on to us throughout the generations of Man, and it is through the Holy Bible that the nature of true faith is revealed to us."

"Now I used the words, 'fundamental interpretation of the Bible,'" Prescott said. "Do you have any problem with being referred to as Christian Fundamentalists? Brother Theodore?"

"We don't generally think of ourselves as Fundamentalists, Sean," Brother Theodore replied. "We simply think of ourselves as Christians. However, if you choose to call us Fundamentalists, I won't dispute your use of the term, in the sense that it helps to differentiate the True Christians from the apostates."

"And by apostates, I take it you mean those Christians who do not conform to Fundamentalist principles and teachings?" Prescott asked.

"That essentially correct, Sean," Reverend Johnson replied, "except that we don't really consider them Christians. At least, not True Christians. An apostate is someone who has rejected the principles and teachings of his faith, and we believe that most people who call themselves Christians these days have strayed from the true path and have abandoned the teachings of the faith."

"So that when you refer to these so-called Apostate Christians," Prescott said, "you're referring to what most people these days would consider to be the mainstream of Christianity, the majority, as it were. Brother Marcus?"

"Well, Sean," Brother Marcus replied, "I believe it was Voltaire who said that if a thousand people say a foolish thing, it is still a foolish thing. Simply because we are, admittedly, in the minority, and the apostates and the heathens are in the majority, that doesn't make them right. Christians have been in the minority before, and they have been persecuted before, but the truth isn't something that can be dictated by the opinions of a majority.''

"Or a minority," Prescott interjected.

"Or a minority," Brother Marcus agreed, "that's quite correct. The truth is simply the truth. It is what is, and whether it's perceived by a minority or by a majority has no bearing on it. God gave us free will, so that we could make a choice about our own salvation. The scriptures give us the wisdom to make intelligent and moral choices.''

"So if I understand you correctly," Prescott responded, "what you're saying is that all those people who don't agree with your beliefs, with your perception of the truth—which is to say, most people these days—that all those people are wrong? Sister Ruth?''

"We prefer to think of them as having made the wrong choices," Sister Ruth replied. "And, in a lot of ways, it's not really their fault. The correct choice is very often not the easy choice, whereas succumbing to temptation has always been easy. Unfortunately, we have a society today that encourages people to succumb to temptations, to make the wrong choices, the easy choices. Take magic, for example. Magic is sinful, it's the work of the Devil, but magic is glamorized in our society today and made acceptable, because it's an easy choice to make, because it's tempting, because it appeals to the sensual, to the corrupt. When you're constantly surrounded by temptation, when you're encouraged daily to succumb by the media and big business, it's very difficult not to give in to that temptation, especially when you're told constantly that it's the right thing to do. The virtue of true faith has never been an easy virtue. The early Christians were thrown to the lions. They were crucified and burned to death for holding to their faith, yet they persevered, and through their perseverance, they were saved.

If the pagan beliefs of the ancient Romans were, indeed, the true faith, then why were they so afraid of the early Christians? Why go to such lengths in an attempt to stamp out Christianity? And if Christianity were not the true faith, then where did those early Christians gain the strength and purpose to die for their beliefs?''

''Well,'' said Prescott, ''I could just as easily say that if Christians got so much strength from their beliefs, then what about all those people killed during the time of the Inquisition in Europe, executed for adherence to pagan beliefs, or often simply because they had been accused of things like heresy and witchcraft, with so-called confessions extracted under torture?''

''I see you've done your homework,'' Reverend Johnson replied, and you could practically hear the condescending smile in his voice as he added, ''however, if you read your history more carefully, you'll see that the Inquisition of the thirteenth century, which resulted primarily from the Albigensian Crusade, and which also resulted in persecutions that echoed throughout the later centuries, was primarily a secular phenomenon, rather than a truly spiritual one. In other words, Sean, it was a question of political power, not of spiritual truth. The Roman Catholic Church was obsessed with many purely secular concerns, a situation that unfortunately persists to this day.''

''I'm not sure I understand what you're saying,'' Prescott replied. ''It sounds to me as if you're condemning the Church—the Roman Catholic Church, that is—and accusing it of being primarily a political rather than a spiritual entity.''

''Well, isn't it?'' Reverend Johnson responded. ''Throughout its history, the Church in Rome has been heavily involved in politics. You have the Crusades, the Inquisition, the behind-the-scenes political maneuverings throughout the centuries, right up to this very day. Frankly, I can't imagine any rationally thinking person believing for one moment that Jesus Christ would have approved of such activities.''

"So you're saying the Roman Catholic Church is and has been acting contrary to the teachings of Christ?" asked Prescott.

"That would seem obvious," Reverend Johnson replied.

"Okay, and with that, we'll take a short musical break while we go to the phones," said Prescott.

It wasn't hard to predict where the program would go from there. Leventhal fast-forwarded past the musical interlude and, when the talk picked up again, Prescott went to the phones and a veritable torrent of hostility against his guests. Things got pretty ugly in fairly short order. I didn't really see any point to it. Humans have been arguing over their conflicting religious beliefs practically since time began, and all too often those arguments had escalated into violence, yet I don't recall ever hearing about anything being settled.

Animals don't have any religion and, if you ask me, we're not missing much. We don't have any need of churches or temples and we don't waste a lot of time arguing over dogma. We don't question our existence, we merely accept it. The way I see it, life's tough enough without worrying about what comes after. But then, according to some people, I'm not supposed to have a soul, so I guess there's no point to sweating the afterlife.

The trouble is, if what you do in this life determines what happens in the next one, then it's probably prudent to make sure you go through life doing the right thing. That can be tricky. Especially when nobody can seem to agree on what the right thing is. And it's apparently not enough to know you're doing the right thing, you gotta make sure that everyone else is doing the right thing, too. And if *their* thing doesn't happen to be *your* thing, then I guess you've got a problem. Don't ask me to figure it out, it's not my thing.

Leventhal just sat there, listening to the tape with his eyes closed, and if it wasn't for the fact that he was smoking, I would've thought he'd fallen asleep. Frankly, I didn't see where listening to this nonsense was going to get us anywhere. If doing programs like this got Sean Prescott his good ratings, then I didn't think much of his audience. It was depressing to think of all those people with nothing better to do at night than call up some radio program to vent their anger and frustration.

Maybe Prescott was performing a public service by giving people an outlet for their rage, but on the other hand, he was also giving them a forum and thereby spreading it around. Maybe calling up the show and screaming wouldn't be enough for some of them. Maybe listening to it all would fire them up and make them want to go out and kick somebody's teeth in. Or maybe shoot someone. Or maybe plant a bomb . . .

The so-called True Christians managed to maintain their composure pretty well throughout most of the abuse the callers heaped upon them, though Prescott did everything he could to bait them and provoke some kind of outburst. He played devil's advocate, no pun intended, and egged on the callers, but though Brother Marcus and Sister Ruth were beginning to show some signs of strain, Reverend Johnson and Brother Theodore kept cool and calm and none of them so much as raised their voice, despite considerable provocation. Perhaps they were coming off as being rather intolerant and inflexible in their beliefs, but it was the callers who were coming across like raving assholes.

I decided that the whole thing was a waste of time and so curled up on the floor to catch a little catnap. I had started to tune out the debate and drift off when Leventhal suddenly turned up the volume with his remote.

". . . Perfect example of how magic is undermining the moral fabric of our society," Reverend Johnson was saying. "As if it weren't enough that thaumagenetic engineers have taken it upon themselves to play God by perverting Nature with their black arts, we are now being asked to give legal and moral sanction to this sinful perversion by granting equal rights to their shameful abominations. I say it's past time for God-fearing people to draw the line, once and for all!''

"Well, admittedly, the ERA proposal is highly controversial," Prescott responded, "and while a lot of people might not necessarily think of thaumagenes as sinful abominations, I think you'll find that many of them might balk at granting them civil rights."

"Perhaps," Reverend Johnson replied, "but the fact that such a proposal is even being made seriously is evidence of just how far our society has fallen. The Lord gave Man dominion over all the beasts of the field. He did not create them to be Man's equal. It's all fine and good to love animals and care for them, but to actually propose elevating them to equal status with humans is nothing short of blasphemy. It only goes to show how far these necromancers and their deluded supporters will go to corrupt humanity."

"Well, now, wait a minute," Prescott said, "you're playing a little fast and loose with the definition of necromancy, aren't you? Necromancy is legally defined as the practice of black magic—"

"*All* magic is black magic," Sister Ruth interjected vehemently. "This whole legal sham of defining black magic as something that entails murder is nothing more than a subterfuge to legitimize sin. Murder is murder, and black magic is black magic—whether you call it thaumaturgy or necromancy, it's all the same. Society has always had laws against the taking of human life, going all the way back to the Ten Commandments. And society used to have laws against the practice of the necromantic arts, as well, only now we're told that magic is only necromancy if it involves the taking of a life. Well, we already have a definition for that. It's called murder, and whether it's done with magic or with a gun or with a knife, it makes no difference. Killing an unborn child is murder, too, but if you call it something else, like abortion, then you start making people think it's more acceptable. It's the same with magic. It's a sin no matter how you look at it, or what you call it."

"I'm not sure most people would agree with that," said Prescott. "I mean, come on, you can't really compare magic with abortion. After all, where would society be today if it wasn't for Merlin—"

"Merlin Ambrosius was the Antichrist," snapped Sister Ruth, no longer sounding so composed. "I'm sick of hearing people refer to him as if he were the Second Coming! He was the Devil incarnate! The Collapse could easily have been Armageddon, but instead it was a warning from God. A *final* warning. Humanity was given a second chance, and look at what we're doing with it! Instead of coming to our senses and embracing God, we have embraced the Devil, and there will be Hell to pay! Don't you understand, there won't *be* any more second chances!"

"Well, now you're being melodramatic," Prescott said. "Are you *seriously* suggesting that Merlin was Satan?"

"The Tempter comes to us in many forms, Sean," said Reverend Johnson, and somehow I knew that he was putting a restraining hand on Sister Ruth's arm as he spoke. I could almost hear it in his tone. "He came to us in the form of the wicked men whose folly led us to the Collapse; he came to us in the form of Ambrosius the Necromancer; and now he comes to us in the form of those who follow in the Necromancer's footsteps, his corrupt disciples, who seek to lead us astray from the teachings of the Lord. They would make the beasts our equals because they would have us be as beasts ourselves, and that way lies the road to our eternal damnation."

"Let's take a call," said Prescott. "Hello, you're on the 'Late Shift.' "

"I think these people are looney tunes," the caller said. "I mean, they're totally out of touch with reality. I don't even know why you're bothering to put these fruitcakes on the air, unless maybe you're going for some comic relief.

Somebody should just tell them to wake up and smell the coffee, you know what I mean?''

''I hear you,'' Prescott said. ''Sister Ruth, this caller thinks you people are a bunch of yo-yos. How do you respond to that?''

''We're the ones who are trying to tell everybody else to wake up, before it's too late,'' Sister Ruth replied. ''In flaming fire He shall take vengeance on them that know not God, and that obey not the Gospel of our Lord Jesus Christ!''

''Flaming fire, eh?'' said Prescott, with a smile in his voice. ''As opposed to fire that doesn't flame, I suppose?''

''You mock the Bible at the peril of your immortal soul,'' said Sister Ruth. ''And those who will mock our Lord and blaspheme against His Word will be struck down and damned to everlasting Hell!''

''Well, if the Lord can't take a joke, I guess I'm in trouble now,'' said Prescott, with a chuckle. ''And, on that rather threatening note, I see we're out of time, and so I'll thank our guests, even if they would see me damned, and hope you'll all tune in again tomorrow night for another edition of 'Late Shift,' assuming, of course, we're all still here. . . .''

Leventhal stopped the tape. He sniffed once, grimaced, and tossed aside the remote control. ''Well, what do you think, Cat?'' he asked.

''Why ask me?'' I countered. ''You're the detective.''

''I'm asking your opinion.''

I got to my feet and stretched to get the kinks out after listening to that long tape. I glanced out the window and saw that it had grown dark. ''Well, they're obviously not sympathetic to the ERA,'' I said, ''but then it didn't sound to me as if there was a whole lot they were sympathetic to. They don't like magic, they don't like the Roman Catholic Church, they don't like people who don't love Jesus . . . reminds me of an old joke.''

"Shoot," Leventhal said.

"Well, there were these two guys drinking in a bar," I said. "And one of them turns to the other and says, 'Hey, tell me something. What do you think about Jews?' And the second guys says, 'I don't really care for Jews.' So the first guy says, 'Well, then what about Catholics?' And the guy replies, 'I don't really like Catholics, either.' 'Yeah?' his buddy says. 'Well, what about Protestants?' 'Don't like Protestants.' 'How about Episcopalians?' 'Don't like Episcopalians.' 'Baptists?' 'Don't like Baptists, either.' 'How about Buddhists?' 'Ain't got no use for 'em.' 'Muslims?' 'Can't stand 'em.' 'What about Jehovah's Witnesses?' 'I hate Jehovah's Witnesses.' 'Well, goddamm it,' says the first guy, 'who *do* you like?' And the second guy thinks about it for a second and says, 'Well . . . I like my friends.' "

Leventhal snorted. "Where'd you hear that?"

"A rabbi told it to me once."

Leventhal smiled. "Well, I definitely see your point," he said, lighting up another smoke. He inhaled deeply and exhaled with a sigh. "They don't sound like a bunch of happy campers, do they?"

"They don't exactly sound like murderers, either," I replied.

"Well, maybe not, but if you could tell by just listening to 'em, my job would be a shitload easier, that's for sure," Leventhal said.

"The point is, we don't really know much more than we did when we started," I said. "It doesn't seem as if we're getting anywhere."

"The night's still young," Leventhal replied. He glanced at his watch and got up, reaching for his leather. "Come on, Cat, I'll buy you a saucer of cream."

Nine

THE huge sign hand-painted on the wall in ornate script said, "Mudd's Occult Café." From the outside, the place didn't look like much. It was a rectangular, two-story building with a flat roof and a wooden outdoor patio attached to the back as if by afterthought. The patio was enclosed by a ramshackle wooden fence made of unpainted, flat boards, so that you couldn't see into it from the street. Behind the fence, there was a dumpster and a small parking lot, with another parking lot across the street. Standing in front of the place on the corner of twenty-second and Champa, you got a good view of the buildings of downtown Denver, all lit up in the night like Christmas trees. Turn around and you could see in through the windows, where people sat at small wooden tables, some with lamps casting a dim and sickly light and some without. The atmosphere inside the place looked dim and smoky. It sounded noisy, too.

The place wasn't exactly in one of the better parts of town. The streets down here looked foreboding, and so did the people wandering up and down. There were several young Rippers outside the front door, standing around or sitting on the sidewalk, leaning back against the wall and smoking, making a hell of a fashion statement in studded, hand-painted leather jackets, punky haircuts, ripped jeans, and clunky boots festooned with metal.

At first glance, they looked like a rough crowd, but a closer look revealed young and relatively fresh-scrubbed faces, some of them trying to look hard, but mostly it was just a pose. People who are really hard don't have to try to look that way. There just isn't any other way that they can look. You can always tell. Their faces have a lived-in look that smacks of the hard lessons of experience. Often, they look older than they really are. But the eyes are always a dead giveaway. They don't stare holes through you, like the poseurs try to do. They just watch with a sort of flat, noncommittal, disaffected gaze. And they don't miss a thing. No, these weren't tough characters, they were just kids. Probably nice kids. Maybe some of them had received a few hard knocks, and maybe a couple of them carried boot knives they probably didn't know how to use, but mercifully, they'd been spared life's tougher lessons. So far.

They knew Leventhal and a couple of them greeted him as we approached. He gave them a grin and a curt, "Hey, how's it goin'?" as we went in. The entrance was one of those alcove things, where you walk in through an exterior door and opposite you there's a wall with another door to the left. The wall had a bunch of leaflets and posters tacked to it, advertising bands playing in local clubs, poetry readings, and various used items for sale. We went in through the heavy black door and through the rest of the alcove, a short corridor ending in another wall festooned with leaflets and posters. There were ratty old drapes hung over another doorway to the right. Leventhal pushed aside the drapes and we went on through.

To our immediate left was a row of bookshelves crammed full of used books in hardcover and paperback. To our immediate right was a wooden staircase leading up to a loft where there were more shelves full of used books for sale.

On the other side of the stairs, to the right, was a small alcove containing more bookshelves. Directly in front of us was a small glass-fronted cabinet containing cigarettes and various items of jewelry. An old, antique cash register rested on top of it, and a bored-looking girl in shorts and a ripped T-shirt about eight sizes too big for her sat on a stool behind the register. Behind her was a partition that ended a foot or so above her head, and behind that was an espresso bar and soda fountain, elevated above the rest of the place. There was a short stairway leading up to it at either end of the partition. The main room was to the left, and to the right was a hallway leading back to the kitchen, the back room, and the outdoor patio.

A guy with a full, bushy, dark brown beard and shaggy hair sat on a stool in front of us, collecting the cover from people as they came in. And beside him, coiled on the floor, sat something that made the fur on my back bristle. It was a snog. The biggest, ugliest, meanest-looking snog I'd ever seen, and, fortunately, I hadn't seen that many. There weren't that many of them around anymore, largely because they hadn't been much of a sales success. They were truly vile creatures with spectacularly mean dispositions, and they were so ugly they were enough to put you off your feed. They'd largely been replaced by dobras, which were ugly enough all by themselves, but generally regarded as more manageable and efficient. This was the other side of the coin. It was another hybrid of a snake and dog, only, unlike dobras, which had the bodies of dogs and the heads of giant cobras, the snog had the body of a giant snake and the head of a dog. This one was an old rattler, with a body as thick as Leventhal's thigh and the head of a Rottweiler. It was covered with iridescent scales and it had a rattle on its tail the size of a man's fist. Coiled up the way it was, it was hard to judge its length, but it had to be at least twenty feet or more. Our eyes met and I arched my back and hissed.

"Hey, Dan," said the bearded guy on the stool.

"How's it goin', Steve?" said Leventhal, as Steve waved him through without bothering about the cover. I hung back. Leventhal turned around and saw me all bristled up, eye to eye with that big snog.

"Ahhhh," the snog said, throatily, as it licked its chops and stared at me malevolently. "Dinner."

Leventhal gave it an open-handed whack on the head that didn't even make it blink. "Cut it out, Smaug," he said. "The cat's a friend of mine."

Steve grinned and said, "Don't worry about ole Smaug. He just likes to rattle the newcomers."

"Steve, meet Catseye Gomez," said Leventhal. "Cat, this is Steve Wiley. And this ugly section of radiator hose is his buddy, Smaug."

Steve grinned at me and Smaug said, "Pleased to meet ya, little fella."

"Likewise, I think," I replied, bristling down.

"Don't worry about Smaug," said Steve, "he only eats dog food and the occasional hamburger. But he does help keep the customers in line."

"Yeah, I'm sure," I said, as I edged past him uncertainly.

"Heh, heh, heh," Smaug chuckled, throatily. "Cat's got spunk," he said to Steve. "Didja see that? He was ready to go for me. You're okay, Cat. Anybody gives you any grief in here, you just call old Smaug."

"Thanks, big fella, I'll do that," I said.

He gave me a little rattle with his tail and I returned the compliment by giving him a twinkle with ole Betsy. It caught him by surprise, the way it always does, and told him there was more to me than met the eye, that maybe I could take him, if it ever came to that, and he just grinned at me with that big, old Rottweiler maw of his and went "Heh, heh, heh" and shook his head, and I knew we understood each other. We were both old troopers who'd seen our share of scraps and if there wasn't any good reason for the two of us to dance, we wouldn't. I felt I'd made a friend, the first thaumagene friend I'd made since I arrived to Denver, unless you wanted to count Princess, and frankly, I wasn't sure of that one at all. Pampered little society pussies have never been my dish. Smaug was a different kind of breed entirely. Him I could understand.

We entered the main room and it immediately became clear that Leventhal was a regular here. A number of different people waved and nodded and spoke greetings as we threaded our way between the tables, toward a booth against the wall, below the raised bar section where the wait station was. I had to watch myself to make sure nobody stepped on me, because it was pretty crowded. The tables were all crammed together and packed. The booths against the bare, brick wall were all crowded, too. There was artwork hanging on that brick wall, and I knew it was artwork because of the little labels with the prices on them. Otherwise, I might've thought that somebody had vandalized a perfectly good wall.

The air was heavy with cigarette smoke, which was in itself sort of unusual. Most places didn't allow smoking anymore, even though there was now a cure for cancer—in a manner of speaking. If you felt like trashing your lungs, you could always buy yourself a set of new ones, assuming you could afford it, since that was a procedure not covered by your health insurance. Still, most people found cigarette smoke offensive and smoking wasn't the big business that it used to be. However, here in Mudd's, smokers were in nicotine heaven. Practically all the Rippers smoked, maybe because it was self-destructive, or maybe because it allowed you to do all sorts of little physical bits of business with your cigarette. And the antique Zippo lighter was a coveted accessory, as well. I guess there was something satisfying in that little, metallic snick of its cover as you flipped it open. Or maybe it was just nostalgia, who knew? Humans get into all these little tribal bits of behavior that have always seemed incomprehensible to me.

There was a raised section at the far left of the room, and
running all the way across to the back wall. There were
some tables up there, but part of it, and the left corner, had
been cleared to make a sort of stage for the live entertainment. There was an old piano pushed up against the wall in
the corner, and there were some amps and microphones set
up. At the moment, there were three people up there
whaling away on keyboard instruments, making a noise that
sounded like a twenty-car pileup on I-25. A young woman
dressed all in black stood behind a mike, and I suppose she
was singing. Anyway, that was my best guess. It was hard
to tell with all the processing the electronics were doing to
her voice. She was doing a chant of some sort, or maybe
she was reciting poetry, or perhaps having a nervous break-
down, take your pick. Her hair was black, her leather jacket
was black, her sheer and skin-tight top was black, her tights
were black, her boots were black, and her eye shadow was
black, and she had enough rings on her fingers to make a
punch from her seem like a decidedly unpleasant proposition, for all her ethereal and fragile appearance.

Leventhal waved at her and she gave him a bored-looking
nod as she continued whatever it was she was doing. We
made our way over to the crowded booth.

"Okay, like, we're gonna take a break now," the female
vocalist said, as the noise stopped with a reverberating echo
that shook the walls. "We're Blackie Dawn and the Scum.
Trish is gonna be up here in a few. Party till you puke.
Catch ya'll later."

"Hey, Dan!" said a young Ripper with long, spiky blond
hair that stuck out in all directions.

"Hey, Rob, how's it goin'?" said Leventhal. He said
hello to the other young men at the table. "Jesse, Isaac. . . ."

"Hey, man."

"Meet my friend, Catseye Gomez," he said.

A round of greetings followed, with more or less the
same, minimalist approach.

"Do me a favor, guys, and let us have a little privacy, will ya? I need to talk to the Baghwan."

"Yeah, sure, man," Rob said. "We'll catch ya later, Baghwan."

The man to whom that last comment was addressed was sitting quietly against the wall, smoking an unfiltered cigarette. He merely nodded in reply. Unlike the others, he wasn't wearing any leather, but a black cloth sport jacket over a rumpled, dark green, button-down shirt. He had on a black wool beret and black-rimmed glasses. One of his eyes looked a little funny and out of focus, what they called a "wandering eye." He had a wispy, black goatee and the face of an ascetic. Leventhal slid into the booth and I hopped up beside him after the others left.

"Evening, Dan," said the Baghwan. He glanced at me and smiled. "Catseye Gomez, eh?"

"Just Gomez will do," I said.

He nodded once. "Pleased to meet you. Why don't you hop up on the table here, so you can see okay?" He slid aside some cups and glasses to make room.

"Long as the management doesn't mind," I said, jumping up on the table.

Oh, they're pretty loose around here," said the Baghwan. He crushed out his cigarette butt and immediately took out another one. Leventhal lit it for him with his Zippo. "Thanks."

A pretty, dark-haired waitress came up to the table and set a cup of coffee down in front of Leventhal.

"Thanks, Becky," he said. "And can we get a saucer of cream for my buddy, Gomez, here?"

"Sure," she replied, with a dazzling smile, as if she served cats every day. Around here, maybe she did. I'd noticed more than a few thaumagenes around the room, perched atop tables and on chairs and on people's shoulders. I decided I could get used to this place.

"I could use a little information, Baghwan."

The Baghwan merely nodded.

"You hear about anybody dealing in explosives lately? Something unusual? Maybe somebody who doesn't normally handle that kind of commodity?"

"You mean like C-4?" the Baghwan asked.

Leventhal raised his eyebrows. "Word gets around fast," he said. "Or do you know something?"

The Baghwan shook his head. "We're talking about the Susan Jacobs murder, right?" he said.

"Yeah. How'd you know?"

"Hell, don't you people talk to each other?" the Baghwan asked. "Or is this some kind of new, double-redundancy investigative technique?"

"What are you talking about?" Leventhal said, frowning.

"I've already been braced tonight on that one," the Baghwan replied. "I told them I didn't know anything about it, but I guess they didn't believe me. So what's this, the good-cop/bad-cop routine? They figure I'll talk to you because we've got some history? Hell, you should have come around up front, Dan, I'd have given it to you straight, you know me."

Leventhal took a deep breath and drew his lips together into a tight grimace. "Let me guess," he said tensely. "Chavez and McVickers."

The Baghwan frowned. "You telling me you didn't know?"

"No, I had no idea they were sniffing around on this. Those fuckers."

"What's going on with you guys?" asked the Baghwan. "It sounds like the right hand doesn't know what the left hand is doing. Who's checking up on whom?"

"I don't know," Leventhal replied, in an annoyed tone. "I was told I was going to have a clear field on this one, but either they fed me a line of bullshit or the commissioner is talking out of both sides of his mouth. Shit. I'm sorry about this, Baghwan. They give you a rough time?"

The Baghwan shrugged. "No more than usual. They came sauntering in, looking tough and talking tough and making threats, and then they sauntered out again, dragging their knuckles on the ground. Even if I knew anything, I wouldn't have told those turkeys, anyway. So what's going on? You being double-teamed?''

"Looks that way," said Leventhal. "Either that or they're doing this on their own, which I wouldn't put past them. Don't worry about it, I'll take care of it. I'll make sure they won't bother you again."

The Baghwan made a dismissive motion with his hand. "Not to worry. Those bozos couldn't find their dicks with a magnifying glass. So what's the story? They played it pretty close to the vest. All I know is this broadcaster lady got blown up in her car in front of her building, where the commissioner also happens to live. Something about the ERA?''

"That's the way it's being played," said Leventhal, "but I don't know that for a fact. For all I know, maybe somebody had a hard-on for the lady. Maybe it was just personal. Right now, I haven't got a lot to go on."

The Baghwan nodded. "So what do you need?"

"Okay. The job was done, as you've already gathered from the Bobbsey Twins, with plastique, C-4. That stuff hasn't been made since the Collapse, so the lab boys think somebody stumbled on a cache that was buried in one of those survivalist safes or something. They figure it had to be a recent find, otherwise it would have shown up somewhere before now. I don't know, it's possible that maybe somebody was sitting on the stuff for a long time, but I'm inclined to agree with their theory. So, what have you heard?''

"Not a thing," said the Baghwan, with a shake of his head. "But I'll ask around and see what I can come up with. Anything else?"

"Yeah, maybe. What do you know about the Tabernacle of True Faith?"

The Baghwan smiled. "You mean the true believers?" He shrugged. "Small bunch of die-hard Fundamentalists.

They've got a church over on the corner of Eighth and Ogden. Looks like just a plain old white mansion from the outside, nicely tended and kept up, wrought-iron fence all around it, very low profile. But they've got a state-of-the-art security system and on the inside, it looks like a biblical wet dream. Fancy chandeliers, gold candle sconces and braziers, religious murals all over the place, meditation rooms, library, study rooms, the whole ball of wax. They run a Bible college out of the place, too."

"You've actually been in there?" Leventhal asked, with surprise.

"I'm a man of diverse interests," the Baghwan replied, with a shrug. "I'm always open to a new educational experience."

"So what's your impression?"

"They're very serious and earnest, but essentially harmless," the Baghwan replied. "They're not terribly political, but there's a faction in there that thinks they ought to be. It's like about seventy percent of them think the world is going to hell in a handbasket and only the righteous will be saved, and the other thirty percent think maybe they ought to do something about it."

"What about that thirty percent?" asked Leventhal.

The Baghwan shrugged again. "Who knows? If you're asking me are they militant enough to make bombs, I'd say no, but you can never really know for sure, can you? I'd say it was a long shot." He grimaced. "I wouldn't think so. They're pretty serious about their beliefs, and the Bible says "Thou shalt not kill.""

"It also says something about an eye for an eye, doesn't it?" Leventhal said.

"True," said the Baghwan. "But they didn't really strike me as a bunch of desperate individuals. Fanatical, maybe, but violent? Possibly, but I rather doubt it. Why, you got anything firm?"

"No, not really," Leventhal replied wryly. "I guess I'm

just reaching. But somebody out there seems pretty intent on the media getting the message that this is a religious killing, knocking off a blasphemer and all that. I don't know, maybe it's a smoke screen, but I've got to check out all the angles. Right now, I haven't got shit to work with, and the pressure's on.''

''You know, it's interesting,'' the Baghwan said, ''but before this killing, the ERA wasn't all that big a deal. Lot of people here were into it, passing around petitions and all that, but now it's suddenly a hot issue and it's getting a lot of press. If your killer was out to squelch it, it would seem he's accomplished exactly the opposite.''

Leventhal frowned. ''So what are you suggesting? That maybe someone in the ERA decided they needed a martyr? I don't know, Baghwan, that seems pretty farfetched to me.''

The Baghwan shrugged again. ''Hey, you're the detective. I was just thinking out loud.''

Leventhal nervously tapped his Zippo on the table. ''I need more than I've got, Baghwan. I need some help on this.''

''I'll do whatever I can.''

''No offense, old buddy, but that may not be enough. I'm groping in the dark here, and I need to cast some light on this situation, real quick.'' He pursed his lips thoughtfully. ''You think you can set up a meeting with the Mystic?''

The Baghwan raised his eyebrows. ''The Mystic, huh?'' He nodded. ''It's possible. But are you sure about this?''

''Hey, I'm grasping at straws here,'' Leventhal said. ''I'll take whatever help I can get, even if I can't use it in a court of law. And word has it the Mystic gets results.''

''Oh, he gets results, all right,'' the Baghwan nodded, ''but they might not be the results you're looking for. With the Mystic, there aren't any guarantees. Especially for cops.''

''Hey, look, I know the Mystic's not a certified adept,'' said Leventhal. ''I couldn't give a shit, you know? I'm not a

BOT agent, I'm just a street cop trying to do his job. Hell, you know me, Baghwan. You can put in a good word. I'm not out to bust him, I just want some information."

The Baghwan gave a small snort. "Oh, I don't think the Mystic's worried about being busted. It's been tried before, you know. And nobody who's tried has ever been seen again. If you want me to try to set up a meet for you, I'm willing, but I'm going to be straight with the man. The Mystic's not somebody you want to cross. I'm going to have to tell him you're a cop."

"So? Tell him."

"Okay. But if he agrees, from there on in, you're on your own, Dan. I wash my hands of the whole thing."

"Fair enough," said Leventhal. "And you can tell him I don't expect any freebies. I'm willing to pay, or trade, or whatever he wants."

"Be careful about that 'whatever he wants' part," said the Baghwan. "I'd think very carefully about any bargain I made with the Mystic. Because he *will* hold you to it, whether you like it or not."

"Hey, if I say I'm gonna do something, I do it," Leventhal replied. "You know me, Baghwan. I've never gone back on my word."

"No, you never have." The Baghwan nodded. "Okay, I'll see what I can do. But no promises, you understand?"

"Just give it your best shot, that's all I ask," said Leventhal.

"Right," said the Baghwan, getting up from the table. "Let me go make a few calls. You stay right here. This could take a while."

"Thanks, Baghwan," Leventhal replied. "I owe you one."

"If I come up with any information for you, *then* you'll owe me one," the Baghwan said. "This one I'm doing for old times' sake. And not without a few reservations, I might add. I'll set up a meet if I can. Whatever happens after that, I don't want to know about it, understand?"

"Got it," said Leventhal. "And thanks again."

As the Baghwan left to make his calls, somebody took the mike and made an announcement.

"Okay, people, it's that time again," the announcer said. "Ladies and gentlemen . . . give it up for Trish!"

The announcer stuck the mike back into the clamp on the stand and walked over to the piano. Amid sporadic applause, a woman walked up to the stage . . . no, she floated up to it, with moves a jungle cat might have envied. Every man in the place was suddenly staring at her hungrily, and not a few women, too. Full, light brown hair cascaded down to her shoulders, framing a face that was enough to take your breath away. One look at that face and you could tell that she'd heard every story, every line, and every promise the mind of man could manufacture. She'd heard and seen it all and found most of it amusing. But she could be polite and listen to it all again. Not that it would get you anywhere.

She had a lush and voluptuous figure packed into a tight, black dress you could have washed in a martini glass. It looked like it was painted on her. She looked out at the audience, which had suddenly gone real quiet, and as her gaze traveled slowly in our direction, she smiled slightly and whispered into the mike, "Hey, Dan . . . this one's for you."

And as the piano player started doing bluesy things with the keys, she launched into "I Only Have Eyes for You." And every guy in the room turned around and stared at Leventhal, hating his guts.

"Friend of yours?" I said.

Leventhal cleared his throat awkwardly. "Uh . . . yeah. Guess you could say that."

"I just did."

"Right," said Leventhal. "Shut up and drink your cream."

I gave him a wink with ole Betsy and busied myself with the nice cool saucer of cream Becky had brought me. Yes, sir, I thought, friendly atmosphere, pretty waitresses to bring me nice, cool drinks, a sexy lady with a lot of cat in her to sing the kind of songs I like, and nobody getting all bent out of shape because I'm sitting on the tabletop. This was definitely my kind of place.

"Excuse me, are you Detective Leventhal?"

I glanced up to see two women standing by the table, looking at Leventhal uncertainly. One was dark and kind of short, a little on the heavy side, with dark hair and a wide, pleasant-looking face. The other one was a tall strawberry blond, lean and leggy, with sharp features and a slightly turned up nose.

"I'm Leventhal."

"I'm Dana Cain and this is Christy Ivers," the dark one said. "You were pointed out to us. . . . You left messages on our machines. . . ."

"Yes, of course," said Leventhal. "Thank you for coming. Please, sit down."

They slid into the booth, opposite him. Becky came to take their order and they both asked for coffee.

"This is my partner, Catseye Gomez," Leventhal said, indicating me.

"Ladies," I said.

They stared at me. "Your partner?" Christy said, with surprise.

"Sort of unofficially," I explained. "I'm supposed to be representing animal interests in this case. Actually, I think I'm just along for the PR value."

Leventhal gave me a wry look and I backed off. This was, after all, his show. I went back to my saucer of cream.

"I still can't believe Susan's dead," said Dana, getting a bit misty around the eyes. "We were supposed to get together tonight . . . right here as a matter of fact. . . ."

"Yes, I know, I heard your message," Leventhal said.

"Oh, yes . . . of course."

"We'll do whatever we can to help," said Christy, "but I'm not sure that we can really tell you very much. The TV news reported that Susan had received some death threats. She didn't even tell us about that. The whole thing comes as a complete shock. I . . . I still don't think it's really sunk in."

Leventhal nodded. "Well, I just wanted to speak with you two so I could ask some routine questions. You know how it is, you were friends of hers, and at this point, anything that I can find out about her and what was happening in her life would be helpful. It's just like on TV, you know, cops ask a lot of questions, trying to put the pieces of the puzzle together. You never really know which piece is going to fit in where."

"I suppose you're going to want to ask us about our alibis," said Dana.

Leventhal smiled. "Well, that may be a bit too much like television," he replied. "I don't really have any reason to suspect anybody yet, and frankly, neither of you two looks like a mad bomber to me, but for the record, we might as well get it out of the way."

"Well, I was at work," said Christy, and she gave us the name and address of the legal firm she worked for. Then Dana did the same. In spite of the unpleasant circumstances, and their being clearly nervous and upset, there was still something about the situation, "being grilled by a police detective," that was fascinating to them. Spillane, MacDonald, Chandler, Hammett, and those other guys would have understood. The Big Sleep had passed them by, but it had struck close to home and there was a heady fascination to that, maybe the same kind of fascination a small rodent feels when it stares frozen into the unblinking eyes of a rattlesnake. The death of Susan Jacobs had been, for them, a grim reminder of their own mortality, a sudden and graphic demonstration of just how quickly life can be snuffed out. Yeah, they were upset and frightened, and they were doubtless grieving for their friend, but at the same time, there was that adrenaline rush of vitality flowing through them. It

could have happened to them, but it had happened to
someone else instead, somebody close, close enough to
make them shudder and feel the shadow of the Reaper, but
the bottom line was that it was someone else, not them.
They had survived.

Leventhal took notes on his little pad while they answered
his questions. Their alibis for the time of the murder
sounded solid. Both women were at work, where others had
seen them and spoken with them. Their alibis for the night
before the murder, however, when the bomb might have
been planted in the victim's vehicle, weren't quite so solid.
Dana Cain had been at home, taking a bath, washing her
hair, and then settling down in her bathrobe and fuzzy
slippers to TV and some pizza. Christy Ivers had gone out
on a date at about eight o'clock, to dinner at a local
restaurant and then some dancing, then back to his place
and, after that, she was a little fuzzy on the time she
eventually got home. As she had said before, neither of
them knew anything about the death threats—or so they
both claimed—and, while it may have seemed unusual that
Susan wouldn't have mentioned them to two of her close
friends, if she had, in fact, written them off as just crank
calls, the sort of thing that happened to people in her
business all the time, perhaps she simply hadn't thought
enough of them to think they were worth mentioning.

"What about her personal life?" asked Leventhal casual-
ly. "What can you tell me about that?"

"Well, she was all business," Christy replied. "Or just
about all business, anyway. We'd go out on occasion, just us
girls, you know. We'd come here a lot and hang out and just
talk, but Susan wasn't really what you'd call a social
butterfly."

"Well, there was Mark," said Dana.

"Mmmm," said Christy. "There certainly was."

"Christy!" said Dana, giving her friend an astonished
look.

"Sorry," Christy said, recalling herself and what the discussion was really all about. "It's just that she had him wrapped around her little finger, this really great guy, and she wasn't doing anything about it."

"You're talking about Mark Michaels?" Leventhal asked. "The general manager at her station?"

"Yes," said Christy. "You've met him?"

Leventhal nodded and indicated for her to proceed.

"He was head over heels in love with her," Christy continued. "And I guess she was in love with him, too, only he wanted to get married and Susan wasn't ready for that."

Leventhal nodded. "Yes, that's what he said."

"She saw marriage as a trap," said Dana. "She said she didn't want to have children, and her career was very important to her. She thought that maybe she'd consider marriage at some future point, when she'd realized some of her political ambitions—"

"She had political ambitions?" Leventhal asked.

"Oh, yeah, absolutely," Dana said. "She had it all planned out. She was going to work her way up at the station, then use that as a springboard to run for office."

"What sort of office?" Leventhal asked.

"She planned to run for Congress eventually," Christy said.

"Really?"

"Oh, she was a real political activist," said Dana. "She was always involved in something—campaigns, working for candidates—and then there was the ERA thing. . . ."

"Tell me a little more about that," said Leventhal. "I understand she pretty much started the whole thing. How'd that come about?"

"She said her cat gave her the idea," Christy said.

"Princess?" I said, glancing up from the empty saucer.

"Yeah," said Dana. She grinned at me. "You'll appreciate this. She hated for anyone to refer to Princess as her cat. She said it implied possession."

"So how were they supposed to refer to her?" I asked.

"As her feline *friend*," said Dana, with a faintly mocking smile. "I mean, she goes out and buys Princess at a thaumagene shop, picks her out and everything, and then she's not her cat, but her 'feline friend.' And she'd get really bent out of shape if anybody teased her about it. She'd give 'em the whole lecture on animal rights...." Dana sighed and her eyes got all misty again. "Oh, God, Susie, you were such a flake," she said, with a catch in her voice. "I'll really miss you."

She swallowed hard and the tears started. Christy put her arm around her friend, sympathetically.

Leventhal said nothing, but merely waited for a moment.

"I'm sorry," said Dana. "I'll be all right in a minute."

"It's okay," said Leventhal. "I understand."

"It's like I told your partners, we were really very close," said Dana.

Leventhal stiffened. "My partners?"

"Those other two detectives," Dana said. "Oh, what were their names?"

"Chavez and McVickers?" Leventhal asked tensely.

"Yes, that was them. They came by to ask some questions, too."

"I see," said Leventhal, his tone flat. "Just a few more questions. Did Ms. Jacobs get you two involved in this ERA proposal?"

"Oh, well, she tried," said Christy, "but I was just too busy with work and all, you know. But I did sign her petition. I just didn't have the time to do any volunteer work, you know, like lobbying for support."

"I helped a little," Dana said. "I mean, at first I didn't really take it seriously, you understand—" She glanced at me apologetically. "No offense, but it did kind of sound like a weird idea at first."

"None taken," I replied.

"Anyway, the more I thought about it ... well, actually, the more I listened to Susan, the more sense it made. Well,

Susan always could put up a good argument, I mean, she was a communicator, after all, and she was real good at it, but the thing was, it didn't actually take much to make me see that what she was proposing really made a lot of sense."

"I'd be curious to hear her arguments," I said.

"Well," Dana replied, "I don't think I can put it quite as well as she did, but the way she explained it was that what had gotten us into trouble in the first place—into the Collapse, that is—was this whole idea that we could be the masters of nature, as opposed to being its stewards. And throughout humanity's existence, animals have always gotten the short end of the stick. She wasn't a vegetarian, you understand, so she wasn't one of those people who don't believe in eating animals for food or wearing leather or anything like that, she always said that was a part of the balance of nature, but that we'd upset that balance, that through our carelessness and sheer selfishness, we had been responsible for the wanton killing of millions of animals as a result of pollution and development and things like that, and that we'd been responsible for the extinction of entire species. Only now that magic had given us the capability to create new forms of animals, intelligent and reasoning animals, we had a chance to make up for a lot of the damage that we'd caused, but we weren't taking the proper attitude. We were trying to act like the masters of nature again, that same attitude that had gotten us all in trouble in the first place. We had created thaumagenes who were in many cases our equals in terms of intelligence, but we were still treating them like dumb beasts and like possessions, there simply for our amusement."

"She drew a parallel with slavery," Christy interjected. "I mean, the way she put it, it did sort of make sense. Thaumagenes are thinking, reasoning, feeling beings, and we are treating them like . . . well, like animals."

"And she said it wasn't right for intelligent, reasoning beings not to have a voice in their own welfare," Dana said.

"We'd spelled out civil rights for people, why not for thaumagenes, as well?"

"And I take it she was pretty vocal about this," Leventhal said. "That is, she was a real activist, as you put it."

"Oh, yes," said Dana. "She saw it as a real cause célèbre."

"And something that might get her a lot of attention in the media," I put in, "which couldn't hurt if she was planning to run for office."

"Well, there was that," Christy replied, "but the danger was, of course, that it would be the wrong kind of attention. A lot of people thought it was a screwball idea at first, but if Susan had a chance to put her point of view across, they generally started to at least think about it seriously."

"Can you think of anyone offhand who may have been extremely hostile to the idea?" Leventhal asked.

"Well . . . extremely hostile? No, I wouldn't really say so," Dana replied. "Some people just laughed it off and said that it was crazy, but I can't think of anyone who reacted with what I'd call extreme hostility. Certainly not anyone who'd want to . . . to kill her for it."

"I see," said Leventhal. "Well, thank you, ladies, I guess that's about all for now." He reached into his wallet and took out a couple of cards, then passed them across the table to them. "I may be in touch again, but if you happen to think of something, anything, that you think might have some relevance to the investigation, I'd appreciate it if you gave me a call at that number."

"Of course," said Christy. "We'll do anything we can to help."

"Thanks," said Leventhal. "And don't worry about the coffee, I've got it."

"Thank you," said Dana. "God, I hope you catch whoever did this awful thing."

"I'll do my best," said Leventhal. He slumped down in

his seat after they left and exhaled heavily. "Well, that wasn't terribly productive, was it?"

"At least we know that she was planning to run for office," I said. "That could have made her some enemies."

"Those kind of enemies generally assassinate you politically, not literally," said Leventhal. "Nah, I just don't buy that as a motive."

"Do you buy religious fanaticism?" The voice sounded familiar, but I didn't recognize the face of the dark-haired, husky man who slid into the booth. And then his next words gave me the answer. "You're Leventhal, right? The guy at the door pointed you out. I'm Sean Prescott. I would've come up earlier, but I saw you were busy."

"Pleased to meet you," said Leventhal, shaking Prescott's hand across the table. He indicated me. "My partner, Catseye Gomez."

Prescott raised his eyebrows. "Your *partner*?"

"Yeah, you got a problem with that?"

"Not me. I was just wondering where he keeps his rod."

"You'd be surprised," I answered, giving him a brief sparkle with ole Betsy.

Prescott raised his eyebrows. "An enchanted stone, huh? And they say if looks could kill. I never met a loaded cat before. What do I call you . . . Officer Gomez?"

"Just Gomez will do," I said. "I'm not a cop."

"He's sort of unofficial," Leventhal explained. "But he's kinda helping me out."

"ERA all the way," said Prescott, giving me a thumbs-up sign.

"You a supporter?" I asked.

"Hell, yes," said Prescott. "Susan got me on the bandwagon early on. I think it's a great idea. We were supposed to do a program about it together. It's a damned shame about what happened. I take it that's what you wanted to talk to me about."

"That's right," said Leventhal. "Just some routine questions."

"Shoot," said Prescott. "Only don't take that literally," he added, gazing at the bulge of Leventhal's shoulder holster.

"Cute," said Leventhal. "You'll pardon me for saying this, but you don't seem too broken up about Ms. Jacobs's death."

"What do you want me to do, break down in tears?" said Prescott. "Susan was a friend of mine, all right? We worked together and I liked her, just ask anybody. I'm really sorry that she's dead, but I'm just not that emotional a guy. In my line of work, that tends to be a handicap. And if you want an alibi for when it happened, I can provide that, too. I was home in bed and I got two ladies who can testify to that."

"Two, huh?" Leventhal said. "You're an energetic guy, Sean."

"Hey, if I get tired, I can always take a break and watch," Prescott replied. "You want their names?"

Leventhal took out his notepad. "Sure. Why not?"

"Bambi and Debbie," Prescott said. "I don't happen to recall their last names, but I got their phone numbers written down here. I thought you might want some corroboration." He passed Leventhal a folded slip of paper. Leventhal opened it and gave it a quick glance. "Tell 'em Sean sent you," Prescott added. "They'll probably go for you."

Leventhal grimaced. "I'm sure they're reliable witnesses," he said wryly.

"You could check with my building security, too," said Prescott. "They've got a guard on duty twenty-four hours a day. I got off the air at two A.M. and we went back straight to my place. The limo dropped us off at the front door, so I know the guy saw me."

"Limo, huh?" said Leventhal.

"One of the perks of the job," said Prescott. "I got the

number one rated program in town, and Michaels pays to keep me happy."

"He must pay pretty nice," said Leventhal.

"Nice enough. But it's not my salary you wanted to discuss, right?"

"Right," said Leventhal. "How well did you know Ms. Jacobs? You said you were friends. Close friends?"

"You mean did I fuck her? No. You mean did we hang out together and tell each other the stories of our lives? No. You mean did we do lunch? Occasionally. You mean did we have a warm and cordial working relationship? Yes, we did. But you gotta understand something about Susan. She was all business. Career, career, career. I don't know what the hell she did with those two bimbos you were sitting with before, Chrissy and Prissy or whatever their names are, I'd seen 'em around before, they'd show up and take her out to lunch a couple times a week, but you'll notice they weren't exactly nuclear scientists, you know what I mean?"

"Unlike Bambi and Debbie, I suppose," I said.

"Whoa, the cat's got some claws," said Prescott, with a grin. "Look, I get off the air, I like to let my hair down. I take a lady back to my place, we're not gonna play chess or discuss philosophy, all right? I got other friends for that sort of thing. But Susan, man, all she ever wanted to talk about was business, issues, ratings, politics . . . it's like, if she had a personal life beyond that, maybe she spoke about it with Michaels, I don't know, but that sap was so in love with her, he would've listened to her babble on about anything. And he's not exactly the world's most well-rounded individual, either."

"What makes you say that?" asked Leventhal.

"You met him, right? Did he strike you as Mr. Charisma? That guy only cares about two things . . . well, cared about two things, I should say. Susan and that radio station. He's one of the owners, as well as general manager. I'd say that if the two of them had anything in common, it was that they both lived for their work, only in Susan's case, her ambition was much greater. To her, broadcasting was only a step up on the ladder. The lady had her eye on a political career."

"That's what I heard," said Leventhal. "She was planning to run for Congress?"

"She would've made it, too," said Prescott. "She was getting a really solid reputation in this town. My money would've been on her."

"Speaking of money," I said, "running for office would take quite a lot of it, wouldn't it?"

"Money's never a problem, if you've got the right connections," Prescott said, "and Susan was making all the right moves. Michaels isn't exactly a pauper, either, and he's got influential friends in this town. Like I said, she was making all the right moves. And as far as I know, she was clean as a whistle. If there were any skeletons in that lady's closet, I'd sure as hell be surprised. She simply didn't fit the profile. She was all business, she had one steady guy who's a prominent, respectable figure in the community, and she didn't play around. She was sharp, good-looking, stylish, and articulate. She'd have made one hell of an attractive candidate for the right people to back."

"Even with something as off-the-wall as ERA?" asked Leventhal.

"Think about it and you'll see it's not so off-the-wall," said Prescott. "It was shrewd political planning, as well as being basically a good idea. Hell, thaumagenes are smart. Smart enough to work in places like this, like that fucking reptile over by the door, smart enough to take care of people's kids while they're at work, smart enough to help them in their businesses in many cases . . . smart enough to assist on police investigations," he added, with a glance at me. "It's a good idea to have their rights spelled out somehow, their legal situation more clearly defined. I'm not saying they need to have absolutely equal rights with people in all cases, but that's the kind of stuff that gets hammered out in subcommittees. The point is, it's a fascinating issue. It's interesting, it's controversial, and it's just the sort of thing the media can really have a ball with. And Susan was smart enough to realize that and get in on the ground floor. It would've got her a lot of publicity." He grimaced. "Hell, even dead, she's the most talked about name in town right now. And the ERA's the number one topic on everybody's minds."

"Only the key phrase is that she's dead," I pointed out.

"Yeah," said Prescott grimly. "Ain't that a bitch? But who would've figured anybody would be crazy enough to kill her over something like this?"

"We still don't know that's the reason she was murdered," Leventhal said.

"Well, if she had any enemies, I sure as hell didn't know about it," Prescott replied, "and I knew her about as well as anybody, except for Michaels, of course. She wasn't the type to excite a lot of passion in anyone, except someone like Michaels. Hell, when the two of them looked at each other, they probably saw themselves. I wouldn't be surprised if they took the newspapers to bed with them. Basically nice folks, you understand, but not the sort of people who'd provoke the kind of reactions somebody like me would."

"She provoked somebody," I said.

"Yeah," said Prescott, "or the ERA did. And if you ask me, it was those Tabernacle freaks, or somebody who buys into their kind of bullshit."

"I heard the tape of that show you did with them," said Leventhal. He shrugged. "It sounded pretty innocuous to me."

"Yeah, well, you weren't sitting there in the studio with 'em," Prescott replied. "They knew what to expect from me, they'd heard my show. They came expecting hostility, they came expecting to be baited, and they were ready for it. All things considered, I'd say they kept their cool pretty well, but then, you didn't see their faces.''

"What do you mean?" I asked.

"Oh, they kept their voices nice and calm throughout most of the program," Prescott said, "but when some of those callers started getting heavy with them, and I kind of egged them on, what came out of their mouths and what came out of their eyes were two very different things. Especially when the ERA came up. It was like that tricky little magic eyeball of yours. If you'd have been there in my place, and if looks could kill, you would've used up every one of your nine lives.''

Ten

MOMENTS after Sean Prescott left, Bobbie Joe approached our booth. She slipped off her jacket and tossed it on the bench seat.

"I saw you sitting with the Late Shit and I figured I'd wait till he split," she said.

"Not one of his fans?" I asked.

"Prescott?" She snorted with derision. "Are you kidding? The guy gives me the creeps. I did a piece on him for Westwind about a year ago and, ever since, he's been badmouthing the paper on the air every chance he gets. I'm not exactly one of his favorite people."

"It wasn't exactly a flattering piece," Leventhal said.

"Hey, I just told the truth," Bobbie Joe replied. "I held up a mirror and I guess Prescott didn't like what he saw."

"I find that hard to believe," I said.

She grinned.

"Whatcha got for me, B.J.?" asked Leventhal.

"Bobbie Joe," she said wryly, as if reciting a tired, age old litany. She opened her shoulder bag and took out a large manila envelope.

"Yeah, right, whatever." He took the envelope from her and opened it.

"My notes on the ERA piece I was preparing," she replied. "You can keep those, they're photocopies. I'm still going through with the piece, only now that a murder's tied into it, I'm going to hold off awhile until I get some more information. So, have you got some information to trade?"

"Seems like Susan Jacobs was your standard, upwardly mobile, young professional," said Leventhal. "Very career-oriented, with political ambitions. Dated one guy, Mark Michaels, and word has it she didn't play around. You listen to the people who knew her and worked with her, she comes off as squeaky clean, with no enemies and no reason why anyone should want to kill her, except perhaps for her involvement with the ERA thing."

"That's *it*?" said Bobbie Joe. "That's all you've got?"

"Well, so far."

She snorted with derision. "Hell, I could've told you all that."

"Why didn't you?"

"Because you were in such an all-fired hurry to run off and play supercop," she replied. "Some supercop. You better not be holding out on me, Leventhal, because if I find out you are, all bets are off."

"I did check out a few other things," said Leventhal, a touch defensively. "So far, all the people I've talked to claim to have alibis for the time she was killed. Alibis that sound as if they're probably going to hold up. So that brings us back to the religious fanatic angle."

"Have you talked to those people yet?" she asked.

"Not yet. Tomorrow. Tonight, there's still something I want to check up on."

"Hi, Dan."

I looked up and saw Trish standing by the table and smiling down at Leventhal. Up close, she was even more impressive. She had a smile that made her look like the cat that had swallowed the canary, and eyes that were absolutely luminous, not that anyone would be looking at her eyes. Not in a dress like that, they wouldn't.

"I just came over to say hello," she said. "I won't interrupt if you're busy."

"Uh . . . yeah . . . actually, Trish, I am. Nothing personal, it's police business. Uh . . . you know Bobbie Joe Jacklin? She writes for *Westwind*."

"Hi, I'm Trish."

"Pleased to meet you," Bobbie Joe said flatly, shaking Trish's hand.

"I've read your stuff," said Trish. "It's really very good. I wish I could write like that."

"Honey, trust me, you don't have to," Bobbie Joe replied dryly.

Trish just smiled and let that one slide by, like water off a duck's back. "Well, I just wanted to say hi. I have to go sing again. It was really nice meeting you, Bobbie Joe."

"Yeah, likewise," Bobbie Joe replied, with a strained smile.

Leventhal just looked down into his coffee cup. Bobbie Joe took his pack of cigarettes, removed one, and lit up.

"The both of them were very nice, weren't they?" she asked me, rhetorically.

"Meow," I said.

"Lay off, B.J.," Leventhal said. "She was only trying to be friendly."

"Well, I'm sure she's a very friendly girl," said Bobbie Joe.

"You didn't have to be so bitchy," Leventhal replied. "She didn't do anything to you."

"No, not much she didn't," Bobbie Joe replied. She glanced at me. "You ever get the feeling like the world was a tuxedo and you were just a pair of old, brown shoes?"

"What's wrong with brown shoes?" I asked her.

"Maybe they're great for cats to play with," Bobbie Joe

replied, "but men tend to like high-heeled pumps . . . and the equipment that goes with 'em. Right, Danny boy?"

"Don't call me Danny boy. I hate that," Leventhal replied.

"So don't call me B.J., Danny boy." She got up. "Give me a call when you come up with something I can use. Otherwise, have fun watching the scenery."

And she was gone, leaving behind a small black cloud lingering over the table.

"Women," Leventhal said sourly. "I'll never figure 'em out."

"What's to figure?" I asked. "She's obviously in love with you."

He stared at me as if I'd just suggested he was sleeping with his sister. "*B.J.?* You've gotta be kidding!"

"And you've gotta be blind," I said. "I have to make a confession, partner. So far, as a detective, you're not exactly impressing the shit out of me."

"Fuck off."

"Snappy comeback," I said. "Why don't you give the girl a break?"

"What's *that* supposed to mean?" said Leventhal irately.

"It means you're being an asshole," I said. "You're stringing her along, engaging in all this snappy repartee, all that half-joking, sexual innuendo—hell, you're jerking her around. If she was built like Trish, you'd be on her like a fox on a duck. Only she's not, and you rub her nose in it by getting all awkward and flustered when Trish stops by to say hello. You looked like you got caught with your zipper down. The truth is, you know damned well how Bobbie Joe feels about you, and you're taking advantage of it. That's why you got that dumb, guilty look on your face when Trish came over. Bobbie Joe's not blind, you know."

Leventhal stared at me for a long moment. He looked as if he were about to say something, but at that moment, the Baghwan returned from making his calls.

"Okay, I've set it up," he said. "And it wasn't easy, let me tell you. There's good news and there's bad news."

"Give me the good news," Leventhal replied. "At the moment, I could use some."

"The good news is, the Mystic will meet with you," the Baghwan said.

"Great. So what's the bad news?"

"The bad news is, he wants me to come along," the Baghwan replied wryly. "And it's gotta be tonight."

"Tonight?" said Leventhal.

"Yeah. Like, in about fifteen minutes," said the Baghwan. "That's how it is, take it or leave it. I guess the Mystic wants to make sure you haven't got a chance to set anything up."

"You talked to him?" asked Leventhal. "What did he say?"

"The Mystic doesn't use telephones. He considers them 'negative energy.' You don't talk to the Mystic on the phone. You deal with intermediaries. And it's complicated, let me tell you. I had to make about half a dozen calls, and use up a few favors. You owe me for this one, Leventhal. You're going to owe me big. I didn't want any part of this, only now I'm roped in."

"Okay, a deal's a deal," Leventhal replied. "I'll play it any way the man says. So what's the setup?"

"The setup is a limo's going to pull up in front of this place in about fifteen minutes," the Baghwan replied. "Nobody's getting out to come in and get us. It'll be out there for precisely thirty seconds. If we're not there to get in, it'll be gone and there won't be any do-overs. It's now or never. And we do what the limo driver says. Period. We ask any questions, we say so much as *one word,* and he pulls over to the curb and lets us out and that's that."

Leventhal pursed his lips thoughtfully. "Sounds like the man's being careful," he said.

"Dan . . ." said the Baghwan. "I'm telling you straight.

You don't want to cross him. If you've got anything in mind you haven't told me about, now's the time to cough it up. You don't want to play games with this guy. Trust me. My ass is on the line here. And so is yours.''

"Square business, Baghwan," Leventhal replied. "I just want to talk to the man. I'll play it any way you like.''

The Baghwan nodded. "Okay. Here's how it is, then. In about ten minutes, we're going outside. We'll just stand on the sidewalk and have a smoke or two until the limo shows up. Then we get in, and you don't say another word, not one fucking word, until somebody tells you to.'' He glanced at me. "That goes for both of you. Understood?''

"Understood,'' said Leventhal, and I echoed his response.

The Baghwan sighed heavily. "I sure as hell hope you appreciate this.''

"I do,'' said Leventhal. "I've never been anything but straight with you, Baghwan, you know that.''

"Yeah, I know that,'' the Baghwan replied. "I also know that, right at this moment, I'm scared shitless.''

"You?" said Leventhal.

"Yeah, me,'' said the Baghwan. "I've played about every angle there is to play in this town, but I've never gotten in this deep. The Mystic is heavy, believe me. I've never even met the man, but from what I've heard, I know enough to be seriously nervous.''

"Why?'' asked Leventhal. "I mean, we're not playing any games here. There's no hidden agenda. I just want to talk with the man. I'm not out to make a big, glamorous bust, Baghwan, honest to God. I wouldn't set you up like that.''

"Yeah, I know,'' the Baghwan said. "If I didn't trust you, I never would've gone through with this. I've never actually met the Mystic. Part of me's always wanted to, you know, but the other part, the part that knows what's good for Number One? That part has always told me to steer clear.'' He exhaled heavily. "I should've just kept my mouth shut.''

"You're getting all wound up," Leventhal replied. "Okay, so the guy's got a heavy rep, but he's just an unregistered adept with money and some heavy connections, right? I mean, come on, what's the big deal?"

"You don't really understand, do you?" the Baghwan replied. "The Mystic isn't just some unregistered adept practicing without a license from the BOT. He's a whole different ball of wax. He's the *real thing,* you understand what I'm saying? The man's a witch, a magician in the classic sense, like Aleister Crowley was, and like Cagliostro and Saint-Germain."

"Who?" asked Leventhal.

"Hey, read a book," the Baghwan snapped nervously. "You're dealing with serious *power* here, you understand what I'm saying? We're not talking about some guy who picked up a little thaumaturgic knowledge on the side, okay? We're talking about the real thing, *arcane* knowledge, man, the kind of sorcery that goes back to the days when Merlin was teaching Arthur how to go potty. Let me make this as clear as I know how to make it, all right? You do one wrong thing tonight, one little fucking thing, and it's a good bet that neither you, nor I, nor Gomez here will ever be seen again."

"Well, I must say, I'm intrigued," said Leventhal. "This isn't like you, Baghwan. I've never seen you sweat before."

The Baghwan lit up one of his unfiltered cigarettes, and I noticed that his hand was shaking. "Let me put it this way," he said. "If I come back from this one, I'm going to be a lot more than just a guy who's got a few connections. A hell of a lot more. I'm going to be *the* guy. But . . . and this is a very big but, my friend . . . if we don't play this one *exactly* by the rules, that limo ride we're going to take in about ten minutes is going to be the last ride we ever take. And if you're not ready to deal with that, now's the time to tell me."

"It's your show, Baghwan," said Leventhal. "You call the shots."

The Baghwan took a deep breath and let it out slowly. "Okay," he said. "I hope you mean that, Dan. I sure as hell hope you do. Because from here on in, whatever I say, goes."

"You got it," Leventhal said.

The Baghwan stared at Leventhal for a moment, then nodded. "All right." He glanced at his watch. "We've got a little less than ten minutes."

The man was clearly more than a little nervous. Making a connection and setting up a meeting was one thing, but now that he was actually going to be involved himself, he was scared. Interesting. Very interesting, indeed. What Leventhal thought, I couldn't be sure of, but he seemed fascinated by it, as well. One way or another, we would soon find out.

I thought of all those scenes in Spillane's books, when Hammer knew he was heading into trouble . . . deep, deep trouble, and he just bulled his way on through, because that was the only way to get the answer. You gotta bring some to get some, I thought. That was one lesson I'd learned the hard way, and I'd learned it long ago. But lessons that you learn the hard way tend to stick. So Leventhal and I had both been warned. Okay. The rules had been spelled out. What remained was to play out the remainder of the game. I could deal with that. And my instinct told me that Leventhal could deal with it, too.

While we waited, Leventhal had another cup of java, and that dark-haired angel, Becky, brought me another dish of cream. I lapped it up to the last drop. What the hell, I figured, if there was a chance it was going to be my last drink, I might as well enjoy it.

The long black limo pulled silently up to the curb and settled to the ground. The windows and the windshield were tinted dark, so it was impossible to see inside. A door in the passenger section opened and we got in. There was no one in there waiting for us. As soon as we got in, the door swung shut again, all by itself, and the limo rose up off the ground and silently skimmed off. The windows were black on the inside, as well, so we couldn't see out. We had no way of knowing where we were going. And there was a partition between us and whoever was in the front seat, so we couldn't see them, either. The inside of the limo was nicely insulated from outside sounds. It was quiet as a tomb.

A little tray compartment opened in front of us and slid out, like a drawer. "Please deposit your pistol in the tray," a voice said, over an intercom.

For a second, Leventhal looked as if he were going to give the guy an argument, but he glanced at the Baghwan, who swallowed hard and nodded; Leventhal did as he was told. The tray retracted and then, a moment later, it slid out again, empty.

"And the knife in your boot, as well, please," said the voice.

Leventhal raised his eyebrows at that, but complied. The boot knife was whisked away, as well. I half-expected to see the little tray come sliding out again, and to hear the voice on the intercom ask me to drop my magic eyeball in there, which would have been a problem, as I've grown sort of attached to ole Betsy. However, the tray did not come sliding out again and the voice on the intercom merely said, "Thank you. Your weapons will be returned to you later, the same way. You will find refreshments in the bar cabinet in front of you. You may not speak, but you may smoke, read, or enjoy a musical selection available through the headphones. Relax and enjoy the ride."

Leventhal gave me an amused glanced, then lit up a cigarette and slipped on a set of headphones. I saw him frown and fiddle with the controls, and then an expression of pleased surprise crossed his face. He cranked up the volume knob all the way, settled back against the seat, and closed his eyes, bobbing his head in time to the music, which he had turned up so loud that both the Baghwan and I could hear it through the headphones. A guitar wailed a bluesy riff and the singer pleaded with some woman to let him be her "Forever Man." The Baghwan and I exchanged glances. He looked even more nervous than before. He fidgeted for a few moments, and finally surrendered to the whiskey from the bar cabinet.

The ride took about an hour and a half, though it was impossible to tell if we were going straight to our destination, or if our chauffeur was simply driving around in order to confuse us about the distance. Leventhal seemed content to simply smoke and listen to the music. The Baghwan chain-smoked his unfiltered cigarettes and worked on the whiskey supply. I simply curled up on the seat and ran the events of the past day through my mind.

In any killing, there has to be a motive. In this one, at least so far, we hadn't been able to come up with any sort of personal motive. Perhaps Susan Jacobs had had no enemies, but then, she hadn't had many friends, either, and none of them seemed to have any motive for wanting to kill her. One phrase kept cropping up whenever anyone described her. "She was all business." A woman with ambition, yet apparently, not much in the way of personality. In other words, a perfect candidate for public office. No one had testified to her having any vices, and indeed, if she'd had her eye on a political career, it would have been in her best interests to remain, as Leventhal had put it, "squeaky clean." Aside from that, she didn't seem to fit the profile of someone who'd have secrets. Her personality, according to Sean Prescott, had been rather bland, and while she'd been an attractive woman, she had cultivated a businesslike, professional attractiveness, not one that was seductive. Her friends seemed to match the profile, too. Nice, pleasant, attractive women, but hardly temptresses; women with good, respectable positions in the business community, whose idea of a good time was going out for a night of girl talk at an "unconventional" local coffeehouse. The man in her life was much the same, a good, solid, local businessman, clean-cut and attractive, but hardly a thrilling kind of guy. He was well off, and what they'd had in common had been their occupations in the media and a mutual interest in current events and politics. We didn't exactly have the ingredients for a major potboiler, here.

Unless there was something we hadn't yet uncovered, or the people we had spoken with were very good actors, none of the classic emotional motives for murder seemed to apply. Passion, jealousy, revenge, they all seemed terms that were much too strong for someone as apparently colorless as Susan Jacobs. Possibly, money could have been a motive. We hadn't yet checked on the angle of who would benefit the most from her death, although we'd have that information soon. Still, the most likely motive seemed to be her involvement with the ERA proposal. So far, that was the only element of this case that seemed to generate any kind of strong emotions.

That, of course, brought us back to the religious fanatic angle. And it wouldn't be the first time. One of the risks in being a celebrity, as Susan Jacobs had been in her role as a broadcaster, was that one can become the target of all sorts of kooks out there who have an ax to grind. Small-minded, petty, ignorant, and insecure, such people often need only a focal point for their frustration to have their rage cut loose. It didn't necessarily have to be one of those Tabernacle people, it could be anyone to whom their message would appeal, and when you have a situation where that message was being widely broadcast, the list of suspects became positively endless.

I knew that Leventhal was hoping that wasn't the answer, that Susan Jacobs had been murdered by someone much closer to home, because otherwise, the odds of finding her killer became damned near impossible. But there was still the fact that whoever had phoned in those death threats had known her private number. And the possibility, as yet unconfirmed, that the bomb might have been planted while her car was still in the garage.

I had looked over the parking lot across the street from the building where K-Talk had its studios. It was open and, in the morning hours, it would certainly have been well lit. There hadn't been an attendant on duty—it was one of those drop-a-bill-in-a-slot affairs—and there was a sign warning that vehicles improperly parked there would be impounded. Anyone could've gotten in there and had access to any of the cars, but, on the other hand, during the time that Susan Jacobs was on the air, doing the morning news and feature show, the city was just coming awake and there was lots of traffic in the streets, both vehicular and pedestrian. It would've taken a pretty cool customer to plant a bomb in that lot, with cars and people going by all the time. Which wasn't to say that wasn't how it was done. But if it had been me, I would've wanted some more privacy.

If there was a personal angle to the murder, then someone had to have benefited somehow from her death. That was the part we couldn't see yet. But the more I thought about it, the more certain I became that it was there. Maybe it was no more than a hunch, but it was pretty strong. The answer had to be there, someplace. It was just a matter of looking under the right rock.

My thoughts were interrupted by the car slowing down, then nosing down a slight incline. After a few more minutes, it came to a stop and gently settled to the ground. The door unlocked and then swung open.

"You may exit the car," the voice on the intercom said.

I was the first one out. Leventhal and the Baghwan followed. As I dropped down to the ground, my paws contacted bare earth and grass. The cool, crisp air told me that we weren't in Denver anymore, but somewhere up in the mountains.

I could see better in the darkness than the others could, and what I saw around me were thick stands of evergreens and aspen, a couple of large rock outcroppings off to the side, and a small clearing just ahead of us where the dirt road winding through the woods led down a slope into the little valley and up to a large, rough-hewn stone house that looked almost like a small medieval castle. It lacked only towers, barbican, and moat. If there were any electric lights in there, they were off, and all that was visible was the soft glow of candles through the windows. Behind us, the limo rose up about two feet off the ground and silently glided away into the darkness, leaving us alone out there.

"Will you look at this?" Leventhal said softly, staring at the stone mansion nestled in the clearing. He glanced around. "Hell, I can hardly see a thing out here. I wonder where we are?"

"Sshhh!" hissed the Baghwan.

"Hey, lighten up, all right?" said Leventhal. "We're here. Let's go knock on the door and see if anybody's home."

As if it had heard him, the massive, wooden front door suddenly swung open with majestic slowness. It didn't creak ominously on its heavy hinges, but I felt it should have to make the effect complete. The effect was further ruined when we walked up and saw that it was a man who'd opened it, and not some mystical, unseen force. Large candles placed in wall sconces provided illumination in the corridor behind him. The wooden floor was covered with a long runner of beautiful, handwoven carpet, and there was a pleasant smell of incense in the air.

"Welcome, gentlemen . . . and cat," he said, with a smile in my direction. "Please, do come in."

He appeared to be in his early to mid forties, perhaps a little older. It was difficult to tell exactly, because he had a

very youthful-looking face. His hairline was receding and
he had a bald spot at the top of his head. Everywhere else,
his light brown hair was long, cascading down his shoulders
in the manner of an adept. He had a full beard, neatly
trimmed and going white around the chin. But the face was
the face of a young man, or perhaps it was just something
about the expression, which conveyed an intense vitality.
The color of his eyes might have been blue or green, it was
difficult to tell, because he wore a pair of small, round,
rose-tinted, gold-rimmed glasses. He was dressed in black
wool slacks and soft, well-made, black western boots, a
black sport jacket, and a white, button-down Oxford shirt
that was open at the neck to reveal a silver pentacle
encircled by a serpent eating its own tail, hanging on a chain
around his neck.

"Follow me, please," he said, leading the way down the
corridor. We started walking after him, and then, with him
already about six or eight steps ahead of us, we heard the
front door close behind us. The Baghwan moistened his lips
nervously and glanced at Leventhal, who simply shrugged.

The man led us to a room that was set up as a den and
library. The walls were covered with bookshelves and the
books they held looked ancient. A marvelous Persian carpet
was spread out on the floor. It was so soft, I couldn't resist
digging my claws into it a little. There was a large,
well-upholstered reading chair by an oil lamp in a corner, a
large desk made out of dark mahogany, and two cloth-
upholstered, straight-back chairs placed in front of the desk.
I also noticed a small settee with a cushion on it thoughtfully placed between them. Our arrival had obviously been
anticipated.

There were some interesting items on the desktop. One
was a large crystal ball, about the size of a honeydew
melon, resting in a silver stand carved in the shape of a
large claw. Another was a large, leatherbound book, ancient-
looking, resting on a corner of the desk. The binding was

old, black leather, and there was no lettering on the cover. Beautiful, antique candelabra made of brass, silver, and gold held white candles that provided the flickering illumination. One corner of the room held a small altar, an intricately carved wood table covered with a black velvet cloth on which rested a number of items in a purposeful placement. At the top left corner of the table was a dark green candle in an ornate brass holder. At the top right corner was a matching holder, with a red candle placed in it. Between the two candles, and slightly in front of them, near the center of the table, was a lovely, golden censer, and in front of that, lying flat in the exact center of the table, a circular pentacle of blue and white stained glass. To the left of the pentacle was a beautiful silver goblet, with a stem carved into the shape of a knight holding a sword. To the right of the pentacle, a small black cauldron, filled with salt. And in front of the pentacle, placed so that their blades angled up toward it, were two knives. On the left, a curved, white-handled blade, and, on the right, a straight, double-edged one, with a black handle. I felt as if, somehow, I'd stepped back into medieval times.

The man who had brought us to the room went around the desk and sat down in the chair behind it, clasping his hands on the desktop before him. He smiled enigmatically.

"So, what was it you wanted to see me about, Detective Leventhal?"

Leventhal stared at him. "You're the Mystic?"

Again, that strange, disarming smile. "I am called that, yes."

Leventhal glanced around. "What's the matter, you don't believe in electricity?"

The Baghwan rolled his eyes and caught his breath, as if expecting to be struck down. The Mystic merely smiled again.

"This is an isolated area," he said. "We don't have

electricity out here. And I rather prefer it that way. I have no real need of it. Its energy can be distracting."

"But you have a telephone," said Leventhal.

"No, as a matter of fact, I do not."

"Then how... I mean, when the Baghwan called..."

"How was I contacted to arrange this meeting?" asked the Mystic. He smiled again. "Telephones are certainly involved, Detective Leventhal, but not at this end. I have ways of maintaining contact with the outside world, but then you didn't come here to question me about my lifestyle, did you? You came seeking help in your murder investigation."

"What are you, psychic?" Leventhal asked.

Again, that smile. "I can be, but in this case, no. It was merely a matter of logical deduction, based on some inquiries I made about you, and about the case you are currently working on."

Leventhal merely grunted, and glanced at the Baghwan.

"Well, I had to tell 'em what it was all about," he said defensively.

"Do not blame the Baghwan," said the Mystic. "He was not, by any means, my sole source of information. I take care not to invite just anyone to my home."

"Is that right?" said Leventhal. "So what makes me so special?"

"Absolutely nothing," the Mystic replied. And then he glanced at me. "It was your feline companion I was anxious to meet. Catseye Gomez, isn't it?"

"Just Gomez will do," I replied, staring at him with some confusion, which I no doubt shared with the Baghwan and my partner. "I'll repeat what my friend here said. What makes me so special?"

"Oh, I've heard a great deal about you," the Mystic replied. "Especially about your involvement in a certain case in Santa Fe. And with certain individuals."

I knew whom he was referring to. Merlin and the others. "You know them?" I asked.

"I know only one of them personally," he replied. "You might say we've had sort of a professional relationship in the past. I often think about him, in my dreams."

The reference to dreams was what told me whom he meant. He meant Modred, better known by the code name he had worked under for many years—Morpheus. The God of Dreams. An appropriate alias for someone who had made a living putting people to sleep . . . permanently. I wondered how much he knew. I certainly couldn't ask him, not with Leventhal and the Baghwan there. The world at large had no idea that Merlin was still alive, only transmogrified by an incredibly powerful spell that had fused his spirit and persona with the immortal shade of his own father, and a cocky kid from England by the name of Billy Slade. The three of them were one now, and together with the "others" the Mystic had referred to, they were engaged in a quest to find and neutralize the Dark Ones, the necromancers once more loosed upon the unsuspecting world. No, I couldn't talk about that with the others present, and the fact that the Mystic knew something about it, or had been involved with Modred at the very least, told me a great deal. I looked at him with new respect.

"Seems like we have at least one friend in common," I replied. "Assuming, of course, that he *was* a friend."

"Oh, yes, he was, a very good one," said the Mystic. And then he smiled cryptically. "And still is, I might add."

I nodded. That meant he knew as much as I did, because the rest of the world believed that Morpheus was dead. I was becoming very much intrigued with this man, and I had a lot of questions I wished I could ask, but under the circumstances, I couldn't ask them. What passed between us was a look of understanding. Leventhal, of course, had no idea what we were talking about, and the Baghwan couldn't care less. He didn't want to know.

"Am I missing something here?" asked Leventhal.

"Yes," replied the Mystic, "but it does not concern you.

Suffice it to say that were it not for Gomez, you wouldn't be here now. So . . . what is it I can do for you, detective?''

The Mystic leaned back in his chair and steepled his fingers while Leventhal replied.

"I'd like to ask a favor," Leventhal said. "I'd like you to perform a divination."

The Mystic frowned. "The police certainly have their own adepts, who are quite capable of performing divination rituals," he said.

"Yeah, but not like you," said Leventhal. "Divination is always an iffy business, at best, which is one of the reasons it can't be used as evidence. But word on the streets has it that you're the best, that you always get results, and right now, I need results."

"However, as you quite correctly pointed out," the Mystic said, "you would not be able to use these results in a court of law. So of what use would they be to you?"

"They might at least point me in the right direction," Leventhal replied, "and I could take it from there. Our lab adepts didn't come up with anything beyond routine forensic evidence, and not much of it, at that. I've got a situation with a lot of pressure here, one that's getting a lot of press, and I'd like to resolve it before it gets worse. Like I told the Baghwan here, I couldn't care less about your being an unregistered adept. I'm not a BOT agent. I'm willing to pay for this, or trade, or whatever you like, within reason, of course."

"And you are quite sure you can afford my price?" the Mystic asked, with a smile.

"No, I'm not sure of that at all," said Leventhal. "But I'm willing to kick in as much as I can afford, providing you're willing to negotiate."

The Baghwan had his eyes closed.

"I never negotiate, detective," replied the Mystic. "I merely name my price, and you are either willing to pay it, or you are not." He glanced at me and smiled. "However, in this case, I am disposed to be somewhat charitable. My price is a favor for a favor. I will perform this divination for you, but at some point in the future, perhaps next week, perhaps next month, perhaps even years from now, I will ask you for a favor in return, and you will grant it. That is my price."

Leventhal cleared his throat. "That's a pretty vague sort of price," he said. "It's not that I'm unwilling in principle, you understand, it's just that—"

"Relax, detective," the Mystic said, with a dismissive motion of his hand. "I can assure you that I shall not compromise your position on the force and ask you to do anything illegal. Well, at least not any more illegal than the sort of things you have already done. Does that help clarify things for you?"

Leventhal hesitated slightly, then decided. "Okay, fair enough, in that case, I accept."

The Mystic nodded. "Very well, then. What, exactly, is the nature of this divination you wish me to perform?"

Leventhal reached into his pocket and pulled out something I couldn't make out. He placed it on the desk before the Mystic, and then I recognized it. It was a piece of the bomb left behind after the blast. I'd seen it before in the police forensics lab, but I hadn't noticed him sneak it into his pocket.

"This is part of a bomb that killed a woman named Susan Jacobs," said Leventhal. "Somebody planted that bomb in her car. I need to know whatever you can tell me about it."

The Mystic looked down at the piece of debris without touching it and nodded. Then he rose and moved over to the altar in the corner of the room. He took the objects from it, the candles and the cauldron, the goblet and the stained-glass pentacle, the censer and the knives, and placed them in identical positions atop his desk. I noticed that both the desk and the altar were positioned similarly—facing north, I guessed. He lit some incense and placed it in the censer.

Then he poured some water from a carafe into the goblet, and added a pinch of salt to it from the cauldron.

"Please take that object and place it in the center of the pentacle," he said to Leventhal, who did as he was told. Then the Mystic took the crystal ball and placed it before him, between the two knives. "I will ask you to remain seated," he said, "and completely silent from now on."

Leventhal nodded. The Baghwan nodded, too. He would probably have done backflips if the Mystic told him to.

"Gomez, I shall ask you to assist me," said the Mystic.

"Me?" I said. "What can I do?"

"A great deal," said the Mystic, with a smile. "The enchanted stone in your eye socket...Even if I did not already know the nature of its enchantment, its trace emanations are like a signature. It can provide energy to augment my own, and it would be a privilege to employ it, if you are willing."

"What do you want me to do?" I asked.

"At a certain point, I shall give you a nod," the Mystic said, "and you will direct a beam of force toward my upraised blade. Not a very strong beam of force, if you don't mind," he added, with a grin. "I do wish to survive the experience."

"Okay," I said. "I'll try my best."

"Good. And now we shall begin. Please remain silent and motionless for the duration."

First, he took the censer and, carrying it, walked slowly clockwise in a circle around the table, a circle that also encompassed us. Then he took the goblet and did the same, dipping his fingers into the water and sprinkling it around the same circle. I recognized the procedure. It was similar to one that I'd seen Paulie do from time to time. He was casting a magic circle.

When he'd finished with the water, he replaced the goblet in its former position, then used a match to light the candles. First the green, and then the red. Then he took the black-handled knife and held it up before him. He closed his eyes as he brought it up level with his face, holding it with both hands, and his lips moved soundlessly for a moment. Holding that same position, he stood facing us for a moment, his eyes closed, and his lips moved silently for several seconds. Then he did the same thing again, facing in the three other directions, turning clockwise as he did so. I knew that he was silently invoking the spirits of the four directions, North, East, South, and West—Earth, Wind, Fire, and Water.

It was witchcraft in the classic form, magic of a sort not usually practiced by most modern registered adepts, who did not go in for much ritual or ceremony. Paulie had done it occasionally, partly out of his personal interest as a scholar of the Old Ways, and partly out of family tradition. Paulie's mother had been a witch, only his rituals had been different, more vocal and elaborate, drawing more on his mother's Native American tradition, mingled with his studies of ancient Celtic lore. This was a more intense, more inner-directed approach. I knew what the Mystic was doing, in general, but I did not know what his specific ritual was. It appeared more Celtic than anything else, or perhaps Saxon, I wasn't sure. The Mystic had his own, idiosyncratic methods.

When he finished invoking the spirits of the four directions, he stood facing us again, still holding the knife—the athame—before him, at the level of his face. He opened his eyes and stared at it intently. His eyes seemed to unfocus, almost to glaze. And as we watched, a faint blue glow appeared around the blade, an aura that grew in intensity until it was blindingly bright and we couldn't look directly at it anymore. Then, the Mystic held the knife away from him, in his right hand, and pointed it toward the floor, toward the point at which he had started making the circle.

What looked like blue lightning lanced out from the tip of the blade, struck the floor, and ignited. A trail of blue flame, like fire following a trail of fuel, raced around the circum-

ference of the circle he'd described before, until we were
sitting in the center of a ring of fire. I glanced at Leventhal,
who sat there motionless, with his eyes wide. I saw him
swallow hard. The Baghwan sat there gripping the arms of
his chair, his eyes squeezed tightly shut, all the color
drained out of his face.

Gradually, the flames died down until we were surrounded
only by a circle that was emitting a soft, blue glow. The
Mystic held the knife before him once again. He moistened
his lips slightly, took a deep breath, let it out slowly, then
looked at me and nodded once.

Okay, I thought, here goes. Not too hard, now. I sure
hoped the guy knew what he was doing. But then . . . so far,
he'd displayed ample evidence of *that*. I stared at his upraised
knife and cut loose with ole Betsy.

A pencil-thin beam of thaumaturgic force shot out from
Betsy like a blue laser and struck the knife. It flared, its aura
growing even brighter than before, and the Mystic jerked
violently, as if struck, and used the knife blade to deflect the
beam down to the crystal ball on the desk before him.

Hell, I'd never seen anything like *that* before. I didn't
even know that it was possible to deflect the force like that.
I watched with fascination as the crystal flared with bright
blue light that seemed contained inside it, as if a fire were
raging in its core. The Mystic then put down the knife and
sat down in his chair, placing his hands over the ball.
Slowly, the glow subsided, as if he were absorbing it from
the ball into himself. He took his hands away and the ball
was left with a faint glow, like bright blue eddies swirling
around in there. It felt very warm and close within the
circle. I glanced at Leventhal and saw that perspiration
stood out on his forehead and his upper lip. The Baghwan
was sweating freely, still sitting there with his eyes squeezed
tightly shut, his lips trembling.

The Mystic picked up the piece of bomb debris from
where it was lying on the pentacle and held it in his left

hand. His right hand, he placed gently along the side of the crystal ball as he stared into it intently. I could see the reflection of the swirling eddies in the ball on the lenses of his glasses. I saw his eyes glaze over as he started entering a trance state. A moment later, he started speaking . . .

And even before he was finished, I knew who had killed Susan Jacobs.

Eleven

FOR the first few miles of the return trip, it was all Leventhal could do to get the Baghwan to relax. He didn't see any reason not to talk now, but the Baghwan resolutely kept his mouth shut all the way back to Denver—that is, when he wasn't filling it with the entire contents of the limo bar. And every time Leventhal opened his mouth, the Baghwan had a nervous fit, so Leventhal, though he was clearly anxious to talk, gave up and settled back to listen to the headphones and think. I settled back to think, as well, only not exactly to myself.

Our chauffeur, though the others didn't know it, was the Mystic. He must have been our driver on the way up, too, which would explain the rule about keeping silent. When people are sitting quietly, drinking or reading or just listening to music, their minds are easier to probe. It also added to the dramatic tension, and the Mystic certainly understood about drama. As we drove back, we had quite a conversation, the Mystic and I, only it wasn't happening out loud. And it was very interesting. Very interesting, indeed.

Once we got back to Mudd's and were deposited on the curb outside, the Baghwan opened up with a vengeance. Having kept his mouth shut . . . and his eyes . . . throughout most of our visit with the Mystic, now he could hardly shut up. It all came spilling out of him, the nervousness and the anxiety, like a torrential verbal flow released suddenly by a stress valve.

"Okay, so we got out of there in one piece, but I swear, Leventhal, no way are you *ever* going to get me to go back again, so don't even ask, all right? No way, no way, José! That's it! Finished! *Finito!*"

"Will you calm down, for cryin' out loud?" said Leventhal, with exasperation. "You're okay! Nothing happened! Nobody turned you into a toadstool or a frog, all right? The guy wasn't even all that scary."

"Well, he scared *me* plenty!"

"He was polite, and he was civil, and he gave us what we needed," Leventhal replied. "Now shut the hell up and let me think about how we're going to prove it."

"That's not my problem," said the Baghwan. "From now on, I'm out of it, you understand? I don't want to know. I don't even want to talk about it."

"Fine! So shut up already!" Leventhal snapped.

"Just remember that you owe me for this one," said the Baghwan. "You owe me big!"

"Okay, I owe you! Now get lost!"

He turned to me after the Baghwan had stalked off in a huff. "You knew right away, didn't you? I could tell."

"Not right away," I said. "But it didn't take long."

"I've never seen a divination performed that way before," said Leventhal. "It was certainly impressive. I got to hand it to the guy, he sure is a showman. It was like . . . he picked up that piece of the bomb and got right into the killer's mind. Putting it together, thinking about how he was going to do it, and what the effect would be . . ."

"When he started taking us through it, step by step, actually going down the stairs to the garage, I began to suspect," I said. "And then, while he was going through planting the bomb, and wiping his hands on the black sweatshirt, that's when I knew it was Rick."

"I should've figured it," said Leventhal. "Now that we know, of course, it all falls into place. Or almost all of it, at any rate. There are still a few loose ends. The question is, how do we prove it in a way that'll stand up in court?"

"If your lab team found some kind of traces in the garage that would indicate the bomb was planted there, you could get a warrant to search Rick's apartment."

"Maybe," Leventhal replied, "but it would be a little shaky. It's not really enough grounds to get a warrant. Besides, there's no guarantee that we'll find anything in there, unless he's really stupid, which he doesn't seem to be. He's pulled this whole thing off without missing a step."

"And it still doesn't tell us who hired him to pull it off," I said.

"My money's on those Tabernacle people," Leventhal replied. "He must've been part of their crowd all along. They got him to get next to Susan Jacobs and pretend to support the ERA, then boom. The vengeance of the Lord."

"I don't know, Dan," I said. "Somehow, I just don't buy it. He seemed pretty sincere about the ERA."

"All part of the act," said Leventhal. "We lean on him, he'll roll over and give us the rest of it. You watch."

"You're going to confront him?" I said. "What if he calls your bluff?"

Leventhal shook his head. "My instinct says he won't. He's not a hardened pro. Right now, he's probably all balled up, tense, hair-trigger, wondering if maybe he slipped up somewhere and if we're onto him. He's dying to get the hell out of there, but he's got to sit tight in order to make it look good, and the longer he sits, the more wound up he's going to get. I'm betting that if we hit him with it hard and fast, he'll break."

"What if he won't?" I asked, playing devil's advocate.

"Then that just increases the pressure on him," Leventhal replied. "He'll know we know, and he'll know we're looking for a way to prove it so we can tie him in all nice and legal, that we're just waiting for him to make one fucking mistake, and you can bet your ass he'll make it. Or he'll run, which'll be just as good.''

We walked over to his car and got inside. Leventhal started it up and we pulled off. He was so keyed up that he didn't even bother with his internal-combustion-engine sound effects. He was thinking out loud, playing it all out in advance and trying out the angles to see how they'd come together.

''We'll touch base with Sharp first, and see if she's heard anything from Eggleston. If they can prove that bomb was planted in the garage, that's one more thing we can hit him with. And even if we can't prove it, we'll bluff him with it.''

''Let's hope he bluffs easy,'' I said.

''Hell, he'll fold,'' Leventhal replied. ''Faced with taking the fall for it all by himself, he'll want to deal.''

''Maybe not, if he's a religious fanatic,'' I said. ''What happens if he's got a martyr complex?''

''Then I'll fucking beat it out of him, if I have to.''

''Chief Moran will love that,'' I said.

''Moran,'' said Leventhal contemptuously. ''That's the other thing. I want to know what the hell those two bastards, Chavez and McVickers, have been doing mucking around in my case. Those assholes are liable to screw everything up. So much for your friend Solo's promise to keep them off my back.''

''Maybe Solo didn't know anything about it,'' I replied.

Leventhal's face grew grim. ''Yeah, maybe. That would figure. Moran knows that if I solve this one, then I'm the fair-haired boy and I'm back on Homicide for keeps and he's behind the eight ball. But if Chavez and McVickers take the credit, then that means Leventhal screwed up again and I'm back to chasing hookers and bunco artists. Well, that's not going to happen, Cat. This one's mine and if Moran doesn't like it, he can shove it up his ass.''

We drove straight to Karen's place, in an apartment

complex overlooking Washington Park. The buildings loomed over the surrounding real estate, affording a good view from their balconies of the park and the mountains in the distance. Leventhal parked the car and we got out. It was a quiet night. The park was closed and the streets were deserted.

"It's kinda late, isn't it?" I said.

Leventhal glanced at his watch. "It's almost four A.M.," he said.

"She'll probably be asleep."

"So I'll apologize for waking her up," said Leventhal, as he hit the buzzer for her apartment. "Hell, she's a cop, she knows what—"

"Who is it?" Her voice over the intercom sounded alert, and not at all sleepy.

"Leventhal."

"Christ, where the hell have you *been*?" she replied. "Get your ass up here!" She buzzed open the front door.

Leventhal glanced at me and grinned as we went inside. "Think maybe she missed me?" he said.

"No, I think it's more like *you* missed something," I replied.

The elevator doors opened. "Floor, please."

"Nine," said Leventhal.

"Thank you," said the elevator. "Kindly extinguish your cigarette in the receptacle by the doors."

"Oh, fuck off," said Leventhal.

"There is no smoking in this elevator. Kindly extinguish your cigarette in the receptacle by the doors."

"Right," said Leventhal, leaning out the doors toward the ashtray. "All right? Ninth floor."

The elevator doors slid shut and it started to ascend. With a schoolboy grin, Leventhal produced the cigarette he had palmed. There was a loud beeping sound and the elevator came to a sudden stop between floors.

"Nice going, Ace," I said.

"All right, all right," said Leventhal, dropping the cigarette to the floor and stepping on it.

The beeping stopped and the elevator resumed its ascent. When we reached the ninth floor, the elevator stopped, but the doors remained closed.

"Well?" said Leventhal impatiently.

"In consideration of the other tenants, please keep this elevator clean," the elevator said.

"Oh, for cryin'out loud . . ." said Leventhal, and he bent down to pick up the cigarette butt.

The doors slid open. "Thank you. Have a nice day."

"I hope your cable snaps," said Leventhal.

Karen was already looking out for us from the open door of her apartment. "Where have you been all day?" she demanded. "You were supposed to keep in touch!"

"Well, like, excuse me, sarge," said Leventhal, "but there was a little matter of a murder investigation to attend to. And wait till you hear the news—"

"Wait till *you* hear the news," she said, as we entered her apartment. She was wearing an orange and blue football jersey that hung about halfway down her thighs, and she quite obviously had nothing on underneath it. It was a considerable improvement over her police uniform and gun belt.

"Very nice," said Leventhal, giving her an appreciative once-over. "Who gets to take the snap?"

"Chavez and McVickers," she replied wryly. "They've arrested Rick Daniels. They've got him down at headquarters right now."

"*What?*" said Leventhal, his jaw dropping open.

"If you'd been keeping in touch with me like you were supposed to," Karen said, "I could've told you that forensics found small traces of plastique and wire insulation shavings in the garage, right on the spot where Susan Jacobs parked her car. And they were able to come up with a decent, enhanced voice-print off those answering-machine tapes, as well. And guess who was Johnny-on-the-spot when that came down?"

"*Son of a bitch!*" said Leventhal. "I don't believe it!"

Princess came out from a back bedroom, looking sleepy and trailed by two, furry, wriggly little snats. "I heard voices," she said, pausing to stretch languidly. "What's going on?"

"Looks like they've got the murderer," I said. "They've arrested Rick."

"*Rick!*" said Princess. "No! I can't believe it!"

The two little snats squirmed over my way, sniffing around. "Hello," one of them said, in a voice that sounded like a cross between a purr and somebody gargling with mouthwash. "You want to play?"

I hissed at them and they both curled up into little balls. I never did like snats. Nothing looks sillier than a cat with no legs, crawling across the floor like a damned inchworm, and those stupid, slimy-looking antennae give me the creeps.

"I can't believe those bastards beat me to the punch!" said Leventhal. "When did it go down?"

"About four hours ago, maybe a little more," said Karen. "They were thoughtful enough to call and let me know, so I could tell you when you checked in. So, hotshot, you want a towel to wipe that egg off your face?"

"Son of a fuckin' *bitch*!" said Leventhal, smashing a fist into his palm. "Come on, Cat, we're taking a ride down to headquarters."

I had to run to catch up with him as he stormed out of the apartment and back down the hall, to the elevator. He stabbed at the call button furiously.

"That bastard Moran's behind this," Leventhal said through gritted teeth. "What do you want to bet Eggleston came up with more than he gave me, but held back on Moran's orders?"

"Maybe," I said. "On the other hand, you did neglect to check back in with him."

"I was going to do it first thing in the morning," Leventhal said. "Of course, I didn't know until tonight that Moran had Chavez and McVickers working the same side of the street. *Damn* him! Come *on*, you stupid box!"

The chime rang and the little red arrow above the doors lit up. The doors slid open and the elevator said, "Floor, please," as we got in.

"Lobby," Leventhal snarled.

"Thank you."

The doors slid shut and the elevator started to descend. Suddenly, it dropped with alarming speed and then jerked hard to an abrupt stop, knocking Leventhal right off his feet onto the floor. I barely kept my own balance.

"*What the hell—?*" said Leventhal.

"Sorry. The cable must have slipped," the elevator said.

Leventhal took out his huge gun and aimed it at the speaker.

"Dan . . ." I said, as he thumbed off the safety.

"The problem seems to be under control now," the elevator replied, and started a smooth descent again. Leventhal holstered the gun and we reached the lobby floor without further incident. The doors slid open and we went out into the lobby.

"Thank you. Have a nice day."

Leventhal's lip dropped in a sneer and he turned back toward the elevator again, reaching for his gun, but I caught his pants leg with my claws.

"Dan . . . . Headquarters?"

He drove like a madman all the way to Cherokee Street, and I had to run to keep up with him all the way to the squad room of the Homicide Division. He came bursting into the interrogation room, where two well-dressed but tired-looking detectives stood over Rick Daniels, who was seated at a table, smoking a cigarette. The tall, dark,

Hispanic-looking one had to be Chavez, and the big blond guy built like a pro athlete was obviously McVickers. The two detectives looked a little haggard. So did Rick Daniels. He also looked tense, and anxious, but he didn't look very scared. He glanced up as we came in, noticed me, and looked a little surprised.

"You scumbags," Leventhal said.

"Leventhal! What the hell are you doing here?" said Chavez.

"Like you didn't know," snapped Leventhal. "Like you didn't call to rub my nose in it! This was supposed to be my case, you son of a bitch!"

"Watch your damned mouth," said Chavez. "And since when do you decide who does what around here? Just because you brown-nosed your way back onto Homicide, don't think you—"

He never got any further, because Leventhal hauled off and decked him. Chavez went back against the wall, blood spurting from a broken nose, and collapsed onto the floor. McVickers was on him in a second, grabbing him and pulling him back, but Leventhal broke free and shoved him away.

"Are you nuts?" shouted McVickers.

"Come *on*!" Leventhal shouted back. "Come on, McVickers, you want a piece of me? *Come on*!"

"You stupid son of a bitch," McVickers said. "You really blew it this time, Leventhal. Get the hell out of here!"

"Bastard broke my nose," said Chavez, getting to his feet and trying to staunch the flow of blood with his handkerchief.

"You'll be lucky if you're writing parking tickets after this," McVickers said. "You stupid jerk, you just flushed your shield right down the toilet!"

A couple of other detectives came in, having heard the ruckus, and McVickers said, "Get this dumb fuck out of here!"

They grabbed him, but he shook them off furiously and left, with a baleful stare at McVickers. I followed him out the door.

"You'll get yours, Leventhal!" Chavez shouted after him. "Your *hear* me, you bastard? You're going to get yours!"

Leventhal knew he'd gone too far. He walked out of the squad room without a word as the others on the night shift just stared after him. As we went out the door, somebody behind us mumbled, "What a jerk."

Leventhal didn't even bother with the elevator this time. He took the stairs and I followed him. He stopped on the second floor and simply sat down on the landing, his feet on the first step down. Silently, he flipped out his pack of cigarettes and lit up a smoke. The snick of the Zippo sounded loud on the landing. He inhaled deeply and let the smoke out in a heavy sigh.

"He was right," he said, finally. "I *am* a jerk."

"Well, I don't know about that," I said, sitting down next to him. "A little temperamental, maybe..."

He snorted and shook his head. "Yeah. I really lost it back there, didn't I? Oh, man. I guess I really did it this time. I just handed Moran my badge on a fuckin' platter." He sighed and rubbed the bridge of his nose wearily. "What the hell. I was getting tired of this gig anyway."

"You haven't been kicked off the force yet," I reminded him.

"Moran'll have my badge before ten tomorrow morning," he replied glumly. "I just had to hit that asshole, didn't I?"

"I'll bet it felt good, though," I said.

He grinned at me. "Yeah. It felt great. I'm only sorry I didn't nail McVickers, too."

"He would've mopped up the floor with you," I said. "He's twice your size."

"I would've got in a couple of good shots."

"It's not over till it's over," I replied.

"What's that supposed to mean?"

"Well, why don't you just wait and see what happens tomorrow?" I said.

"Thinking of putting in a good word for me with the commissioner?" asked Leventhal. He reached out and lightly scratched me behind the ears. "I appreciate the thought, pal, but I wouldn't bother if I were you. I crossed over the line this time. Solo's not going to look too kindly on this little episode. He won't go against the chief for the likes of me. I mean, let's get real, here." He threw down his cigarette and crushed it out, then stood. "Fuck it. It's late, and I'm tired. I'm going home."

"You want some company?"

He smiled. "Thanks, I appreciate it, but no, I think I'd rather be alone. If you don't mind, I'll drop you off at Karen's place. No point in disturbing the commissioner at this hour. He'll be annoyed enough with me when he wakes up."

He took me back to Karen's apartment building, and she buzzed us in. He walked me through the lobby and called the elevator for me. When it arrived, he said, "Tell Karen I'm sorry I screwed up her first homicide case." He grimaced. "She didn't get to do too much on this one, but at least she'll get another chance. It's been good working with you, Cat. You're okay."

"And so are you," I said. "Even if you are a screwball. Go home and get some sleep."

"Yeah. Right."

I took the elevator up to the ninth floor and Karen let me in. She was still up, and anxious to know what had happened. I filled her in while Princess listened and the snats kept their distance from me. When Karen heard about Leventhal breaking Chavez's nose, she shook her head sadly.

"Well, he's screwed himself now," she said. "That's all the excuse Moran will need to have his badge."

"That's what he thinks," I said. "Maybe he's right. Maybe not."

"Loyalty to your partner is always commendable," said Karen, with a smile. And then she sighed. "It's too bad, though. He should have kept his damned temper."

"I still can't believe that Rick had anything to do with this," said Princess. "There must be some kind of dreadful mistake!"

"There isn't, kitten," I said. "He did it, all right."

"I don't believe it. How can you be so sure?" Princess asked.

"Before this whole thing went down, Dan and I attended one hell of an impressive divination ritual," I said. "And there's no question in my mind but that Rick planted the bomb."

"But . . . isn't divination inadmissible in court?" asked Princess. "I seem to remember hearing something like that, anyway . . ."

"No, you're right, Princess, it isn't," Karen said. "But they found evidence that the bomb was planted in the garage, and they have a voiceprint off those threats on the answering-machine tapes."

"I don't understand," said Princess. "How could they tell that was Rick? I mean, what makes them think so? I know what his voice sounds like better than any of them, and *I* certainly didn't recognize it."

"They enhanced the tapes in the police lab to get a decent print," said Karen, "and they'll probably be able to match it to Rick's voice. I'm sure they have solid grounds on which to charge him, Princess, otherwise they wouldn't have arrested him. I'm sorry."

"I still can't believe it," Princess said, sounding stunned. "I mean . . . he was *with* us on the ERA! He cared! I know he was sincere! *Why* would he want to kill Susan? *Why?*"

"That's what I keep asking myself," I said. "Leventhal figured it this way: Rick was never in your camp at all. He never supported the ERA. He only made you think he did, so he could get in close, close enough to do what he had to do and establish a good cover for himself, so that when he made his move, he wouldn't be suspected. When we got here tonight, before we found out he'd already been arrested, Leventhal was planning to head over there and bust Rick himself, brace him, and get him to spill the beans. He figured Rick couldn't have been working on his own, that he was tied in with those Tabernacle of True Faith people, and that if pressed with what we knew, he'd break down and talk.

"It would've been a bluff, of course," I continued, "because you're right, Princess, a divination isn't admissible in court. We'd have required corroborating evidence. However, there was a good chance Rick wouldn't know that. Most people don't. But like I said, the divination ritual we had performed for us was pretty damned impressive, and it was done by a guy who really knew his stuff. You'll have to take my word for that part, but trust me, there wasn't any doubt about it. Rick was the one who planted the bomb, all right, and what we got from that divination would have been enough to shake him up pretty badly if Leventhal had confronted him with it. Or at least he thought so.

"The only thing was, Chavez and McVickers beat us to the punch and busted Rick first. They were following pretty much the same course we were, only they kept a couple of steps ahead of us. I figure they'd put it together pretty much the same way we did. Maybe they even had a divination of their owned performed, I don't know, but it's a safe bet that if they did, whoever they found to do it wasn't as good as our guy was. I seriously doubt they had any more than we did, which means they didn't have anything solid, nothing that would really nail it down unless Rick confessed.

"The only trouble was, Rick hadn't done that. They'd had him down there for at least four hours by the time we got there, and it didn't look like they were getting very far. They still had him in interrogation. Rick looked a little nervous and anxious, and he looked a bit shook up, but he didn't look scared. That bothered me. Rick's just a kid. He's not a hardened, professional killer, and he'd just been arrested for murder. So why didn't he look scared?''

"What are you getting at, Gomez?" asked Karen.

"I'll tell you," I replied. "See, I didn't put it all together until just a little while ago, and a lot of it's still guesswork, but I'm betting that when all the facts come in, they'll bear me out. What we've got here is an almost perfect crime. There isn't really any way to tie Rick into it for sure in a manner that will guarantee a conviction. There's no way to trace the explosive that he used, unless somewhere down the line somebody comes forward with that information, and there's not much chance of that. Nobody saw him do it. He made damned sure of that. At best, all we've got is circumstantial evidence.''

"We know the bomb was planted in the garage," said Karen.

"That's about all we know for sure," I said. "And even then, it could've been anybody. People manage to get into security apartment buildings all the time.''

"We've got the voiceprint," Karen said. "And the fact that the caller knew Susan's home number. The manager would know that.''

"So could almost anybody else," I said. "You know how easy it is to get unlisted numbers? You could call the phone company and represent yourself as a police officer on an investigation, or a member of some government agency, or another operator investigating fraudulent charges, or any of a number of other cons. For that matter, for all we know, it could've been someone who worked for the phone company, or maybe a computer hacker who managed to break into their data base. Sean Prescott had this fan who kept getting his home number every time he changed it. But the voiceprint, that's the interesting part.

"Rick knew about voiceprints. It's part of the security

system in this building, built into the elevator computer. So why would Rick leave threatening messages on Susan's answering machine if he knew a voiceprint analysis could tie him into it? Unless he *also* knew that by disguising his voice, muffling it somehow, they'd have to do enhancing on the tapes at the police lab in order to get a decent print, and a good lawyer could cast a lot of doubt on that sort of thing. On top of which, it still didn't prove he was the killer. At best, it might only prove he'd made the threatening calls. Without a confession, we simply wouldn't have a case. Solo could tell you better than I could, because he used to be the D.A. in this town, but frankly, I don't even think the D.A.'s office would bother to prosecute on evidence as flimsy as that. And Rick knows that, he knew it all along, which is why he was a bit shook up down at police headquarters, because two big cops were leaning on him pretty hard, *but he wasn't scared*. He knew that all he had to do was keep his mouth shut and refuse to talk without a lawyer present and he'd skate. So in a way, although he doesn't realize it yet, Chavez and McVickers did Leventhal a favor. Instead of letting him take the risk of making a shaky bust, *they* took it, and it backfired on them. Rick Daniels didn't bluff, and he won't. He'll be out by tomorrow afternoon.

"But that's not all of it," I went on. "What I kept coming back to was the motive. There had to be a motive. If Rick was tied up with the Tabernacle of True Faith, then maybe that was it. Or, possibly, he was just some screwball religious fanatic who was set off by them, maybe when he heard the program with Sean Prescott, who knows? It's tempting to try tying in that kooky bunch with this whole thing, but there's just one thing that doesn't fit. Those people might hold views that are unpopular, and maybe they're intolerant and inflexible in their beliefs, but when it comes right down to it, *they don't believe in murder*. It's a sin. They believe in the sanctity of human life, they're opposed to abortion because they believe it's murder. They believe in a fundamental interpretation of the Bible and the Bible says, 'Thou shalt not kill.'

"Okay," I said, "maybe a few of them went off the deep end and found some way to rationalize killing Susan Jacobs, but it just doesn't seem very likely. They may be narrow-minded, they may be simple, but deep down, they believe they're doing the right thing. 'Vengeance is mine, saith the Lord.' That seems pretty clear. And if maybe one of them was fanatical enough to think the Lord had somehow appointed him as the instrument of that vengeance, then it would fit that he *would* confess, and proclaim proudly that the Lord had told him to do it. Only Rick hasn't done that. And he won't. Because Rick simply doesn't fit the profile of that kind of fanatic. But maybe he's another kind.

"It all comes back to what his motive was. If he really thought the ERA was blasphemy and he thought killing Susan Jacobs would kill the ERA, then he couldn't have been more wrong. Ever since the murder, the ERA's gotten more publicity than ever before, and a lot of people are starting to think very seriously about it. The news media's dying to interview you, Princess, which is why we've had you hidden out here, but when this is over, you'll be the most sought-after cat in town. A real celebrity. And then you'll really have a platform, won't you?"

"Gomez! What are you saying?" Princess said.

"You know exactly what I'm saying," I replied. "For Rick, there were two motives. He really does care about animals. He cares about them a lot, probably likes them more than people. He went out of his way to make things easier for the thaumagenes in his building. I think he really was committed to the ERA, passionately committed, fanatically so, and that's where the first motive comes in. It's political. He knew the murder of Susan Jacobs would make her a martyr for the cause and catapult the ERA into the headlines, and it did just that. The way the media's been playing it up, I wouldn't be surprised if it got on the ballot in the next election, and maybe it's even got a better than fair shot of passing. But the second motive, and this is where the guesswork comes in, had to be money. Probably a lot of money. And part of that money would come from the life-insurance policy on Susan Jacobs, and I'm betting that when we get a look at that policy, we'll find out that you, Princess, are the chief beneficiary. Maybe even the sole beneficiary. Susan didn't have any kids. She was all business. But not quite all business, because whatever maternal feelings she might've had, she bestowed on you, Princess, and I think that when we look at all the paperwork, we'll find out that she'd set up a legal guardianship for you that would probably allow you to live pretty comfortably on your own. And you knew that, too, didn't you, which is why not once during this whole thing did you express any anxiety about what was to become of you. What did you do, promise Rick a share of the loot?''

"You're crazy," Princess said. "I've never heard anything so ridiculous! How *dare* you suggest such a thing? It's absolutely outrageous!"

"Is it? You're spoiled rotten, Princess, I knew that when I first met you. And when I didn't trip all over my tail trying to get in your good graces, you got all frosty and contemptuous, because you're used to getting your own way. Hell, you were the one who came up with the whole idea of ERA in the first place, and Susan ran with it for you, both because she saw where she could make some political gain from it and because she loved you. Yes, that's right, she loved you, the way women who often insulate themselves from real emotion love their pets, but you despised her, didn't you? You hated her guts, because despite insisting that everyone refer to you as her 'feline friend,' everything that Susan did for you reminded you that you *were* a pampered pet, and you just couldn't stand that. I know exactly how you felt, because I know myself what it feels like to be proud. When I was young myself, I couldn't stand

ιe thought of being bought by somebody and owned, so I
ιd something about it. But you never had the moxie to
ιtrike out for yourself and try to make it on your own. You
ιad to have it all given to you, but you'd hate the hand that
ιd the giving. And there's the real motive, Princess. Yours,
ιecause you're the one who planned the whole thing and
ιalked that poor sap Rick into doing it. For you, it was a
ιrime not only of greed and political fanaticism, but it was
ιlso a crime of passion. The perfect crime. Only not perfect
ιough.''

"Stop it!" Princess shouted. "I don't want to hear
ιnymore! How can you be so abominably cruel? Karen,
ιake him stop!''

Only Karen didn't say anything. She was watching me,
ιer eyes wide, glancing from me to Princess and back
ιgain. She was taking it all in, and it made sense, and she
ιnew it. I had no proof, but her cop instincts told her I was
ιight.

"I'll stop it, kitten, but not yet," I replied, "because you
ιtill haven't heard it all. The guy who did our divination
ιr us was a fella called the Mystic. A very powerful witch,
ιnd a gifted psychic, to boot. He was able to reconstruct for
ιs much of what went down, by holding onto a piece of
ιebris left over from the bomb and getting impressions of
ιhat Rick was thinking when he planted it. He didn't tell
ιe others everything that he picked up, because some of it
ιonfused him, but he told me, because we've got some
ιutual friends in common and, well, I won't go into all that
ιow. It doesn't matter. What does matter is that on the way
ιack, he was in contact with my mind, and he told me
ιomething he didn't tell the others. He said that Rick had
ιept thinking about 'all the little animals' while he was
ιanting that hellish device, thinking that he was doing it for
ιem, and that he was thinking one more thing. The Mystic
ιld me that he got the distinct impression that the killer
ιept thinking about royalty, and that was what confused

him. 'It's for the Princess,' Rick kept thinking. 'For all the
little animals, and for the Princess.' The poor sap loved you
too, didn't he? The kid who cared so much about all the
little animals, but didn't have a thaumagene of his own
because he couldn't afford one. Did you promise him that
too, Princess? Did you promise him that you would be his
pet?''

Her eyes were twin slits of loathing as she hunched over
glaring at me with her ears pinned back. "You can't prove
any of this," she said, her voice almost a hiss. "And even if
you could prove it, what good would it do you?"

"It would do me a lot of good, kitten," I said. "Personally
it would make me feel just fine. And it wouldn't do you
much good at all, because maybe there's no provision in the
law for sending a cat to prison, but I'm sure the insurance
company would disallow your claim as Susan's beneficiary.
You'll never see any of that money. And whoever Susan had
appointed to act as your legal guardian—Mark Michaels
maybe, or perhaps one of her girlfriends—will cut you loose
without a dime and with no roof over your head. And you'll
have to either find somebody to take you in or live out on
the streets and eat from dumpsters. Either way, I doubt your
haughty pride would survive it, kitten.

"As for proof," I continued, "you're right, I haven't got
any. But that doesn't really matter, because you're going to
give it to me. You're going to confess, Princess, and you're
going to give my partner the proof he needs to nail down
this case and send Rick Daniels to jail for murder one. As
for what happens to you after that . . . frankly, kitten, I don't
give a damn."

She snarled at me with contempt. "You're a fool, Gomez.
A dumb, arrogant, fool tom. What makes you think I'm
going to confess to anything?"

"The ERA makes me think that," I replied. "The fact
that our civil rights aren't really legally defined. You know
it's a damned shame, but there just isn't any law against

cat fight. And if you don't give me what I need, kitten, I'm going to claw your pretty little hide to shreds."

The look of contempt was suddenly replaced by one of fear. She took one look at me and knew I meant every word of what I said. "Karen," she said, fearfully, "you can't let him do this!"

"Oh, no?" said Karen. "Just watch me."

I started to move toward her purposefully. With a yowl of fear, she leaped off the couch and snatched up one of Karen's stupid little snats in her teeth. The snat gave a high-pitched, gargly, mewling sound as Princess raced with it in her mouth out to the open balcony. She leaped up onto the wall and looked back at me, wild-eyed, holding the wriggling snat in her teeth, threatening to drop it nine stories to the ground.

"Don't!" Karen cried. "Don't, *please*!"

People really do love their pets. It's true, I thought, sometimes people care for animals more than they care for other people. But I've never had that problem. I try to keep things in perspective. I moved toward the balcony.

"Gomez, don't!" Karen cried. "She'll do it!"

"So let her. What the hell do I care?" I said, keeping my eye on Princess as I closed the distance between us. "I never did like snats, anyway."

"Gomez . . . *please*!"

"Go ahead, Princess," I said. "Go ahead and drop it. Makes no difference to me. On the other hand, I kind of like Karen, and I'd hate to see her upset. So I'll make you a promise. If you do drop that snat, I'll take every one of your nine lives. Or maybe I'll just leave you half a one. Half a life. Just barely kicking."

I kept moving closer.

"You'll look like you got center-punched by a Pontiac. Your legs will be broken, your tail will be chewed off, your pretty face will be clawed to pieces, and by the time I'm done, you'll be begging me to take that last little half a life

I've left you, only I won't. I'll just leave you lying there, squirming on the floor and leaving a trail of blood and guts behind you. So go ahead, Princess. Drop the snat. Give me a reason. Make my day.''

The first gray light of dawn was showing in the sky, and the birds were starting to sing. It was a brand-new day, but Princess had run out of time and she knew it. She let go the snat and let it drop back down to the balcony, where it immediately curled up into a quaking little ball. Behind me, I heard Karen sigh with relief. I stood looking up at Princess, trembling there on the ledge.

"Don't come any closer, Gomez," Princess said. "I'll jump."

"No, you won't," I said. "You haven't got the nerve. Now get your tail down here before I get really mad."

For a second, she actually considered it, but I knew she didn't have it in her. Pampered. Spoiled rotten. Always had it easy. Too damned easy. With a pathetic little whimper, she obediently got down off the ledge.

"That's better," I said. "Karen, why don't you give Leventhal a call?" And with a grin, figuring that he could use some motivation, I added, "Ask him if he'd like to come and get a little pussy."

Twelve

SOLO came in and tossed a paper down on the coffee table. "You're getting to be famous," he said. "Not bad after less than a week in town."

I glanced at the cover of *Westwind*. It featured a large, close-up photograph of me on the cover, and the prominent headline, "Catseye, P.I." Byline, Bobbie Joe Jacklin. She'd wound up the whole story of Susan Jacobs and the ERA, the murder, and the solution of the case, with me cast as the hero. Somewhere in there, Leventhal was mentioned once or twice.

"Leventhal's going to love this," I said wryly.

"He's lucky he's still on the force," said Solo. "If it wasn't for you saving his bacon by breaking the case, he'd have been out on his ear. As it is, Moran will be gunning for him. One mistake—he so much as spits on the sidewalk—and he's out."

"Come on, Solo, he did most of the work on this one and you know it," I said. "If wasn't for Dan, we'd never have wrapped the thing up so fast."

"You mean if it wasn't for *you*," said Solo. "Leventhal was on the right track, but you're the one who put it all together. You're a good detective, Gomez. I ought to offer you a position on the force.''

''I'm sure that would make Chief Moran real pleased,'' I replied.

Solo grinned. ''You mean you'd consider it?''

''I dunno. Blue's not exactly my favorite color. Besides, where would I carry my badge?''

''Oh, I'm sure we could have a special one made up,'' said Solo jokingly. Or at least I hoped he was joking. ''Maybe a small one, like a medallion, hanging from a nice black leather collar.''

''You try to hang a collar around my neck and I'll scratch your eyes out,'' I warned him.

There was a knock at the door and Solo went to answer it. ''You expecting company?'' he asked me.

''Karen and I are going out to dinner at Mudd's,'' I said. ''Leventhal's supposed to meet us there. Although after this article, I'm not sure if I want to go.''

Solo opened the door and Karen came in, wearing civvies. ''Good evening, Commissioner,'' she said.

I noticed Solo casting an appreciative eye over her tight breeches. ''Evening, Officer Sharp,'' he said.

''I hope I'm not disturbing you. I came to pick up Gomez. We're going down to Mudd's.''

''Well, you kids have fun,'' said Solo, with a faintly mocking tone. ''Don't stay out too late, now.''

She grinned. ''Gomez, have you seen . . .'' and then her gaze fell on the paper lying on the coffee table. ''Oh,'' she said, sounding slightly disappointed. ''You've already seen it.''

''Yeah,'' I replied, with a grimace. ''Just what I need. My puss plastered all over town. I'll probably get quite a ribbing down at Mudd's. And I was just beginning to like Bobbie Joe. 'Catseye, P.I.,' for crying out loud.''

''What's so bad about that?'' asked Karen. ''You know, maybe it's not such a bad idea.''

"What?"

"Being a private investigator," she replied. "You've already proved that you're a good detective, and the publicity you've gotten would certainly get you clients. If the ERA goes through, you could get a license. And you seem to have some pretty good references," she added, with an amused glance toward Solo.

"A feline private eye," said Solo. He chuckled. "That would really take the cake."

"You know," I said, "maybe I'll think about it."

"Are you serious?" said Solo.

"Why not? The way Leventhal's going, who knows how long he'll remain on the force? He'll probably need a job before too long. And he's really not all that bad a partner, you know. Maybe I'll even get Karen to quit her job and be my secretary."

"That all depends," she said. "How much are you going to pay?"

"You guys *are* joking, aren't you?" Solo said, uncertainly.

"Oh, I don't know," I replied. "I've always thought it would be a blast to be a private eye, just like Mike Hammer. Hell, why not?"

"What about Santa Fe?" asked Solo.

"It'll still be there," I said. "Denver's actually not that bad a town, once you get used to it. And I've got some friends here, now. Think maybe I'll stick around awhile."

The phone rang and Solo picked it up. He listened for a moment, then rolled his eyes and turned to me. "It's Channel 7," he said. "They're interested in doing a feature on you."

"Hell, tell 'em I just left," I said.

"I'm afraid he must have stepped out for a while," said Solo, into the phone, "but I'll be sure to give him the message."

He hung up. "You know, maybe you're going to need a secretary," he said irritably.

Yeah, maybe, I thought. I thought of Mike Hammer's lovely secretary, Velda. Karen would fit a role like that real well. And, of course, if she wasn't a cop anymore, then there'd be no problem if Solo decided to take her out to dinner sometime . . . . Whoa, I thought. Let's not go putting the cart before the horse. Take things one step at a time.

"So, you ready to go?" asked Karen.

I gave her a sparkle with ole Betsy. "Sure, kid. Let's go out and do some yowling."